A Wi

The Chronicles of Brawrloxoss, Book 5

By

J. R. Knoll
Vultross@aol.com

Artwork is the amazing talent of
Sandi Johnson
goldenSalamander.deviantart.com

A few dedications...

This book is dedicated to mothers, fathers, grandparents, aunts and uncles, healers, good friends and all of those who would go out of their way to help others. For every wound tended, every boo boo kissed, all of those encouraging words, those who simply helped in any way they could, pints of blood donated or even a shirt for someone's back. Even if it's to say "Good game" or "you did a good job" this book is for you.

You know who you are.

Those of you who don't do this, start, or no book for you!

CHAPTER 1

Middle Summer, 989 Seasons

A small village was usually one of peasants, those who worked the land to support a kingdom. One village deep in the Western Abtont forest was different. Most villages resented their kingdoms for demanding taxes and tributes for protections they only rarely provided, but resentment was low in this village as the kingdom was a prime location for trade, and the modest village had hidden wealth that the kingdom would not know of.

Over two thousand people lived and worked here in huts, houses and multi-level dwellings, running shops of all kinds that made fabrics, metal works, many different kinds of foods, clothing, jewelry and the like, and the village sprawled in a huge clearing in the forest and well into the forest itself. In fact, many homes were concealed there, hidden from sight but for the roads that led to them.

This was also a village with a problem. In the canyon where copper and other metals were found and from where over half of the village made their living, one of the deep mines had been taken over by a dragon. This area was desolate, though surrounded by the wealth of green things that was the Abtont Forest. Thanks to the villagers, little would grow in this canyon as the rock was continually hacked away, quarried for building stone and the metals that could be found there. And, of course, the dragon was the problem.

They quickly learned that the dragon could be placated with sacrifices. Sheep were offered at first, and this seemed to keep him in his lair and away from those who sought their fortunes down there. Then, of course, came the first attack. A few miners ventured too close to his lair and out he came. A battle erupted between three men armed with picks and shovels and a dragon that was over ten paces long with a slender, almost serpent like body and short, thick legs. With a head as large as a man and teeth as long as a man's hand, this was a formidable beast, the color of the copper that the miners sought with metallic scales that would prove to be very hard and resistant even to the hard swing of a pick. Bronze colored dorsal scales ran from between his dark, serpentine eyes to the end of his long slender tail, and here his armor was the strongest.

It is this kind of dragon that is most common in Abtont, and on the whole continent, really. Flightless but extremely fast, it hunts game where larger dragons cannot and can run down almost anything, even humans, horses and deer, though it will stay clear of unicorns, a known enemy of all dragons.

After this incident with the miners, tensions ran very high. More sheep were offered and it took them, and once it took the woman who was bringing the tribute to it, and this, they eventually thought, would be the key.

First, it was time to call in favors from the kingdom. The mayor himself made the trip to appeal to the king to send knights and soldiers to dispatch the troublesome beast, but he was not allowed to see the reigning monarch there and his pleas fell on deaf ears.

So, it was back to the village where he would revive the age old practice of offering higher quality sacrifices. Blessed sheep would go first, and as the dragon grew more demanding, a lottery was held, and on the morning after the last full moon, a young maiden, a virgin, would be prepared and taken to the canyon where she would be bound to a specially carved, ritual post to await the dragon, and most of the villagers would go to watch the grisly outcome.

This macabre ritual would be repeated for almost five seasons. Those who tried to hide their daughters and sisters were executed and their bodies given to the dragon, or they were given a crude sword, a wooden shield and a little armor to face the dragon in one on one combat that never ended well for the human. Once in a while, a knight or warrior would appear on the day of the sacrifice, seeking to be a hero and attain the title of dragon slayer, but all fell as one would expect, killed by fire or brute force by a beast they had no business challenging.

As humans do, most began to grow weary of losing their people to this dragon, and demands were made of the mayor to rid them of it. Brute force had failed. More appeals to the kingdom had failed, and now the task would fall to a lonely mage who lived in a small house at the very edge of town.

Ellianta was a young woman who had just turned twenty-six. Not married and still unknown by men, she was almost always alone but for the people who ventured her way in need of her services, or when she would venture out herself for supplies or to render aid to the sick. For this reason, many feared her, but she enjoyed many friendships. In appearance she was a very attractive young woman, though her features were what many would consider ordinary. High, full cheeks still clung to the round features of her girlhood and her deep blue eyes shrouded by very long lashes were the envy of many women and the allure of every man who saw her. A beautiful face, one so pure and free of blemish, made one wonder why she did not have a man at her side, though she had plain features that could make her disappear into a crowd of others. Her body also clung to its youth as she was perfectly muscled in arms and legs. A lean waist and round backside were proof of her active life and wholesome diet. Womanhood had changed her body seasons ago, broadening her hips and endowing her with a bosom that completed the curves that would catch the eye of every man who looked her way, though she was not as generously busted as most. There was something graceful and dainty about her and her movements were almost like those of a cat.

Sharp vision over a distance had abandoned her many seasons ago, but a craftsman in the village had fashioned oval lenses for her to correct this which she wore in snug fitting, copper frames that hooked behind her ears and kept the lenses at an appropriate distance before her eyes.

Most days, her long, dark brown hair would be restrained behind her. She washed daily and washed this long hair every three days, more for a need of cleanliness than to attract a mate. In the confines of her small house, an open structure on the inside that was ten by seven paces exactly, she did her work from the time she awoke to the time she slept. And this was a woman who slept very little. None in her village resented sleep as much as she did, as she considered it a waste of her time, time which was best consumed with her studies or with making potions or powders. When she was not doing this, she loved to sew, and all of the clothing about her small house was that which she had made.

Most of the house was devoted to her work. In one small corner was her simple bed with a wooden frame and a feather mattress, a wash tub that was a full pace across, and a small table with a basin of water. Hanging over the bed where her head would be was a painting that was the width of an arm length and about half that high. It was of a white unicorn running across a grassy field in some magical forest. A gift from her late mother, who had died from illness eleven seasons past, it was one of only a few comforts she owned, and it was a picture she admired every day when she awakened and every night before she slept. *Someday,* she would sometimes think, *perhaps I will actually see one.* Many candles lit the place and a smoky haze lifted slowly toward the ceiling and out the many vent holes along the peak of the house. The center of the house was consumed by a long work bench that was laden with many flasks and buckets and other containers full of stuff she had collected over many seasons. Shelves lined two walls and a fireplace consumed most of another. She worked here tirelessly when she was not out in the forest collecting things to use in her work.

Such was the life of a Wiccan healer.

With so many candles burning and the fireplace burning, drying out things that hung close by, the small house would grow hot within, as Ellianta kept her shutters closed for privacy. Preferring to work unencumbered for the most part, she did not dress in the mornings, and often would wander about the forest naked, but for a cape in the winter, as she searched for the things a Wiccan would need for her potions.

And on this day, she would be hard at work as usual. An unfinished dress lay on her bed and the wash tub was still full of water. Many things were half tended as she stood at her work bench and watched a bubbling glass flask that she held over a thick candle intently, her dark blue eyes dancing behind the lenses of her spectacles as the bubbles rushed to the surface of the orange liquid within. Holding it with wooden tongs of her own construction, she swirled it slowly, then lifted it from the fire and examined the liquid closely as the bubbling stopped. Ever so carefully, she moved it to a glazed clay bowl and slowly emptied the contents into the pure water within the bowl, then she set the flask down and gently stirred. A pinch of red powder here, a pinch of green powder there and she sniffed, then added something else, and something more. Satisfied, she plucked a few red berries from a bowl and held them over the mix, squeezing some of the juice from them and slowly mixing the concoction as she did. Drawing a breath, she dropped the squeezed berries back into the bowl she had gotten them from and groped for a rag to wipe the juice from her hands. She had been hunched over the bench for a time and slowly rolled her head back, arching her back forward to stretch. Pushing her spectacles up slightly for a quick rub of her eyes, she picked the bowl up and looked down into it, taking a sniff of the concoction within, and then she held it to her lips and took a sip, smacking her lips a few times as she pondered the flavor. An involuntary raise of her brow showed that it was what she had wanted and she drank more, then more, and finally emptied the bowl. A satisfied sigh and a smile followed.

Setting the bowl down, she reached for the nearby notebook and plucked her pen, made from a turkey feather, from the inkwell and went about making notes. All of her writings were in Latirus, as few people from the village knew that language and her secrets would be safe that way. For some time she stood at her workbench, in the nude, leaning over it as she scribbled her notes, her eyes following the words she scribed on the pages. One foot was perched atop the other as she wrote and her mouth silently made the words as she did.

Her inner senses were very sharp and she knew there were people approaching her house long before they got there. With an impatient sigh, she finished a few last thoughts, then put the pen back in the inkwell and turned toward her bed. A light robe, sky blue in color, hung beside it, one made of thin linen that was just enough to cover her, and she slipped into it, pulled it tightly against her and tied the sash off with quick movements as she slowly padded back over to her workbench. She knew who was coming, knew they would enter without knocking, and always hated it.

When the door burst open, she was already writing in her notebook again and didn't look up as three men entered, but she did greet in a young voice, "Good morning, Mayor."

Mayor Trogden was a hefty fellow, dressed very formally as he always was in public. His hair was thinning and had abandoned much of his head. Dark eyes glanced about her small house as he stopped only a couple of paces inside the doorway and set his hands on his hips, his heavy, polished boots sliding to a stop on the wood plank floor beneath.

Two men entered behind him, each armed with a sword and each wearing a steel breastplate and helmet, black riding trousers and black boots.

As they looked around her house, she just kept writing, but dryly offered, "How may I help you today?"

"You know of our woes," was his reply.

"The dragon," she confirmed as he strode slowly around her workbench and toward her. The last words inked, she stabbed her pen back into the inkwell and stood fully, turning toward him. She was not tall, not quite average height for a woman, but looked up at him fearlessly and folded her arms. "I've told you many times what to do, you only have to listen."

He looked to her work bench and absently picked up a container of small bones, looking it over as he said, "Yes, the advice you so strongly placed before us was determined to agitate and provoke the beast. I would prefer that he be kept at bay where he is and out of the village itself."

She plucked the container from his grasp and put it back in its place on the bench, countering, "Just quit feeding it and it will go away. Why is that so difficult to understand?"

With a raise if his chin, he also folded his arms and looked down on her with narrow eyes. "Such insights from a witch can only raise suspicions from the people."

"I'm a Wiccan," she corrected. "If you didn't come here to listen to me, then why are you here?"

"I am charging you with the disposition of this beast," he announced, looking to her work bench again. "Surely some of these powders and potions can concoct some kind of lethal response to him."

Ellianta looked away and set her jaw, drawing a deep breath to calm herself before she replied. "Mayor, I am a healer. I don't concoct poisons or magic potions in here."

"But you do control magic," he countered. "I've seen it myself. That weave of twigs you wield as a weapon could cause this dragon all kinds of harm, much like it did those men in the village last summer."

"I was defending myself and you know it."

"Of course you were," he drawled. "The lottery is losing favor among the people."

Her eyes shifted back to him and she informed, "It should never have had their favor. Now if you will excuse me, I have much work to do before the winter sickness returns to the village. Good day."

He did not take the hint and just shook his head. "That sickness you speak of is no doubt of your own design to keep people dependant on you."

"It plagued the village for decades before I was born. You know that as well as I."

"No one knows how old you truly are," he observed. "A witch who is a hundred could look as a young woman in her prime, just like you."

"I'm a Wiccan," she corrected again.

"Of course you are," he said with a nod. Raising a hand to her face, he gently stroked her lips with one finger. "You've never married. You've never even lain with a man."

She turned her face from him and took a half step back. "I've no time for a husband. I'm the only healer for twenty leagues around here."

He nodded again. "I see. No time for a husband, and no time for a suitor. No time to lay with a man…"

Her eyes widened a little and darted among the cluttered work bench. Somewhere there was the wand she had crafted many seasons ago out of twigs from the forest and a red gemstone woven into the end of it. With a hot piece of metal, she had scribed tiny Latirus words on it in carefully selected places. It was to wield the power of the forest, to defend herself when she had to. And now, it would have to be called on for that once again.

"You claim to be how old?" he asked.

"Twenty-six," she replied, her eyes finally locking on the wand she sought.

"And still a virgin," he observed. "A pretty little virgin at that." He looked over his shoulder at the guard who stood behind him. "Do you think our dragon would like this one?"

The guard smiled and nodded. "I would. Anyone would."

Looking back to her, something sinister took the Mayor's eyes and he announced, "I think there will be no lottery this month. No, I think a virgin of our village has committed crimes against the people and the dragon shall be offered instead a pretty little criminal."

Slowly pulling her arms apart, Ellianta stared up at him

and shook her head. "I've done nothing wrong. I've been the village healer since I—"

"Living here alone," the Mayor interrupted, "plotting who knows what kinds of mischief, perhaps plotting to bring down a plague on the village that only you can cure."

Shaking her head, she insisted, "That isn't true!"

"Someone's baby disappeared," he informed, glancing about her house. "Will we find the poor infant's corpse here?"

She backed away a few steps, a little panic surging forth as she cried, "That is a lie! You know I don't—"

"I know no such thing," he informed straightly. "You, my dear, are guilty of heresy, and after your trial you will make a fitting sacrifice to the dragon you have refused to rid us of."

She took another step back away from him and held her hand toward the work bench, and her wand responded by flying right to her palm. The red stone flashed to life and she swept it toward the mayor and his guard, a crimson light spraying forth and slamming into them with enough force to knock them down. Sensing the man behind her, she tried to spin around but was too slow and her wrist was caught in his hand and twisted brutally behind her as he plucked the wand from her. Twisting and wrenching her body to free herself, she saw her wand tossed toward the Mayor right before her other wrist was grabbed and twisted behind her. Her legs were kicked from behind and she was forced to her knees.

The other guard reached her first and knelt down before her, and the Mayor approached from behind him with her wand in his hand.

"Stop this!" she ordered.

"Or what?" was his response. "Now, you've assaulted the Mayor and his guards, all because we came to plead for your help."

The guard in front of her untied her sash and the man behind pulled it from her as he held her wrists together with his other hand. When she twisted and struggled to free herself, the guard before her took her throat and squeezed hard. She felt her sash being wound around her wrists and she struggled harder to free herself. Panic was in her eyes and a whimper escaped her as she fought to suppress it, to free herself.

Taking her chin in his hand, the Mayor forced her eyes to his and shook his head, looking upon her with some kind of mock sympathy. "Shh. There now, stop your complaining." He nudged the guard, who released her throat at the silent command.

As the man behind her finished tying her wrists, she was seized by the arms and forced to stand. Her robe opened slightly and the Mayor took notice, slowly reaching to her again and sliding the robe open a little more. "Such a pity. You are so lovely, so perfect."

She looked away as he slid the robe from one shoulder and his hand glanced across her breast. "Please stop this. Please." Tears blurred her vision and she blinked to make them stop.

"Look at me, girl," the Mayor commanded. She did not and the man behind her grabbed her hair and wrenched her head back, forcing her eyes back to the Mayor. When he had her attention again, he raised his chin slightly and smiled a little. "I so hate to see someone so young turn to a life of lawlessness."

"Okay," she offered. "You win. I'll do what I can about the dragon. I'll try to drive him away. Please, just stop this,"

"Oh, no," he drawled. "It is much too late for that, and I don't believe that you would take care of our problem anyway. You've already assaulted me and made your feelings quite clear. No, you are going to stand trial, you are going to be convicted of attacking me and of heresy, and you are going to be sacrificed to the dragon."

Shaking her head, she pled, "Please don't. Please, my Lord. I... I'll do whatever you want. Please don't do that to me."

"I can't trust you anymore," he said with an almost apologetic tone as his fingers brushed tenderly across her cheek. "If I just let you go now there is no telling what kind of revenge you would bring down on me."

"I won't," she assured desperately as he brushed the robe from her other shoulder. "Please, I promise! I swear! I'll rid you of this dragon. I'll… I'll be your humble servant as I've always been!"

He looked to the man behind her and ordered, "Take her to my carriage, and be sure that when she arrives at the village, she is still a virgin, and a fitting sacrifice for our dragon." His eyes glanced over her body again. "And see to it she is kept bound until her trial. We wouldn't want her to strike a curse upon us now would we?"

She watched helplessly as he turned and made for her door, and as she was forced that way herself, she whimpered, "Please, don't."

**

The cell she was held in was only about three paces by three paces. A wooden plank was mounted in the bare stone wall about knee high to serve as both a place to sit and her bed. But for a little hay on the dirt floor, there were no comforts in here, only four stone walls and a timber roof overhead. The door was also of heavy timber and here is where the only window was, and through it came the only light.

She sat on the plank bed, her hands now bound before her by course rope. She stared at the hay on the floor, trying to reason out how this had come to pass, trying to calm her restless mind.

Most of the day came and went and but for the occasional voices outside she was all alone.

Light poured in through the window and she knew the sun was setting.

Flinching as she heard the clatter of the lock outside opening, Ellianta's eyes snapped to the door as it swung ajar and she raised her chin slightly as Mayor Trogden strode in with his hands folded behind him.

With slow steps, he wandered to the center of the cell and

stopped, staring ahead of him as he seemed to ponder his words.

Ellianta watched him nervously, shrugging her shoulders up slightly as the tension in the small cell grew.

At long last he turned toward her, looking down on her with authority and contempt. He allowed her uneasiness to grow with a long silence, and finally he informed, "You are to be tried in the morning, and executed in the afternoon."

She swallowed hard, trying to suppress her fear and she asked, "If I am already guilty then why bother trying me?"

The Mayor smiled slightly. "A formality, my dear."

"I know how to rid us of the dragon," she informed.

"Do you, now?"

Nodding, Ellianta continued, "I know how. He can be driven off if we can find a unicorn." When he laughed, she found herself growing desperate and tried to explain, "I've read all about unicorns and dragons. They are bitter enemies, and if we can find a unicorn that is powerful enough he might be convinced to attend this dragon. Unicorns can kill dragons."

Shaking his head and wearing a broad smile, the Mayor laughed again and said, "Oh, you are an amazing piece of work, aren't you? We both know that unicorns are made-up stories told to little girls. They aren't real and you would have us find one, anyway."

"They are real," Ellianta insisted.

"Yes, I saw that painting above your bed. Only true believers can see them, I hear, and those of education never will. I wonder why that is? No, little girl, we'll not waste valuable time to try and find one."

She leaned toward him, desperately saying, "But the maidens you've been feeding to this dragon are just what you need to find a unicorn! Unicorns will always—"

"A shame about your little painting," the Mayor interrupted. "It seems that your house was searched for evidence, and someone knocked something over which ignited, and the fire could not be controlled. Oh, it was a horrible mess."

Her lips parted, her eyes widened and she shook her head slowly. "You… You burned my house?"

"Oh, we found what we needed," he informed, "but your house could not be saved. Even if you manage to get out of here, you will have nowhere to go."

"That was my mother's house!" she cried.

"A shame about her, too," the Mayor drawled. "A lovely woman, really. And she died so mysteriously. So fortunate that you were there to claim her house."

Tears filled Ellianta's eyes and she looked away from him.

"Truly a shame," he went on. "Truly. And truly a shame that her daughter, a healer, could not help her."

"I was fifteen," she strained to say through clenched teeth, her eyes locked on the door.

"And a season later you were curing the sick," he continued. "Amazing what one can learn in a season. Simply amazing."

"I did everything for her I could," she spat, trying not to cry.

"I know you did," he drawled, sounding as if he was trying to console a child. "A pity your father could not be there to help you. Oh, but then you never knew him, did you?"

She did not answer, nor would she even look at the Mayor.

He smiled a little. "Of course you didn't. I suppose your mother was both a witch *and* a whore, wasn't she?"

"Please leave," she asked softly.

In three slow strides he was upon her and he took her chin, forcing her eyes to him. Slowly shaking his head, he softly said, "Such a shame."

Ellianta turned her eyes away, then tensed as he stepped even closer and propped a knee beside her and pushed her against the wall. As he bent toward her, she shrank away and whimpered, "What are you doing?"

His grip on her chin tightened and he forced her head back against the stone wall and bent closer to her. With his mouth a finger length from hers, he informed in a low voice, "You don't have to die a virgin tomorrow."

She raised her bound hands to his chest and tried to push him away, but he took her wrists and forced her hands back down.

"None of that," he warned. He forced his lips to hers and she shrieked behind the kiss he forced to her. He was a powerful man and she could not hope to match his strength.

Managing to twist free of him, she turned her head aside and warned, "You do not want to do this to me. Please go."

"You wish to die tomorrow?" he asked straightly.

"You mean to kill me anyway. Now stop!"

He took her robe and pulled it brutally from one shoulder. "I am in control here, little girl. You are mine to do with as I please."

She tried to pull away again as his mouth attacked her neck and she warned, "I should be a virgin when you give me to that dragon. He will know! The dragon will know!"

"How is that my concern?" he snarled as he pushed himself closer to her, pulling her robe down further."

"I've read all about them!" she cried desperately. "He will smell you on me no matter how much you wash me after."

He hesitated and pulled back a little.

"If he smells you," she continued, "he will come for you next, and no number of guards or soldiers will stop him."

He pulled back more and looked down into her face.

She glared back. "Go ahead and rape me. Go ahead. You deserve to die with me."

Trogden stood from her and backed away, then he turned toward the door.

Before he left, Ellianta called after him, "My regards to your wife, Mayor."

He hesitated, then departed.

As the door locked behind him, Ellianta pulled her robe back up, and wept.

CHAPTER 2

They came for her early for her trial, but she was already awake. She had not slept. Taken to the spacious town hall, the largest stone building in the village, by four of the Mayor's guards, she was not given the opportunity to change into something more appropriate than her robe, nor did she even have her sash to keep it closed. With her hands still bound before her, keeping it closed was a challenge with each step.

Ellianta kept her head down as she was paraded through the village toward the town hall, and it seemed the whole village was out to jeer at her.

Finally inside, she was taken through the crowd of people who waited inside to see her trial. Escorted to the box for the accused, an elaborate, raised wooden structure less than a pace square and shin high, she was forced up in it and a brass chain was hooked from one side of the opening to the other, seemingly to keep her in.

She kept her eyes down for the most part, but finally looked up as the Mayor, now dressed in black robes and a white headpiece that looked more like something a clergyman would wear, finally entered through a side door and walked behind the wide bench at the end of the room. Two other, similarly dressed men entered behind him.

They took their seats behind the bench, Mayor Trogden sitting in the center, and they shuffled parchments and mumbled amongst themselves as they prepared for the trial.

Against the whole village and the village elders and Mayor, Ellianta would stand alone.

Another man entered, carrying a heavy book that was bound in leather. He was also dressed in black but wore no headpiece. Clearly in his fifties, this was a thin man who was often seen in the company of the Mayor or the village leaders.

As he stood before the court bench, which had the men behind it looming over everyone in the room by half a height over a standing man, he raised a hand and the people who had come to see the trial fell silent. Slowly, he opened the book, and turned a few pages.

Ellianta turned her eyes down again.

Looking back down to his book, the scribe announced, "Be it known that this day the Village Court is convened to hear charges brought against Citizen Ellianta. These charges, brought justly by the Village Elders and the Village Mayor are as follows: Practice of witchcraft, heresy, assault on the Mayor," he turned his eyes to her, "and murder."

Her attention snapped to the scribe, then she saw the men who carried the wooden box into the room. It was a pace long, half that wide and was not covered. As they put it down, her eyes widened and locked on what was inside, and her lips slowly parted.

The scribe continued, "The accused will now answer the charges."

Looking to her, the Mayor ordered, "You will answer the charges. Have you practiced the dark arts?"

She did not answer and her eyes were locked on the box.

"You will answer!" he roared.

Ellianta finally tore her gaze away, turning her eyes down and away.

Another of the elders leaned forward and folded his hands on the bench. He was a far older man and regarded Ellianta cruelly as he demanded, "Do you contest these charges?"

She knew in her heart they would find her guilty regardless. All of the weight was against her. The village was against her. She could find no hope or comfort anywhere. With tears welling up in her eyes, she softly replied in a voice more befitting a little girl, "No."

"Then you admit guilt of heresy?" the same elder pressed.

Still staring blankly aside, she nodded slowly and strained to say, "Yes."

"You admit guilt of witchcraft?"

Again she replied, "Yes."

"You admit guilt of assault on the Mayor of this village?"

With another nod she answered, "Yes."

"You admit guilt of murder?"

She tightly closed her eyes and bowed her head.

The Mayor announced, "Then you are clearly guilty of all of the charges. You are justly sentenced to death and sentence is to be carried out an hour past high sun. We are adjourned."

With that, the three men behind the bench collected their parchments and stood, filing out of the door they entered from.

Taken back to the small stone cell to await her death, she sat quietly on the wooden plank that was her bed and stared across to the wall on the other side. She had been offered no food, no water, and no company. All feared what could happen to them if they listened to her, how her words might influence their thoughts. Rumors grew around her like wildfire, how looking her in the eyes could make one her zombie slave, how her words could melt one's soul, how if she got her hands free she could weave spells of horror and disease from the straw on the floor of her cell. So, she was kept under heavy guard all morning, and she heard outside how the very people she had healed and treated for injury, fed sometimes and advised most of her life had turned so quickly against her.

Some hours later and just after high sun the door opened and several women in white entered. None looked at her and all carried something, one a basin of water, one a plate of food, one a towel. Ellianta did not stand as the first people she had seen since her trial entered. She just sat there and watched them go to task, her eyes glancing from one to the next.

One of them, the oldest of them with graying black hair stood before her and took her chin in her hand. Ellianta recognized this as a woman she had helped through a long night of difficult childbirth some time ago and her vision was blurred by tears.

The woman just stared at her for long seconds, then finally

said, "You will be washed and fed, my dear, and readied for your sacrifice to the dragon. Please know that we are not your enemies, and I wish for your last hours to be comfortable. Please let me make them so."

Hesitantly, Ellianta nodded, and she offered in a whisper, "Thank you."

Some hours later, the women emerged into the sunlight with Ellianta among them. Many guards strode forward and the women in white abandoned her. Two guards each seized an arm and she was brutishly rushed to the waiting wagon, which was adorned with flowers and had a wooden step set in place. It was white and pretty, pulled by a white horse, and was a horrible sight to a young woman who feared the death that was to come. All around her the villagers jeered and mocked her, many shaking their fists and shouting.

The ride to the canyon and the dragon's lair seemed very short and before she realized she was being led by the arms down the trail and to the bottom of the ten height deep canyon. Twice that wide, it was relatively flat at the bottom and had been chiseled away at for many decades. Cut stone still littered the bottom, but a smooth trail was cleared for the purpose of leading condemned maidens to their deaths.

Normally, she would look around her surroundings with great interest, as she had never been here before, but today her eyes were locked on the charred, wooden pillar before her, and she gasped as she saw the remnants of a rope still hanging from the iron ring, a rope that still bound two skeletal hands and the bones of one arm to the elbow still dangling from it. That was all that remained of the last girl to be sacrificed a month ago. The dragon had torn her hands off of her as he had wrenched her from the pillar!

"Oh, no," she wept as they forced her closer.

All around her, villagers watched from the canyon rim and their perches along the walls as she was taken to the pillars, and many mocked her as she began to resist the five men who took her there.

The dragon's lair was right behind where she would be. She would not face the dragon nor would she see him as he emerged, and this fed her growing terror even more.

One of the guards kicked a bleached skull aside as he reached up with his dagger to cut away the rope from the last sacrifice.

Ellianta's robe was cut from her by this same guard, who pulled it from her without gentle movements as another man turned her and pushed her back against the pillar. Another rope was wound around her wrists by this man where her wrists crossed and quickly tied there, then he pulled her hands over her head and fed the other end through the ring above her.

As he worked, she turned her begging, deep blue eyes to him and pled one last time, "Please don't do this to me. Please."

He did not respond as he finished his work nor did he even look at her.

An older man in ornate robes opened an old scroll and recited some Latirus words from it, something he had done many times, then he closed the scroll and led the way back toward the path out of the canyon.

Horns on both side of the canyon began to blow, alerting the dragon that his next sacrifice awaited him.

As she heard the drag of scales and the heavy footsteps behind her, Ellianta closed her eyes and rested her head back against the pillar, took a deep, broken breath, and prayed, "Father Sky, Mother Land, please bring me a hero. Please bring me a brave soul to save me from this horror."

She prayed this over and over, her words finally trailing off to a whisper. She had read stories of maidens such as her, of damsels who were saved from dragons and other monsters by a dashing and handsome knight or some warrior whose goal seemed to be to rescue others.

Hearing the dragon drawing closer, she closed her eyes more tightly and pled, "Please! Please Father Sky! Please

Mother Land! I need you!" She finished in a scream, "Please help me! Please!"

A growl, then a grunt broke her concentration and she slowly opened her eyes, looking to her right. All of the color left her face as she saw the dragon staring back at her. Its head was almost a man's height from the ground and scaly lips drew away from its many hand length, sharp teeth. It was only a pace away, close enough for her to feel its breath on her, breath that stank of its last meal. Orange, serpentine eyes had her in their gaze. The time for prayer was over. Her fate was sealed.

She whimpered and cried, struggling to pull her hands free as her wide eyes were locked on the beast that meant to kill her. Her panic was spent quickly and her heart resigned to the death that was only a pace and a moment away from her, and for this she wept.

Its jaws opened slowly and a forked tongue lanced forth and danced up and down her body.

Screams from the canyon all around usually preceded the maiden's death, and as all those white teeth glistened in the sunlight she closed her eyes and turned her head the other way.

A bang, a crash sent tremors through the canyon and stones of every size cascaded from the walls, rolling to the canyon floor.

The dragon's breath no longer hit her and she heard it take a few steps aside, and it growled.

Opening her eyes, Ellianta looked toward it, seeing it was facing down the canyon.

And then her eye caught the huge black form directly in front of her. She slowly turned her head forward and up, her eyes widening as far as they could go and her lips parting as her mouth slowly opened fully. Her gaze was filled with the biggest creature she had ever seen.

Standing before her and only about sixty paces away, a huge black dragon towered some five men's heights over the canyon floor. His thick arms were folded, his broad wings half spread, and his feet were planted firmly on the rock beneath him, some of which had shattered when he had landed. At the end of his long, thick neck was a head that controlled powerful jaws and black horns swept up and back from behind his pale blue eyes. A long, powerful tail swept casually back and forth behind him as he kept her locked in his gaze. Beneath the heavy armor scales was a network of immensely strong muscles. As the sunlight hit his scales, they reflected jade green and midnight blue back.

A long, tense moment passed.

Finally, the black dragon's body lowered toward the ground, his tail rose up a height, and he strode forward with long, slow steps that shook the ground, his eyes on her as he approached.

The smaller copper dragon opened his jaws and hissed at the much larger one. The black dragon was more than five times his size, and yet he only backed away a step at his approach.

Stopping with his head only two paces away from her, the black dragon's eyes narrowed as he lowered his hands to the ground. The pale blue of his eyes gave way to a red glow that started within the black-red discs at the centers, then an emerald glow as he studied her, and Ellianta could sense tremendous power in him, even as the glow in his eyes faded back to the pale blue there.

Drawing his head back only slightly, the black dragon raised a brow, and a low growl rumbled from him. When the smaller copper dragon hissed at him again, his eyes finally shifted that way, and narrowed again.

The dorsal scales of the smaller dragon stood erect as he arched his back, his jaws opening slightly more.

Other than another soft growl that rumbled from him like distant thunder, the black dragon did not react until the smaller dragon blasted him in the face with a burst of fire. He grunted and flinched back with closed eyes, then looked down to the smaller dragon with a low brow and bared teeth the size of short swords. When the copper dragon still held his ground, the black dragon's jaws swung open and he roared so loud the ground shook.

And the courageous stand of the copper dragon ended with a shriek as he turned almost as a serpent would and scurried back into his lair. In seconds he was gone, not to be seen or heard.

The black dragon grunted through his nose, then he turned his attention back to Ellianta, and stood again, towering over her.

She craned her neck back, unable to look away from those piercing blue eyes of the dragon. Before, she had prayed for a hero, some brave knight or invincible warrior to come to her rescue. That was now a distant thought. No knight or army of knights could stand against a brute of this size and power. Cringing as his hand slowly moved toward her, she whimpered again as she awaited the painful inevitability of her death.

The dragon's hand stopped three paces away and gestured back and forth, and the ropes that bound her crumbled away from her wrists.

Slowly, she lowered her hands, her eyes still locked on the dragon as she gently massaged sore wrists that had been bound for almost two straight days.

Dragon and woman studied each other a moment longer.

He folded his arms again and in a booming voice observed, "Well, you haven't fainted yet. I suppose that's a good sign."

Her chest heaved in a breath when she heard him speak, her lips parting in shock and fear.

Leaning his head, he asked, "Your name is Ellianta?"

Dumbly, she just nodded.

"Excellent. I'd hate to think that I've deprived the wrong dragon of a meal." The dragon glanced up at the canyon rim on one side, then the other. "Looks like the spectators are leaving. Or hiding. No matter. There will be no sacrifice today, anyway." He looked back down at her and reached for her again, this time grasping her around the body and easily lifting her from the ground. The width of his hand engulfed her body from chest to hips and she could feel the strength of his grip. Though she was sure he could crush her with one squeeze, his grip was a gentle one and the true power of this hand was clearly held in check.

A breath shrieked all the way into her as she was swept from the ground and her arms clamped as tightly onto his hand as they could as she watched the canyon floor drop four heights below her. As she looked to the dragon and he opened his wings, she whimpered, "Oh, no," as she realized he meant to fly — with her in his grasp! With two strokes of his powerful wings, the dragon was air born and Ellianta watched the ground grow further and further below, streaking by faster and faster in a dizzying blur. As the wind blew faster across her, she reached to her face more by instinct to hold her spectacles in place, her eyes squinting against the fast moving air.

She did not know how long or how far they flew, but the terror of the first moments surrendered itself to her natural curiosity as they gained more altitude. Far below them was the vast Abtont Forest, a place she had lived her entire life but had never seen from such a perspective. For some time her eyes just swept across the landscape, looking down onto towering trees, into creek and river valleys, over hills and down into clearings and ponds in the forest. In the distance to the northwest a white palace towered out of the forest. Ahead, a vast field of grass was dotted with huge forms she knew were Grawrdox. Steam rose from a place to the south, one that looked as if it was burned right out of the forest itself.

Sometime later the dragon's angle into the wind changed and they began to descend, and her stomach felt as if it was dissolving away within her. Still she fought back the urge to be ill and made her last observations of the land from this angle. She was briefly afraid that he would slam into the treetops, as many of them were only a height or so below them, but she reasoned out that this dragon must have known what he was doing and dismissed that silly fear, instead looking ahead of her at the approaching land. The trees suddenly opened up and she felt the dragon's body change position again. Now the descent was a rapid one and she held her breath until she felt the dragon's feet hit the ground, and she closed her eyes for long seconds as he trotted to a stop. Before she realized he was leaning over to put her down, which he did with surprising gentleness.

Back on solid ground, Ellianta dropped to her knees and settled her behind on her heels as she planted her palms on the ground before her. The grass here was relatively flat, no doubt made so by grazing animals, and where she knelt was a mix of new grass and the soil beneath. It was soft against her and she struggled to collect herself. Drawing a breath, she retreated into her inner senses for a moment, blowing the air from her through pursed lips.

Quickly, reality returned to her and her eyes flashed open. The dragon was still there. Very slowly, she raised her head, her eyes darting to one side to see him standing in the middle of the clearing. He was staring off into the distance with that green glow in his eyes. Seeing him from the side, she got a better look at him. Similar to the copper dragon, this one had heavy dorsal scales that ended in points running from between his eyes all the way down his back and to the end of his long tail. The scales grew larger as they ran down his back, the largest ones right below his shoulders. They grew smaller after. Slightly smaller scales flanked these all the way from his head, down his neck and body, to the end of his tail. From this angle, his muscles seemed even bigger. His armor made him seem invincible; his strength and the bulk of muscle made him seem unstoppable.

Ellianta pushed herself up and stood, looking up at this huge dragon with fearful eyes. There was really nowhere to run here and the trees of the forest were too far away to allow her to hide from him, not that she was confident she could. Swallowing back her fear, she raised her chin and pushed her spectacles up the bridge of her nose. The dragon had spoken to her before, frightened off the other dragon, and seemingly flown her to safety, and what he wanted of her now was a complete mystery.

She drew another breath and held her arms straight down and her palms toward the ground. Hesitantly, she asked, "What will you do with me now?"

His eyes slid to her, then his head turned toward her and down.

She swallowed hard as he just stared at her. "Um," she stammered, "my name is Ellianta."

"We've established that already," he boomed.

Ellianta cringed a little and nodded, drawing another deep breath, this time with some difficulty. "May I ask… Um, what do you…" Her breath escaped her again. She needed to know, but really did not want to. She cringed again as he turned fully and she took a few steps backward.

Sitting catlike before her, the dragon leaned his head and asked, "So how long has your village been doing that?"

She glanced away from him, but only for an instant. "Doing what?"

He turned his eyes up and growled through clenched teeth, "Sacrificing girls to that dragon."

"Oh!" she declared. "Um, almost five seasons, I think."

"Hmm," rolled from the dragon's throat as he looked back to her. "I wasn't aware that anyone still did that. Of course, that species does have a taste for your kind."

She raised her brow, hopefully. "You mean you don't?"

He snarled a little. "Sorry, but I have a much more sophisticated pallet than that. I'm guessing you were chosen in a lottery or some nonsense like that?"

Tight lipped, she shook her head and replied, "I was condemned for crimes that they made up. The Mayor wanted me to concoct something to use against the dragon, but that is not my purpose. I am a healer."

"I see," the dragon said with a nod. "If they wanted rid of the little dragon, why didn't they just quit feeding him? He would have moved on looking for food."

She thrust her hands up at the black dragon and declared, "That's what I kept telling them!"

Raising a brow, the dragon nodded again. "And instead of taking your advice, they elected to placate him by sacrificing their only healer to him. Sounds about like the logic of your kind."

"The Mayor is a short sighted man," she informed straightly. "I've never liked him and I don't understand why he stays in power." She bit her lip and raised her brow a little, and it arched in the middle. "May I ask what it is you want me for?"

"I don't want you for anything," was his reply. "Someone asked me to go and find you."

"That's how you knew my name," she guessed.

"That would be how," he confirmed.

"What do I do now?"

"You wait for him to arrive."

"I'm afraid," she confessed. "I've never been away from home before."

"Then take some time to explore your surroundings." He looked toward the West. "I have something to attend to. Just wait here until he arrives."

When the dragon stood, Ellianta felt a little near panic and her eyes widened. He was a dragon, the most powerful creature she had ever encountered, but in a strange place he was the only thing remotely familiar to her and his presence was something she drew security from. As he began to stride away and opened his wings, she darted after him shouting, "You are leaving me here alone? You... You aren't going to stay with me?"

He stopped and looked down at her. "You're afraid to be left alone in the forest? I was under the impression that you spent quite a lot of time out here."

"That was at my home," she cried. "I don't know what's even out here."

"Good time to find out," the dragon countered, turning to take to the wind again.

"Wait!" she bade, and when she had his attention, she scrambled for some reason to keep him from leaving her. Her eyes darted about as she stammered, "Uh, it… It may not be safe for me here all alone. Someone could —"

"You aren't alone," he cut in.

Shaking her head, she watched as he took to the sky, finally calling after him, "But I'm naked down here!"

"It isn't cold this time of year," he called back.

Now feeling vulnerable as she stood in the middle of the field, she crossed her arms over her chest and looked around her, suddenly aware of the breeze that caressed her skin. Goosebumps raised themselves up all over her as she scanned the forest around her. Anything could be out there, or anyone, and horrible things began to flash through her mind.

She did not know how long she stood there looking about her, but she finally picked a direction and walked hesitantly that way, toward the trees. There were certain parts of the forest she had haunted near her home, but she only rarely strayed beyond them in recent seasons. Now the world seemed much, much bigger, and unknowns teased her imagination without mercy.

Once at the trees, she found a boulder that had been pushed up by tree roots and swept her hand across it to clear away any dust or dirt that might be on it before she turned and sat down on it. Her brow arched with uncertainty, she sat huddled on the knee-high boulder with her legs pressed together and her arms over her chest. Her eyes still darted about and anxiety squirmed within her stomach. This is not how she thought her day would go. At least had the other dragon killed her, the demons that lurked beyond her imagination would be gone. Now they were everywhere, behind every tree, under every stone, in the thick of the grass, perhaps lurking in the treetops. Only one thing was clear: An uncertain future awaited her.

Pushing her spectacles up again, she rubbed her weary eyes, then she pulled them off and bowed her head toward her hand as she ran the fingertips of one hand up and down her forehead. This had always calmed her and helped her clear her mind and soothed the restlessness within her that always seemed to be about. She drew a deep, soothing breath as she sat there slowly massaging her forehead. Life had been so good before. Her work and the people she helped had filled her days with joy and often excitement. How she would miss those days.

For some time she just daydreamed of days past and had almost lulled off into a shallow sleep when her inner senses flashed to life. She slowly lowered her hand and blinked her eyes open again, just staring at the ground as she felt a presence close by her. Very close. Hesitantly looking up, just a little, she saw hooves perhaps three paces in front of her, big bronze hooves, and a surge of fear raced through her again. Raising her eyes further, she saw the blurry image of a bay horse, a big one, standing right before her. She could not make out a rider, but thought she saw one on its back. Her arm rose up to her chest in a futile effort to conceal some of her as she raised her head fully and squinted to try and bring the big form into focus.

It whickered and shifted slightly.

With slow movements, Ellianta raised her spectacles to her face and awkwardly pushed them into position with one hand, and when it came into focus, she lost her breath at the sight she beheld.

It was not a horse at all! It was a unicorn! He was a big, brown-red stallion with a glossy black mane and tail that fluttered ever so gently on the slow breeze, as did the black beard beneath his chin. Brown eyes that looked sharper and more focused than any horse's would studied her and copper ribbons within the spirals of his horn glistened in the scant rays of sunlight beneath the tree she sat under. He was a muscular beast, and much larger than the unicorns she had heard of in all of the legends and all of the scripts she had ever read.

Having never seen a unicorn before, Ellianta found herself completely consumed with the magnificent creature before her and everything else around her washed away as she stared with wide eyes at this magical beast.

The unicorn leaned his head and whickered again.

Realizing that she was struggling to breathe, and doing so through an open mouth, Ellianta found her vision blurred again, this time by tears, but she did not want to risk looking away or even closing her eyes for an instant, lest this elusive creature disappear forever. Reaching under her spectacles, she rubbed the tears from one eye, then the other, never taking her gaze from the unicorn's. For the first time, work did not matter, finding the stuff she needed for her labors did not matter, her whole life did not matter. All that did was the enchanting creature before her, something she had wanted to see for longer than she could remember. She absorbed every second in his presence and memorized every line and detail about him.

Staring at her half a moment longer, the unicorn finally looked out into the field, then he turned that way and paced toward the center.

"Wait!" Ellianta cried, sliding from the boulder and falling to her knees. When he looked back at her, she extended a hand toward him and begged, "Please, wait. Please! I've wanted to see you since I was a little girl, since…" She breathed in gasps and wept a little, slowly falling forward and planting her other palm in the ground. "Please don't go. Please don't leave me out here all alone."

He looked out into the field again, then threw his head up and whinnied.

Somewhere in the distance he was answered by another

whinny, a higher pitched one.

Ellianta looked that way and her breath caught anew as she saw the magnificent white form galloping toward her through the tall grass. Covering her mouth, she saw the unicorn of legend, and saw the unicorn she had sought for more than twenty seasons.

Solid white she was, snow white, white like the clouds above, a white that sparkled in the sunlight. As she reached them and slowed to a trot, then a walk, Ellianta could see brown eyes looking back at her, and ribbons of gold within the ivory of her horn. A long white mane blew lightly on the breeze and a tail that was just as glistening white swished behind her. When the unicorn's eyes shifted to the big bay, so did Ellianta's and she saw him looking to the smaller white unicorn, looking at her with a certain tenderness in his eyes.

The white unicorn turned and approached the big bay, nuzzling him lovingly, then she turned and paced right up to Ellianta, whickering to her. She leaned her head as she just stared back at the girl and whickered again, then she snorted and looked back to the stallion, who was turning to pace their way.

Daring to close her eyes, she called up her inner senses again, and finally lowered her hand from her mouth. What she heard astonished her and her eyes flashed open again, focusing on the little white unicorn and the sounds she made.

"I don't know," the white unicorn complained, looking to the big stallion. "Humans either understand us or they don't."

Ellianta heard the sounds she made, sounds that were much like a horse would make, but in her mind she could make out words spoken, and understood them.

The stallion stopped at the little unicorn's side, his eyes on Ellianta as he informed, "This one has a good heart and is even unknown by her males. I do sense that she is afraid, but something seems to be distracting her from that."

"You are," Ellianta admitted softly, and when both unicorn's were looking to her, she smiled a little and offered,

"Thank you. I'm not so afraid anymore."

"You're welcome," the white unicorn replied. Her voice betrayed youth, as did her eyes, while the stallion was clearly a much older unicorn, wise and experienced.

"Are you comfortable down there?" the stallion asked suddenly.

Settling her behind on her heels, Ellianta straightened her back and raised her head, glancing from one unicorn to the next, and finally just shrugged as she lacked a suitable answer for him.

The white unicorn approached a few more steps, well within touching distance as she assured, "You will be all right. Someone is coming who will take care of you. He asked us to watch over you until he arrives."

Her brow arching again, the girl asked, "Who is coming?"

"A friend," the stallion answered.

Ellianta nodded, then she reached toward the white unicorn, and hesitantly touched her cheek.

Taking a step closer, the white unicorn lowered her head and turned it slightly to bring the girl's hand close to her ears. "Scratch right there," she ordered, and as Ellianta did, she closed her eyes and whickered softly, "Oh, yes. That's the spot."

Ellianta smiled and her heart pounded with joy.

The stallion jerked his head up and looked to one side, then turned that way and whickered, "Predator. That forest cat again."

The white unicorn looked to him, then approached and said, "We should go and —"

"No, Shahly," the stallion corrected suddenly, pushing her head around with his nose. "I'll go and attend to the forest cat. You two mares just wait here and get acquainted." With that he launched himself into a gallop and was out of sight and earshot in short order.

The white unicorn huffed a breath, then shook her head and approached the girl again, lying to her belly beside her and looking toward where her stallion had disappeared as she absently said, "He was overprotective before, but now he's just becoming…" She shook her head.

"Overprotective of you?" Ellianta asked before realizing.

The white unicorn nodded. "It is a long story." Looking back to the girl, she seemed to smile and informed, "He thinks I have a gift for getting myself into trouble, and I suppose I do. But now it is much worse for him."

"Why?"

The unicorn smiled a little more and announced, "Because I'm going to have a baby."

And now Ellianta smiled as her heart was filled with a joy she had never even imagined.

"Are we the first unicorns you've seen?" the unicorn asked.

Ellianta nodded. "I still feel like I'm dreaming. I was supposed to be sacrificed to a dragon but a big black dragon came along and took me away and brought me here. And now I'm actually speaking with a unicorn. I've wanted to see you since I was a little girl."

The unicorn smiled. "I've heard that a number times from your kind."

Sitting back on her haunches, Ellianta pulled her feet from under her and drew her knees to her, wrapping her arms around them and leaning her head a little as she asked, "Did I hear the other unicorn call you Shahly?"

"You must have," the unicorn confirmed. "That is my name. The stallion with me is called Vinton."

Ellianta smiled a little broader. "And he's going to be a papa."

Nodding, Shahly confirmed, "And he is as proud as any unicorn can be."

The young woman just stared at the unicorn before her for a long moment. "You are as magical as I had imagined and more."

"Only the purest hearts see that," Shahly informed. "You are one who is giving even beyond her own needs. That is rare in your kind."

Looking away, Ellianta nodded humbly. Absently, she rubbed one wrist, which was still sore and bruised from her bindings as her thoughts were thoroughly consumed.

Looking to the young woman's wrist, Shahly turned her head just a little and lowered her horn to the bruising and chafing she saw, touching her wrist with just the glowing tip of her spiral and gently moving her other hand aside.

Ellianta watched in stunned amazement as an emerald glow enveloped her wrist. A soothing coldness wringed her wrist almost as the bindings had, then a gentle warmth replaced the coldness. The pain was swept away, and as the glow about her wrist faded, her eyes widened and she raised her arm before her, seeing that there was no trace of the injuries from the ropes. Feeling that similar coolness on her other wrist, she looked to see the unicorn's horn touching that was as well, and in short order that one was healed. Her eyes glossy with tears, she looked to the little unicorn and offered in a whisper, "Thank you."

Shahly smiled. "You are very dear to someone who is very dear to me." Her eyes narrowed slightly and she asked, "What is that on your face?"

Absently, Ellianta raised a hand toward her temple, feeling the earpiece of her spectacles, then she turned her eyes down and answered, "I have weak vision over a distance and this helps me see."

The unicorn leaned her head. "Really."

Ellianta nodded. "I know. They make me look silly, don't they?"

"Not at all," Shahly corrected. "I thought they were an ornament. I've seen your kind wear such ornaments before. I have one, myself." She raised her nose to show her human companion the amulet that hung by a thin gold chain around her neck.

"It's beautiful," Ellianta said softly as she saw the golden raptor's talon gripping the emerald sphere. "Where did you get it?"

Lowering her nose, Shahly replied, "A gift from a dear friend. It was something I needed once, now it is just something I cherish."

"I had never heard of unicorns possessing such things."

"Most don't. I am just a fortunate unicorn, I suppose."

Ellianta smiled. "And I am a fortunate woman to know a unicorn." Something touched her inner senses and she raised her head a little, her eyes darting about. It was a presence, a powerful and familiar presence, one drawing closer. A dragon's presence! The black dragon was coming back!

Shahly saw and felt the fear around the girl and asked, "What is it?"

"You need to go," Ellianta said straightly. Having read every script on both dragons and unicorns that she could get her hands on, she knew they were enemies, and she also knew that this small unicorn had no chance against that dragon when he returned. She sprang to her feet and brushed off her backside, ordering, "You must go! Hide in the forest, quickly."

Shahly looked over her shoulder, out toward the field, then back up at the girl and asked, "What is wrong? I don't sense anything dangerous coming."

Looking toward the field, Ellianta shrieked a gasp as she saw the black dragon sweep in and land on the other side. She heard the stallion whinny and the black dragon turned toward him in response and growled. "Oh, no," she breathed, backing away a step. The dragon was approaching and her mind whirled as she was consumed with how to protect this little unicorn and her unborn baby.

Shahly looked over her shoulder again, right at the approaching dragon, then she stood and turned fully toward him. She raised her head as she watched him draw closer, her ears swiveling that way and she sighed away what could have only been frustration.

Ellianta took the unicorn's side and gently placed a hand on her back, watching fearfully as the dragon approached.

And then she noticed the stallion walking at his side, looking up at him, and snorting.

The dragon looked down at the stallion, and even from that distance Ellianta could make out what was said.

"Allowing such a predator within a league of her is about as irresponsible as it gets, Plow Mule!"

Vinton snorted again and countered, "*You* wrote the book on irresponsible. And I had the cat dealt with!"

"Sure you did. Just like you've dealt with all of the other things that have come along that I had to attend to myself."

"The worst thing that's ever happened to her is you, dung-head."

The dragon looked toward the girl and unicorn. "And once again your memory fails you."

"My memory is just fine!"

"Get fleas and die."

Shahly snorted and stomped toward them. "You two promised that you would not argue around me anymore!"

Ellianta gasped again, raising her hand to her mouth as she made the startling realization that this dragon knew these unicorns.

Ten paces away, the dragon sat catlike in the field and looked down at the little unicorn as he countered, "We aren't arguing. We're debating."

Shahly's eyes darted from the dragon to the stallion and back and she flattened her ears against her head. "I do not want to have an angry foal because you two can't get along around me!"

Dragon and stallion glanced at each other, then Vinton defended, "Shahly, we argue anyway and our baby won't be born angry because of it."

Her eyes narrowed.

Stallion whickered, dragon growled and they both looked away from her.

A voice announced from behind, "It's just something to get used to, my dear."

Ellianta spun around, covering her chest with both arms as she saw the old man emerge from the forest.

He had long white hair and a long white beard, and wore a smile. His ancient eyes were locked on Ellianta with a stare that was not of hungry lust, but one of joy at seeing one who was absent for some time. He wore the green robes of a wizard and carried a walking staff. His bushy white eyebrows were raised high above his eyes as he approached.

The unicorn looked over her shoulder, and when she saw the old fellow she spun around and whinnied, "Leedon!" as she galloped the last few paces to him.

When she reached him and nuzzled his chest and shoulder, he slipped his arm around her neck and hugged her tenderly, asking, "How is the lovely mother-to-be today?"

"I'm great!" she replied.

The old fellow looked back to Ellianta, and slowly approached her again, his eyes on hers as he greeted, "Good day, my dear. I trust the journey here was not too traumatic for you?"

Ellianta found herself unable to respond and just stared back dumbly.

Shahly bounded around him and positioned herself between the old man and the girl, looking to him as she declared, "You should not see her like this! It isn't proper!"

With a soft laugh, the old man stopped where he was and shook his head. "You are right as usual, Shahly. Where are my manners?" He dropped his walking staff, then he made a fist and reached between his index finger and thumb with two fingers from his other hand, then slowly withdrew it, pulling a white cloth from his fist as he did.

As Ellianta watched with wide eyes from behind the unicorn, the old man pulled a white dress seemingly out of thin air, then he held it up for her to see, asking, "Is this to your liking?"

She looked it over, seeing that it was just a simple little spring dress. It was sleeveless with finger width straps that held it up, and it appeared to be the perfect size for her.

Finally recognizing him as a wizard, Ellianta leaned her head over a little, her eyes narrowing as she spat, "Well I hope you got a good look at me, wizard."

He closed the last few paces between them with four strides and held the dress to her, countering with a smile, "You've nothing I haven't seen a hundred times, Ellianta."

Her mouth fell open as she took the dress and she just stared at him as she slowly pulled it over the unicorn's back. Feeling a little frustrated, she asked, "How is it everyone knows me here?"

"I've known you your whole life, child," the wizard replied. "I've been watching you for twenty-five seasons."

"I'm twenty-six," she countered.

He nodded. "I know you are. I also know your gifts have grown wildly since you came of age. I know that you've devoted your life to people who would end up betraying you."

She turned her eyes down to the dress she held as she felt the sting of the last few days.

"Get yourself dressed," the old wizard said sympathetically, "then we can talk at length."

When she raised her eyes to him again, he had turned his attention to the dragon and was walking around the unicorn toward him.

Shahly maneuvered herself around the girl to keep her out of the wizard's line of vision, then she looked to her and asked, "Aren't you going to put that on?"

Looking back to the dress, Ellianta nodded, and then set about the brief task of slipping into it. She discovered that it fit her absolutely perfectly, and she absently smoothed it over her belly and hips. As was the style of the time, the neckline was rather low, but tastefully so and trimmed in a pretty lace. She smiled a little as she saw it, and when she did embroidered flowers of yellow and pink began to appear in a ring around her waist and just under the lace around her neckline. More bloomed along the straps over her shoulders. A little amazed, she spun around and the skirt, which was also trimmed in lace with blooming yellow and pink flowers around it, belled out as she did. Her hair flailed over her shoulder and settled there as her eyes found the old wizard, and she smiled a little more as he looked back to her.

Nodding, Leedon looked her up and down and said, "It suits you well. I hope you like it."

"I love it!" she declared, more a little girl now than a grown woman. She looked down at it and seized the skirt, pulling it up and apart somewhat to see it more, then she turned her eyes back to the old wizard and said in a girlish voice, "Thank you!"

A broad smile and a nod was all the response he would give, but his eyes grew a little glossy with tears.

The dragon boomed, "This is all very touching, but I believe—"

Raising a hand, the wizard interrupted, "I know, Ralligor, I know. Much to do."

"I'll attend to those other matters and meet you later," the dragon informed. He looked down at the stallion and snarled, "Do you think you can handle things without me for a few hours?"

Vinton shot him a narrow eyed glare and snorted back.

As the dragon stood and turned to take flight, Ellianta strode over to the old wizard, her eyes on the winged form that flew away. She puzzled over the events of the day, and as the dragon flew over the horizon, she finally realized that the old man was staring at her with a strange little smile.

The stallion approached and bumped the wizard with his nose, drawing his attention. "Thank you for allowing us to help in this matter. You've always come to others' aid and I consider it an honor to finally be able to help you."

The wizard tenderly scratched him between the ears. "I should be thanking you, my friend."

"You don't need to," the white unicorn insisted. She

glanced at Ellianta and smiled, then looked to the stallion and raised her head a little. "We should leave them to talk."

He nodded to her ever so slightly and informed, "I saw some of those berries you like near a creek on the other end of the clearing."

Shahly's ears perked and she trotted to her stallion. "We'll see you two later."

Leedon raised a hand to them and bade, "Be well, my friends. I'll see you in the morning."

Though she wished they would not go, Ellianta also, if reluctantly, raised her hand to them and bade, "Be well."

The wizard turned to her and folded his arms. "You are hungry, exhausted, and full of questions."

She looked to him and nodded, still not feeling entirely comfortable with him.

He held his hand out and his walking stick whizzed to it from behind her and settled itself into his palm, then he grasped it and turned toward the field, bidding, "Walk with me, child."

Ellianta took his side and they walked in silence all the way to the middle of the clearing. Her mind whirled. So much had happened the last few days. Her life had been ripped apart, the people she had known her entire life had turned against her. And now she was in a new land, speaking to a dragon and unicorns, enemies who seemed to get along…

"You have so many questions you don't know what to ask first," the old wizard observed.

Tight lipped, she nodded, staring down at the tall grass before them as they walked.

"As I told you before," he said softly, "I've been watching you for a quarter century."

"Putting it like that makes me feel very old," she murmured.

He smiled. "You'll not be old for many, many seasons, child."

She looked the other way, still scrambling to organize her

thoughts.

"Were you happy growing up?" he asked suddenly.

"I suppose so," was her answer.

"No special boy caught your eye when you were younger?" She shrugged again.

They walked in silence as she tried desperately to organize her thoughts.

He shot her a sidelong glance. "How did you end up here, you say?"

It was as good a place to start as any, so she looked to him and replied, "I was rescued from a dragon by that really big dragon and brought here."

"You grew up to be a fine young woman," he observed. "You've cultivated your gift, studying on your own, and you've quite the reputation as someone who is giving, someone who strives to help others in need. You must make your parents very proud." When she looked away from him again, he asked, "What happened to her?"

"My mother, you mean?" She drew a breath, a painful memory surging forth. "I was fifteen seasons old. She had taught me everything I knew and I eagerly learned everything. I loved her and cherished every moment with her." She turned her eyes down. "She got very sick one winter and I… I did everything I could, everything I knew how to do."

"And she passed on anyway," Leedon finished for her.

Ellianta nodded, a tear rolling down her cheek.

"And you faithfully devoted your life to healing the sick and cultivating your Wiccan gifts to help others." He slipped his arm around her and pulled her close to him. "You cannot help but make others proud of you, Ellianta. You've grown into such a fine young woman as to make knowing you an honor to anyone."

She still did not feel that comfortable with him as her eyes showed when she looked his way, but she did not try to twist from his grasp. Something was amiss. She sensed that some missing element of her life would soon reveal itself, and he had the answers.

"Did she ever speak of your father?" he asked suddenly.

Shaking her head, she looked down again and replied, "No, not often. She seemed fond of him in some respects, but..." Her eyes widened and she raised her head, then she pushed away from him and backed away many steps, her wide eyes locked on him.

He did not turn to her right away, he just stood where he was, staring into the distance, and finally he said, "Now you have even more questions."

"You!" she cried. "You just left us! How could you just leave us like that? You could have healed her and you..." Slowly, she shook her head. "How could you just leave us like that?"

The wizard slowly drew a breath and turned his eyes down. "I've wanted to tell you everything for many seasons, Ellianta. I've wanted so badly to..." He raised his head again, staring into the forest before him. "If you would truly like to know everything, I will tell you. You must know first that I didn't leave your mother and you. I left you with the woman that you grew up knowing as your mother."

She stared at him in disbelief for a moment, then pulled her spectacles off and rubbed her eyes. Drawing a breath to calm herself, she found her mind an uncontrollable whirlwind yet again. Many emotions battled within and she did her best to set aside anger and all those related to it. After a moment, she was still tight lipped, but finally put her spectacles back in place and raised her head, looking on him with steely eyes. "Very well, wizard. I want to know all that you do."

CHAPTER 3

Part of Ellianta's gift had always been the ability to feel the emotions of others, just basic emotions, nothing like reading one's thoughts. This was something more involuntary like hearing or seeing something absently.

In the waning hours of a late summer day, she felt everything from this old wizard as they walked silently a path in the forest and he hid not a single emotion from her. She did not know where he was leading her, nor did she even think about it. He seemed to be trying in vain to organize his own thoughts and she would allow him time to do so. In the silence between them, she felt from him many things, like regret, anxiousness, a little shame. They were a whirlwind within him, much the way she often found her own thoughts and emotions.

Finally, she found a question to ask him, a hard question for them both. "Can you tell me why you left me with a woman who was not my mother?"

"To protect you," he replied, "from your birth mother. I have two sons, and as things deteriorated between your mother and me, and as we tried over and over to reconcile, she found herself with child a third time." He took many paces in silence before he spoke again. "I had already seen her influence with my sons. She taught them to seek power and little else. Any teachings I had for them were wasted and in time her influence with them greatly outweighed mine." He thought again, just for a moment. "I have one son who is strong with the gift, though his gift is the *sortiri* and I really had nothing to teach him other than those things of manhood and all that. His mother thought otherwise and, well, when I chose another apprentice for the disciplines in the *wizaridi* that I had developed she thought me… Well, long story short we did not see eye to eye when it came to training our son in the craft. She never forgave me."

"And your other son?" Ellianta asked softly.

Leedon smiled slightly. "Fancied himself a great warrior from the time he could hold a stick as a sword, and his mother indulged him so. Sadly, even with enchanted weapons and armor, it was not enough for him. He would eventually abandon his goal of conquest and turn on others. He would seek the title of Dragonslayer."

Her eyes widened a little, her lips parting in shock. "But... But that's so dangerous."

"He thought he had all of the details attended to. And then came the day he challenged the wrong dragon." Leedon shook his head. "His quest for glory and his greed for power would be his undoing."

"Oh, no," Ellianta breathed. "Did he... Was he..."

"No," the wizard assured. "He is still alive, though he may as well not be."

"What happened?"

"He crossed the wrong dragon." He looked to her. "But I'm thinking that you aren't interested in your brothers right now."

"In time I will be, but I would like to know... Well, I would like to know about my mother, about you, about how I came to be here." She grasped his shoulder, raising her brow a little. "That dragon finding me was more than a coincidence, wasn't it?"

Leedon smiled, his eyes still looking ahead of him. "Like I told you, I've been watching, and everything seemed fine until a few days ago."

She nodded. "When the Mayor came to see me."

"I had to do something, so I sent Ralligor."

"Ralligor," she said softly. "The black dragon."

"My apprentice," he confirmed.

She folded her arms, her brow low over her eyes as she complained, "You know, he almost didn't get to me in time. I was seconds away from having my body ripped apart by that other dragon."

Leedon smiled and nodded. "Ralligor has always preferred a dramatic entrance and I can assure you his arrival was perfectly timed to that end."

She huffed a breath through her nose, looking forward again as she grumbled, "I'll live with the image of all those teeth coming at me for the rest of my life thanks to him."

"Demand an apology at your own peril, child," was the wizard's response.

She looked down and nodded, then smiled a little herself. "You should have seen that other dragon scurry away when Ralligor roared at him. I'd seen what he could do to people, even those armed with axes and swords and wearing armor, but he did not seem fond of the idea of fighting something as big as the black dragon."

"Nor will he," Leedon assured. "Very few creatures have been foolish enough to challenge him and most of them did not live to tell the tale."

More long strides passed in silence.

"I must know something," she informed. "Why did you never come visit me?"

"I always wanted to," he said softly. "God knows I wanted to, but I could not risk her finding out about you. She has Wiccan gifts herself and has ways of watching. I simply did not want her to find you, or find out about you."

"Do you think she would hurt me?"

"I don't know for sure, child. I was never willing to take the risk." Tight lipped, he just stared at the ground for a while, then he finally continued. "You were only a baby when I took you to the village where you grew up."

"Um," Ellianta stammered, "she did not notice that I was gone?"

"You were taken in the night," he explained. "You had been sick, and she was away for a couple of days and left you in my care. I tended your illness easily, and took the opportunity to remove you from her madness. When she returned, she found a grieving father, a grave behind the cottage... One of many miscalculations I've made in my life. She was already on the edge of sanity and that pushed her over. Your death was something else she never forgave me for."

"She sounds like she has a lot of problems within her own heart."

"She wasn't always so. There was a time I loved her like I've never loved before. It was sad to see her change, to see her demand more than the fulfilling, modest life we had and much more sad to see her inject this into my sons."

Ellianta nodded and turned her eyes down. "I wish I had gotten to know you many seasons ago, but I do understand why. Part of me still wants to be angry with you."

"If you must be angry, then be angry."

"I can't," she informed softly. "You are... I just can't."

"You have the right to be, Ellianta. The decisions I made for you were brash and hasty."

"And from the heart of an overprotective father," she finished for him.

Their eyes met, and they offered little smiles to each other.

Ellianta took his arm and pulled herself close to him, leaning her head on his shoulder as she asked, "What should I call you?"

"What do you wish to call me?"

She shrugged. "My feelings cannot be tamed right now and I can hardly think." Her eyes slid to him. "I've always wanted..."

His eyes shifted to her and he reached to her and grasped her hand. "You remind me so of your mother when we first met, when she was the lovely young lady that I fell so easily for."

She raised her brow. "Now I just have to not turn crazy."

He laughed under his breath. "Yes, there is that, but a simple living seems to appeal to you better than the pomp of a royal court."

"I wouldn't mind seeing a royal court someday."

"I'll see to it," he assured. "In fact, I've arranged lodging somewhere that you might like."

"And something to eat?" she asked hopefully.

"Of course," was his answer as he patted her hand.

Their trek continued, as did their talk. Leedon generously shared all of the answers she craved, and she was just as generous with tales of her childhood, and of growing to womanhood. In a couple of hours, she felt herself grow very close to him. He held back no secrets, even of his failings and mistakes, and she felt compelled to do the same.

After a time, and after finding some late season pears growing wild by the road side, they neared a bridge that crossed a broad, slow moving river, and they approached it walking hand in hand.

Smiling a proud smile, his eyes slid to her as he confirmed, "So, you taught yourself Latirus? That is a difficult enough language to learn even with a qualified instructor."

She shrugged. "I come from good bloodlines, I suppose. I read everything I could about the Wiccan disciplines, and even a little about the *wizaridi*. I sometimes wish I had that discipline in me."

"The Wicca suits you far better, child."

Fifty paces away from the bridge, a mist poured out of the river channel and Leedon stopped, pulling back on Ellianta's hand to make her do the same.

Her eyes widened as she watched something horrible emerge.

Gray skin contrasted the green of the landscape all around. Two small eyes that were black pits within pools of white locked them in their gaze. A flat head and low brow, a round flat nose, a heavy jaw and one sharp tooth protruding from its thick lips betrayed it as a river troll. Its body was huge, very thick and as it propelled itself to them on short, stout legs, its hands nearly drug the ground, even though it walked upright. It had little hair on its head and a shiny gray body, and what hair it did have grew long and resembled black moss hanging from an old tree.

Approaching with heavy steps, it looked down on Leedon from almost three men's heights high, an expression of contempt as it stopped only eight or so paces away.

"Well," it drawled in a rumbling deep voice with a snarl to its lip. "Look who has ventured this way again."

Raising his brow, Leedon greeted, "Hello Turkott. I thought you had moved on by now."

"Not with such a profitable bridge as this," the troll informed. "You've always chosen your friends well, wizard, and your enemies foolishly."

"I never chose to have you as an enemy, Turkott."

"And yet I am your enemy. Do you mean to use my bridge without paying me a tribute?"

"As I recall, this bridge was built by Caipiervell Castle, so that kingdom seems to own it."

The troll smiled, revealing huge, yellow teeth as he corrected, "Not anymore. You'll pay me my tribute if you wish to cross, old man."

"I don't carry coin on me, so I suppose we'll just have to go around."

When he started to turn and pull Ellianta with him, the troll took a heavy step toward them and corrected, "No, it's too late for that, wizard. You owe me a tribute."

With a patient sigh, Leedon looked back up to the troll and informed, "I have nothing for you, nor do I wish a confrontation today, so we'll just go about our way."

Taking another step toward them, Turkott snarled again and informed, "I see something I like beside you. Give me the girl and you can go about your way."

Ellianta shrieked a gasp and backed away, still clinging to the wizard as her wide eyes were still locked on the troll.

With a smile and a shake of his head, Leedon patted her hand and informed, "You'll be taking no girl today and I'll not have another confrontation with you. Now move aside and allow us to pass."

Smiling back, the troll laughed a deep laugh under his

breath. "I suppose I'll be taking her, then. Do you think your power is up to dealing with the likes of me, old man?"

"It won't have to be. Now let us pass peacefully."

"And if I don't?"

"Perhaps you should look behind you."

The troll laughed again. "Do you think me a fool, old man?"

Leedon raised his brow. "That all depends on the choice you make in the next few seconds."

Ralligor approached from behind the troll with slow, silent footsteps, his eyes glaring down on him as he drew closer. As Turkott laughed again and cracked his knuckles, the black dragon stopped half an arm's reach away, towering more than two heights over the troll as he folded his arms.

"As I said," the troll thundered, "you choose your enemies very foolishly. After I squash you, the girl will be mine anyway."

Raising her chin slightly, Ellianta suggested, "Perhaps you *should* look behind you."

His small eyes narrowing, the troll growled, "So you are both fools. Perhaps I will squash you both, then." When he heard the low growl, he wheeled clumsily around and stumbled a few paces away from the black dragon as he declared, "Ralligor!"

The black dragon raised a brow, his eyes fixed on the stammering gray form before him.

Leedon looked down and shook his head. "Turkott, Turkott, Turkott. I suppose now you can collect your tributes from him.

The troll swallowed hard, his wide eyes fixed on the dragon's.

A long moment passed, and finally the dragon asked, "Turkott, do you like fire?"

A frantic shake of the head was the troll's answer.

Ralligor took a heavy step toward him and lowered his head, bringing him eye to eye with the troll and their noses less than a pace apart. "This wizard's good health is in your charge now. If anything happens to him, *anything*, while he is in this part of the land, I will hold you personally responsible. And believe me I won't be very happy with you."

Turkott nodded quickly, making the fat and loose skin around his throat giggle and he assured, "They will cross safely, Desert Lord. They both will cross safely. Me word on that!"

Ralligor's eyes narrowed a little more. "See to it you don't threaten anyone else in my favor ever again."

Another frantic shake of the head and the troll agreed, "Never again, Desert Lord."

The black dragon stood fully, glaring down at the troll with a snarl that showed many of his long, sharp teeth. After a terrifying moment, he asked, "Why are you still irritating my eyes?"

Moving faster than he looked like he should have been able to, the troll lumbered quickly back to the river channel and disappeared under the watchful eye of the dragon.

Shaking his head, Ralligor looked back to the wizard and asked, "Why didn't you just put him down, *Magister?*"

With a jolly smile, the wizard answered, "Because I did not want to deprive you the privilege, mighty friend."

The black dragon nodded. "Well, they are awaiting you and you're still two leagues away."

"We'll be there in short order," Leedon assured. "No worries."

"Do you need my further assistance with anything?" the dragon asked.

"Not at the moment, mighty friend, but feel free to accompany us if you wish."

"Another time," the dragon sighed. "I'm going to make sure Plow Mule has Shahly well in hand, or hoof, or whatever he has her in."

As the dragon opened his wings and strode past them, Leedon called back to him, "Very good, Ralligor. Keep her out of mischief and I'll see you in the morning." He shook his head and laughed under his breath as he watched the dragon take to the wind, then he turned and continued on his way toward the bridge, mumbling, "Soft hearted drake."

Still a little fearful of the troll, Ellianta clung to the wizard as her eyes darted about nervously.

Leedon patted her hand and assured, "Oh, don't worry over Turkott. He'll not allow harm to befall us today."

She nodded, and wrapped her arms tightly around his arm anyway.

Hours later they were encountering more and more people and the sun was plunging into the treetops. They never really stopped talking the whole journey, but as they rounded a turn on a well kept road through the forest, Ellianta lost her breath at the spectacular white washed castle before her. Like a wide-eyed little girl she scanned the mountainous structure. The wall, four men's heights tall, was an imposing sight in itself, but the towers that were peaked with high battlements and red, cone shaped roofs were spectacular.

As they ventured through the gate and into the courtyard between the wall and the palace, her eyes darted about at all of the activity, the little wagons and booths scattered about where people sold their goods, the people who wandered about, the guards who watched doorways, patrolled the wall and guarded doors to the palace.

Leedon led her between two of these guards and into the palace itself. Ellianta found herself nervous about walking into someone's palace like this and now her eyes darted around, her brow arched in fear as she just knew that they would be stopped and arrested any moment. Still, she trusted the wizard and stayed close to him.

Striding through an ornately carved set of double doors that were made of some dark red timber, they entered a large room with a long table in the center of it. It was covered with a long white cloth and had many candles burning on it. This was a royal dining hall, and Ellianta felt they had no place here.

Someone cleared her throat behind them and a young voice informed, "You are late for dinner, wizard."

Leedon smiled broadly as they turned toward the girl, who was only about sixteen seasons and dressed in a long blue gown with puffy sleeves, a belled skirt with white ruffles and lace and a gold tiara over her brow. Her long, black hair was restrained behind her by silver cuffs that were spaced a hand length apart. She was a pretty girl, but her eyes were held a little narrow, her brow low, her arms folded, and she was tamping her foot impatiently.

She strode right up to him with long steps and stopped an arm's reach away, her eyes still locked on the wizard's as she scolded, "You make a habit of keeping others waiting, and that could be a habit that lands you in my dungeon."

Now, Ellianta's eyes narrowed and she was another word away from putting this little brat in her place when Leedon pulled away from her and folded his own arms.

"No dungeon yet made can hold a wizard of my power," he warned. "Do your worst, Highness. I stand ready."

The girl raised her brow, a little smile trying to break its way through her lips. "Do you, now? And if I feed you so much you'll be too stuffed to move?" She finally giggled and threw her arms around his neck, squealing, "It's so good to see you!"

He hugged her back as tightly as he dared. "Always you warm my heart, Faelon."

Pulling away from him, she offered another broad smile, then she looked to Ellianta and asked, "Is this who we've been awaiting?"

Leedon took her arm and pulled her to him, introducing, "This is Ellianta. Ellianta, meet Princess Faelon of Caipiervell."

The Princess smiled broadly and extended her hand. "You honor me with your visit, Lady Ellianta."

Ellianta took Faelon's hand and bowed her head to her, offering, "I am honored to meet you, Highness, but I am only a humble healer and servant of the people."

Raising her chin, the Princess withdrew her hand and insisted, "In *my* castle you are Lady Ellianta." She turned and nodded to the wizard, who smiled and nodded back.

"As you wish, Highness," Ellianta agreed with a smile.

Taking her hands again, Faelon said straightly, "You must be famished after that long travel. Please, come and sit down and eat something. I wish to hear all about you."

As she was pulled to the table, she glanced back to the wizard to make certain he was following.

Before anyone could even sit down, a tall, blond haired woman dressed in light armor over her shoulders, some of her chest, her upper arms and her left lower arm walked in. Her legs were bare but for the knee high boots and the greaves she wore over them. Hanging on the thick black belt she wore was a broadsword on the left, a dagger and longer sword-breaker on the right, and a few pouches on the front and sides. She was very attractive, her long hair restrained in a pony-tail behind her. This was a woman in her forties, and the tallest and most muscular woman Ellianta had ever seen!

Walking in with long, slow strides, she half smiled and folded her arms as she loudly said, "Well look what the northern wind has blown in."

Leedon turned and offered her a warm smile as he strode toward her, and they met with a big embrace.

Ellianta leaned toward Faelon and asked, "Is there anyone he does not know?"

The Princess shrugged and replied, "I've never met anyone he doesn't know, man, woman, unicorn or dragon." Just a little shorter, Faelon glanced up to her guest and mumbled, "Here it comes," as Leedon and the tall, muscular woman strode toward them.

Looking the blond woman up and down, Ellianta guessed, "You are from Zondae, aren't you?"

The tall woman nodded once to her.

Leedon introduced, "This is Pa'lesh of Zondae."

"I'm a field captain there," Pa'lesh added, then she turned her eyes to Faelon and finished, "and a babysitter here." She raised her brow. "Did we forget about the inspection of the battlements along the perimeter wall?"

Faelon looked away and folded her arms, confessing, "No, but something else came up."

"I've rescheduled it for first thing in the morning," Pa'lesh informed, "So you are getting up way before high sun."

"Okay," the Princess grumbled.

Looking back to Ellianta, Pa'lesh guessed, "You must be Ellianta. We've been looking forward to your visit."

She nodded to Pa'lesh, knowing fear of her and feeling intimidation the likes of which she had never experienced, not even from the soldiers who would visit her village.

"Okay," Faelon declared, "Let's sit down and eat." She looked to Ellianta and insisted, "I want to know all about you."

**

A full meal was served and everyone enjoyed a wonderful time. Pa'lesh dismissed herself early to attend some castle business but everyone else remained behind to converse over wine and enjoy the company at hand.

A couple of hours later darkness had fallen and Ellianta was shown to a room on one of the upper levels by the Princess herself. Lamps were lit, the huge bed was made but for one corner where the covers had been neatly laid back and many comforts were about.

As Ellianta looked about the room, Faelon took her hands and raised her brow as their eyes met. "I know you've had a trying time, and I know you are in a strange place, but I want you to sleep well and be comfortable, and don't emerge from here until you are ready."

Leedon leaned on the doorjamb and folded his arms, a certain warmth in his eyes as he watched them.

Ellianta glanced at him, then turned her eyes down. "Why all this fuss over a renegade Wiccan?"

The Princess took her chin and raised her face up. "You are

the daughter of a man who is very important to me, someone who has always been there for me whether I knew it or not. But for him I would be dead and my snake of an uncle would be on the throne. As far as I am concerned you are my sister."

Tears blurred Ellianta's eyes once again and she whispered, "Thank you."

Faelon grasped the sides of Ellianta's head and pulled her close to kiss her on the cheek, then she hugged her and whispered, "You sleep well, okay?"

Ellianta hugged her back and assured in a whisper, "I will. You, too."

The Princess pulled away and strode to the door, reaching up to kiss the wizard on the cheek as she passed, ordering, "You sleep well too."

"As you wish," he assured. When she was out of the room, he looked back to Ellianta with fatherly eyes. "I trust you are going to be well the rest of the evening?"

Tight lipped, she nodded, then she smiled a little and walked to him, kissed his cheek and slipped her arms around him, whispering, "Good night, Papa."

He hugged her as tightly as he could, laying his cheek on her head. "Good night, my sweet Ellianta."

CHAPTER 4

Ellianta did not remember sleeping so deeply before, but three trying days had surely taken their toll. Her eyes opened slowly and she drew a deep breath, blinking the sleep from her as she raised her arms over her and stretched. The night had been a chilly one, but the beddings were very warm, the mattress very soft, and the sheet she lay on was smooth against her bare skin. The sun was shining into her window and had been up for some time. Normally, she would not have slept so long, as she considered sleep to be a horrible waste of her time, but today that did not seem to matter.

She took her time getting up, and when she did sit up, she rubbed her eyes, then finally stood and looked around at the blurry room for the water basin. She finally sat back on the bed and groped about the night stand for her spectacles, recognizing them by feel and pulling them onto her face. And right there on the night stand was the water pitcher, the basin, and a towel.

After refreshing herself a little and washing the sleep from her face and eyes, she padded over to the wardrobe where she had hung her dress before going to bed. A few other dresses were in there and Faelon had made it clear that she was welcome to any of them, but she wanted to wear the one her father had given her. The flowers on it were gone as it hung there and it was solid white again. Slowly, she lifted it over her head and pulled it on, settling it over her waiting body, her eyes sparkling as the flowers bloomed all over it again. This time even more colorful ones appeared and they drew a smile from her as before.

She sat down at the vanity and looked about at the comb, the brushes and all of the other things a girl would like to see in the morning, then to her reflection in the mirror. Slowly, she reached to her hair and pulled the binding from it, then she spent some time to run a brush through her long hair, very slowly. She was meticulous here as she had been with her work and chose a slightly different style this morning, leaving her hair down and pulled over one shoulder. Finding a barrette among many of them in a drawer, one that was shaped like a butterfly, blue in color and made of some kind of thin glass, she nestled it in her hair over her left temple to restrain those locks and keep them out of her eyes. She smiled as she saw her reflection. Ellianta had never had pretty things before and for the first time in her life she felt a little giddy looking at her reflection.

Turing her eyes to the door, she knew she would have to go out into the world sooner or later, so she took a deep breath and stood, striding gracefully to the door. She still had no shoes, but did not really even care. She had never felt so pretty.

She almost glided down the staircase, which spiraled into the main hall in this part of the castle. Glancing about, she did not see anyone she recognized, but did not become uneasy so quickly. Now was a time to wander the palace—*after* finding something to eat.

Finding her way back to the dining hall, she entered the empty room and hesitantly strode to the middle, nervously holding her hands to her as she glanced around, and finally bade, "Hello?"

A door on the other end swung open and a pleasant looking black haired girl in a simple blue dress emerged. She strode quickly to Ellianta and stood before her with her hands folded in front of her. With a friendly smile, she introduced herself. "I am Cenna. I've been expecting you. Please, come with me." She turned on one heel and led the way back to that door at the other end.

Ellianta followed her through the kitchen and into a narrow hallway. The servant's quarters were behind the kitchen and her heart sank a little. Just the day before she had been an honored guest and now she was to eat in the back with the help. No matter. She was truly a servant of the people, after all, and clearly a servant of the crown of this castle.

They arrived in a small room, perhaps four by four paces with a simple wooden table in the center, a lamp burning in the center of it and several young women in the same simple blue dress sitting around the table in a heated discussion about something, a conversation that stopped as soon as Cenna entered with Ellianta behind her. Everyone stood and greeted the guest and she offered each a friendly smile and a salutation.

As she was offered a chair at the table, she glanced around and noticed someone there who seemed out of place.

Wearing a formal looking yellow dress, Princess Faelon was huddled in a chair in the corner where she could not be easily seen from the doorway, and she offered Ellianta an uneasy smile and a timid wave of her fingers.

Ellianta rested her elbow on the table and her cheek in her palm as she stared back, and finally she asked, "What are you doing down here."

With an arched brow, the Princess replied in a low voice, "I'm hiding from Pa'lesh."

"I can't imagine why," another of the girls there joked. "Just because you missed that inspection again."

"I overslept!" Faelon whined "and now she is going to yell at me again."

Raising her brow a little, Ellianta asked, "Aren't you the Princess here?"

"You would think," she grumbled back. "Believe me, if you were in my position with that big Zondaen looking over your shoulder all of the time, you would have a time pulling rank with her, too."

"She *is* intimidating," Ellianta admitted. "So, what is it you plan to do?"

"Hide here forever," Faelon mumbled.

Turning her eyes up, Ellianta smiled, realizing that she was the oldest and probably the wisest one in the room. "Okay, Highness. What if I can get you out of this?"

Faelon's eyes snapped to her. "I would be in your debt for the rest of my life!"

Shooting her a wink, Ellianta ordered, "Everyone gather around. We'll formulate a plan over breakfast."

Later, high on the perimeter wall, Princess Faelon strode slowly with her hands behind her, looking over every detail of the battlements and inspecting the soldiers who stood watch there. With her were two palace guards, a big, burly soldier from Enulam, and Ellianta.

Stopping by the watch captain, she looked him up and down as he snapped to attention. He was a handsome fellow who seemed a bit too young to be of that rank, though he wore his armor and tunic proudly and had his chest puffed out and his alert eyes staring straight ahead as he stood motionless.

Princess Faelon raised her chin, looking to his eyes as she asked, "How long have you had this post, Captain?"

"Six months, Highness," he answered straightly.

She nodded, looking around him a little. Finally, she patted his shoulder and complimented, "Well done, Captain. You have everything in perfect order up here and I think we are all safer for it. Thank you for your service to the crown."

"It is my pleasure, your Highness," he replied with a bow.

She smiled slightly at him, then moved on, winking at Ellianta as she did.

Below them, in the southern courtyard, she happened to see Pa'lesh leading a group of five soldiers to a post near that gate and was barking orders as she did.

Leaning over one of the blocks of the battlement, Faelon shouted down to her, "Captain Pa'lesh!" When she had her attention, she waved down to her and continued, "Everything is in order up here and I've attended some matters by the servant's quarters. Can you address the horses near the cavalry stable? Thanks." She pushed off of the wall and continued on her way, glancing down at the field captain twice just to see that surprised look on her face and that gaping jaw for the first time.

As they reached the stairs to go down, Faelon leaned back toward Ellianta and murmured, "I am keeping you no matter what anyone says."

They enjoyed a little laugh as they descended into the courtyard, and Ellianta patted her shoulder. "I think you did a fine job."

"There you are," Leedon greeted as they reached the bottom of the stairs. He paused as he saw Ellianta and a little smile curled his mouth. "You look lovely, child."

Faelon folded her hands behind her, cutting her eyes that way as she informed, "Yes she is, and I knew you would go for that blue barrette. Leedon, please tell me that you and Ellianta will be staying for a while."

"A fast friendship, eh?" he observed. "Faelon, you have a gift for that. How long would you like for us to stay."

She shrugged. "I don't know. Three, four… Fifty seasons."

"I'll see what I can do," he assured. Looking back to his daughter, he asked, "You slept well, I trust?"

"I did, Papa," she assured. "It was wonderful." Her eyes danced away from him as thoughts she had been trying to avoid forced their way through.

"You already miss your work, don't you," the wizard guessed.

Her gaze found the ground in front of her and she nodded, her hands fidgeting.

"Your work?" Faelon questioned, her eyes shifting from the wizard to her friend.

"I am a healer," Ellianta explained softly, her eyes still on the ground before her, "and I study the arts of the Wiccan. It is part of the discipline I use to aid those in need."

"I don't know what that is," the Princess admitted, "but I'm sure we could use one here and I know we need a good healer. Would you consider staying? I can provide you with anything you need."

Timidly, Ellianta met the Princess' eyes, just staring at her for long seconds, then she looked to the wizard, unsure of how to answer.

He raised his brow. "You are likely not to get another such offer, Ellianta, and as ruling monarchs go, Faelon is among the fairest and most giving in the land."

Princess Faelon's eyes shifted to him and her mouth tightened to a thin slit, then she looked back to Ellianta and took her hands. "Had I known you were a healer when you got here I would already have asked you. Will you stay?"

"A new start," she breathed. She looked to the wizard once more, then she looked to Faelon and raised her chin. "I would be honored to be the healer for your people." Her eyes widened as the Princess squealed and bounced up and down before her and she raised her brow and looked to the wizard again, who just smiled and shrugged.

"This is going to be delightful!" Faelon announced as she took Ellianta's arm and led her toward the palace. "We are going to make this the best kingdom in the land, we'll stay up late at night talking about boys and drinking wine…"

"I'll have my work to do," Ellianta informed firmly, "and my research, and my studies in the Wiccan arts."

Raising her brow, Princess Faelon looked to her and ordered, "You will still make time for the rest of us. Life is not all about work, that's why I insist that everyone who is employed here has time to enjoy the simple things."

"Like?"

"Well, like wine and boys."

They both giggled and the wizard and guards and soldier with them shook their heads.

Nearly to the door of the palace, they were all startled by what sounded like thunder at the main gate of the perimeter wall, and everyone wheeled around, the guards and soldier drawing their weapons as black smoke poured in and screaming people fled from it. Lightning flashed within the cloud and fire spewed from it randomly, burning out as it tasted fresh air.

Leedon strode out between the guards and the approaching cloud, motioning behind him as he ordered, "Ellianta. Faelon. Stay back. Stay behind the guards."

Pa'lesh came running from across the courtyard and took the wizard's side with her weapon already poised for battle. Baring her teeth as she watched the cloud expand, she shouted over the thunder and other sounds within it and over the wind that began to swirl around it, "What is that thing?"

"Something your sword won't stop," the wizard shouted back. "Go stand with the Princess and let me handle this."

She grasped his shoulder, then backed up past the guards and took her position right in front of Faelon and Ellianta.

Fire and lightning spewed from the front of the cloud, right at the wizard, and he raised a hand and stopped it on an invisible wall only two paces in front of him. Once it was deflected, he held his fist up and a blue light lanced from both sides of it and flashed, revealing his walking staff suddenly in his grip. Grasping it before him with both hands, he lowered his brow and commanded, "Show yourself!"

Lightning spat from both ends of his staff and pelted the cloud randomly, blasting away parts of it and leaving glowing burnt holes on its surface. The cloud struck back as it had before and he blocked the strike as he had before, but this time he raised his hand to the sky, shouting some Latirus words.

Overhead, clouds boiled up out of nowhere and grew heavy and dark. Thunder rolled from them and in seconds they began to spit lightning right at the dark cloud in a devastating barrage that blasted and burned more of it away.

In only a moment of that, the cloud began to dissipate and fade from sight. The wind slowed and died down and the dust and debris it carried returned to the ground.

Silence followed for a moment.

Leedon slowly lowered his staff, his narrow eyes piercing through the settling dust and finding four riders pacing through the gate. They were on massive black horses that wore dark plate armor over their heads and necks. More steel covered their haunches. Their eyes glowed red, and as one snorted, flames erupted through his nose. The riders were all huge men, broad shouldered and also covered in black, rusty steel armor. Helmets of dark, rusty steel covered their skeletal heads and their armored bodies were huge and powerful. No flesh appeared to be between the joints of their armor, though something must have been there. Black riding boots were armored as well and looked very old and tattered.

When Caipiervell soldiers behind began to advance, Leedon gestured for them to remain where they were, then he gestured again for them to back up.

One of the haunted riders carried a crystal spear and this one led the way right toward the wizard, who held his ground and raised his staff slightly.

Stopping less than seven paces away, the haunted rider looked upon the wizard with empty eye sockets, then he raised the spear and thrust it into the ground.

Light flashed from it, then flames erupted from the ground it was stabbed into. The flames gave way to black smoke which rose only a height or so before it rose no more and quickly solidified. A glow started from within and it was overtaken by white smoke which took the form of a cloaked figure with its bowed head covered by a red hood.

Leedon's eyes narrowed more.

The figure in the smoke slowly lifted its head, and all that could be seen of its face were two eyes that glowed blue. In an ancient woman's voice, the form greeted, "Well hello again, dear Leedon."

He also raised his head, but he demanded, "What is it you want?"

"You know what I want, my love," the form replied. "How long did you think you could hide my daughter from me? Did you really think I would not figure out that you lied about her death? Did you think I would never find her?"

Ellianta's eyes widened as she clung to the Princess, and she slowly shook her head.

"You have no claim to the girl," the wizard shouted. "Leave her in peace. Leave us all in peace!"

"That will never happen, my love. You've wasted your life. You've wasted your power and your teachings. One of us should see to it our daughter is not wasted also."

"She has no wish to go with you."

"What she wishes has no consequence. She will do as commanded." The glowing blue eyes turned to Ellianta and the form raised a hand, beckoning to the girl as she ordered, "Come, child. Come with me so that you may be trained properly." When Ellianta timidly shook her head, the form screeched, "You *will* come with me! I will slay every life in my way to get to you!"

Crying, Ellianta turned fully to Faelon and hid her face in the girl's shoulder and the Princess wrapped her arms protectively around her.

Lowering its arm, the form snarled, "So be it. My minions are many, Leedon. Not even you can stop them all, and everyone who gets in my way will die until she is returned to me." Flames exploded all around the form and in an instant it was gone, and not even the crystal spear remained, only a burnt place on the ground.

The four haunted riders drew their weapons, swords and battle axes, and the other three came abreast of the first one. They raised their weapons, and a horrible screech was heard outside of the gate.

Leedon's grip on his staff tightened and he shouted, "Be ready for them!"

Winged demons, a score in number, swept into the gate and began to attack the soldiers there.

The wizard raised his staff and blasted one from the air, then another.

Caipiervell's soldiers fought against them gallantly, but immortal creatures were not so quick to fall by mortal means.

The four haunted riders kicked their mounts forward, raising their weapons.

Pa'lesh started to advance, but the wizard motioned her back again.

Thrusting his staff at the riders, he blasted the first with lightning, but it had little effect other than making it lurch backward. He swept the staff, bringing up a whirlwind to at least confuse them for a moment while he quickly formulated a new plan, and backed up a step or two.

Another demon flew in from one side, landing hard near the Princess and its true target. This was a tall woman figure with bat-like wings and dark gray skin, glowing orange eyes and long black hair. Pointed ears had earrings with black gems hanging from them. It was barefoot, but had the feet of a hawk and the thick arms of a Zondaen warrior. It wore little, a belted tunic that left its arms bare and it had a generous bust line that made her both alluring and ominous.

Faelon screamed when she saw the demon and Ellianta wheeled around, her wide eyes betraying terror, her open lips betraying uncertainty. She knew this creature, knew it as a succubus that would drain the life force of its victims, often quite very painfully.

The succubus smiled, revealing pointed teeth that would remind one of a vampire, but it had fangs on both its lower and upper jaw. She beckoned to Ellianta and assured in a sweet yet raspy voice, "Come, child. I'll not harm you." When Ellianta shook her head and backed away, the succubus took on a much less pleasant expression, and she advanced, assuring, "I will kill everyone here if you do not, and I will bring you pain you've never imagined. Come along before I have to punish you." She stopped as Pa'lesh stepped in front of her.

Poising her sword before her, the Zondaen warrior half smiled and offered, "Come punish me instead, demon, and let's see how fast I can kill you."

With narrow eyes, the succubus advanced, warning, "You cannot kill the dead."

"Won't stop me from trying," Pa'lesh shouted as she

attacked.

A sword lanced out from the demon's fist and met Pa'lesh's in mid-swing.

Leedon more than had his hands full with the creatures that they did battle with. The haunted riders seemed invincible. Nothing he did even stunned them and all of the attacks from the surrounding soldiers, arrows spears and lances did nothing. They continued to slowly advance toward the girl, and Leedon continued to slowly retreat as he struck with everything he had. Looking up, the wizard set his jaw as a flame raptor perched on the battlement wall, killing the men it landed on. It was over two men's heights tall, was made of blood red flames and had yellow flames for eyes. Leedon knew he had not the tools to deal with something like that without casting complex spells, which he did not have time for. Backing up another step, he watched as a dragon of blue flames swept over head and circled around the castle.

More demons charged through the gate, these clad in thick leather and dragon scale armor and wore black helmets with three rows of dragon scales over the tops. They were hunchbacked and each carried a single sided axe. As guards and warriors rushed forward to engage them, the demons hacked their way through them, relentlessly pushing their way into the castle's perimeter.

Barely blocking another strike of the succubus' sword, Pa'lesh called upon all of her strength to push against the demon's blade and force her back, shouting over her shoulder, "Get her into the palace!"

Two young women stayed frozen where they were, unable to move through the veil of fear that surrounded them.

As the Zondaen Captain stumbled and raised her sword to defend herself, another warrior shouted a battle cry and engaged the demon, and Pa'lesh took the few seconds of distraction to regain her footing and her bearing, then she looked over her shoulder and ordered, "I said go! Get yourselves to safety!" She spun back as the other warrior fell and the succubus' sword came at her again.

Leedon had retreated all he dared and stood his ground as more of the axe wielding demons and the four haunted riders closed in on him. He slammed the end of his staff down and raised his other hand, calling on all his power as he declared, "You shall come no further!" Sharp blades of ice blasted up from the ground before the riders, and one impaled one of the hunchback demons and carried his body two heights into the air.

Methodically, the haunted riders began to chop their way through the thick ice, but Leedon had bought himself the time he needed to start formulating a more complex spell to deal with them, but only one at a time, and immediately he began to build his power and channel it into his staff for one massive blow.

Long before he could finish, the flame raptor leapt from the battlement and streaked toward him, screeching an ominous battle cry as it quickly drew closer.

Leedon looked up as it rapidly neared, knowing he would have to turn his built-up power on it just to defend himself, but he would have to wait until the last possible second, and as he watched, a huge black form crashed into the flame raptor's back, slamming it into the ground with killing force.

As the flame raptor exploded into nothingness, the black dragon stood from it, his eyes glowing red as he bared his teeth and looked skyward to the blue flame dragon that swept toward him with a hollow roar, and he roared back in response through bared teeth. Opening his wings, Ralligor leaped upward as the blue dragon tried to veer off and with one mighty stroke of his wings he was high enough to strike, his jaws slamming shut around the fire dragon. Coming back down, he threw his head over and released the fire dragon, slamming it into the stone perimeter wall. It tried to rise up again, but the black dragon was upon it and stomped a foot down on its back and his jaws slammed closed, his teeth plunging deep into his smaller enemy. With a dying screech, the fire dragon's body was ripped apart by the Desert Lord as green and then yellow flames spewed forth, and it was no more.

Leedon smiled slightly as the tide of battle quickly turned, and as the haunted riders crashed through the rest of the ice, he thrust his staff at one and blasted it with white lightning, dismounting it as its armor was blown apart.

Three remained, and one arched its chest and threw its head back as ruby light lanced through it, then again, and again. It burned red from within and it and its horse collapsed in upon themselves as a silver-blue light lanced through another. The last of them turned and raised its weapon, barely turning half way before the ruby light ripped through it, and it burned from within as the others had.

As the last of them fell with ruby fire burning through it and quickly consuming it, the big bay unicorn paced steadily forward, a ruby glow enveloping his eyes and his horn. A slightly smaller silver unicorn with a white mane, tail and beard paced at his side, a silver-blue glow enveloping his horn and eyes.

Still unaware of the turn in the battle, the succubus seemed to be enjoying her battle with Pa'lesh, and the Zondaen was tiring and wounded, holding a hand over her bleeding side. Still, she refused to yield, baring her teeth at her enemy as they circled each other.

Smiling, the succubus made small circles with the end of her sword, taunting her foe as she said, "You should join us, Zondaen. You have wonderful skill and the strength we can give you would make you invincible."

Pa'lesh actually smiled back a little, catching her breath before she countered, "Oh, no. I'm rather enjoying things as they are."

Responding with a little shrug, the succubus conceded, "Very well, Zondaen. Just know I've enjoyed our little game, but I've no time to continue." She held her sword vertical before her in a final salute, then swept it hard. When Pa'lesh responded, the succubus' sword burst into flames and cut right through the Zondaen's blade. She grabbed Pa'lesh's arm and pulled her off balance and toward her, slamming a knee into her gut.

The wind exploded from Pa'lesh and she dropped to her knees, dropping her hilt and the melted remains of her sword as consciousness began to abandon her.

Shaking her head, the succubus looked down on Pa'lesh with a little pity in her eyes as she drawled, "How I wish you would join us. No matter." She seized the Zondaen's arm and hoisted her easily from the ground, then turned and hurled her into the palace wall where she hit with brutal force and crumpled unconscious to the ground.

"No!" Faelon screamed as her friend and bodyguard lay unmoving. She ran to her, placing both her hands on the Zondaen as if to look for some sign of life in her, then she turned fearful eyes to the succubus.

With Pa'lesh out of the way, the succubus turned her eyes to Ellianta and leaned her head. "Coming quietly now?" When her prey started to back away, she shook her head and informed, "I was hoping you wouldn't." She extended a hand toward the young woman and opened her fingers, a thin gold colored chain lancing from her palm.

Ellianta shrieked a gasp as the chain wrapped around her neck and squeezed down on her throat and she raised both hands to try to pry it off. It was already so tight she could barely get her fingers between it and her skin. It tightened more and in a second she could not breathe. Blackness began to close in and gray spots obscured her vision. As she fought to remain conscious, she sank to her knees, her mouth gaping as she struggled for air.

Faelon took Pa'lesh's sword-breaker and charged the succubus, screaming as she did and thrusting it up at the demon's body.

With her free hand, the succubus knocked the sword-breaker away and in a quick sweeping motion clamped her hand around the Princess' throat, smiling as she slowly turned her eyes on the girl. "Well, now, what have we here? A little pest." She picked Faelon up easily and hurled her back-first into the palace wall.

Faelon's breath exploded from her and her head hit the stone very hard before she crumpled to the ground, holding a hand to the back of her head. Pushing herself up with her free hand, the Princess looked up at the demon with narrow eyes, her lips curling back from her teeth as she shouted, "You will not take her!"

Smiling back at her, the succubus leaned her head and drawled, "Who will stop me, little girl?"

"I will," Shahly replied from behind the demon.

The demon wheeled around, her eyes now wide with fear as she declared, "Unicorn!"

Shahly paced slowly toward the demon with her head low, her ears laid flat, and a bright emerald glow enveloping her horn. She had approached unnoticed through the fray of demons and men and only announced herself about five paces behind the succubus, who now retreated.

A green glow overtook the unicorn's narrow eyes and she ordered, "Release Ellianta."

Baring her teeth, the succubus hissed, "Never."

Shahly lunged forward with amazing speed and her head slammed right into the demon.

Screaming, the succubus staggered backward, the chain that held Ellianta crumbling to black dust as she raised her other hand to the hole in her chest. An emerald fire erupted from it, consuming the demon from within.

Shahly watched with narrow eyes as the succubus collapsed. The hole in the demon's chest burned wider and her body arched upward and began to collapse in on itself. More green fire erupted from her mouth, her eyes, and soon it engulfed her and she burned to ashes. Shaking her head the unicorn mumbled, "Silly demon."

Drawing a desperate breath, Ellianta coughed and fell

forward, catching herself with one hand as her other was around her throat. She coughed more and struggled to regain her breath and struggled more just to regain her full consciousness.

Faelon and Shahly rushed to her, but the unicorn paused as she saw the unmoving Zondaen and went to her instead.

With the black dragon in the fray and on the attack, the battle took a decisive turn against the demons. With emerald glowing eyes, he looked skyward, toward a group of flying demons, and as he swept his hand they were all torn apart by explosions of emerald fire, all but one. This one attacked him from his right and he turned and met the demon head-on, gaping his jaws and blasting the demon with a short burst of orange and green fire, and the demon was gone.

The ground demons were more than a match for any human, but two powerful and experienced unicorn stallions slashed through them with a fury rarely seen in their kind. Ruby and silver-blue light lanced from their spirals and blasted through dragon scale armor, burning the evil within them to nothing until only dust remained.

Not known to retreat, the demons fought to the last, but up against unicorns and a wizard trained dragon and a wizard *magister* they had no chance.

When the last fell, a quiet moment seized the courtyard as all looked around them, trying to realize the battle was over.

Her breath finally returned, but Ellianta's neck and throat were hurting, and breathing was still difficult. She felt the Princess slip an arm around her back, and she raised her head to look into the girl's eyes.

"You're all right now," Faelon assured. "They're gone. We've fought them off."

With her hand still over her throat, Ellianta looked beyond the Princess, out into the battlefield where dead and wounded men lay, where smoke rose from many fires. The destruction was not like anything she had seen before.

Leedon rushed to her and knelt down, dropping his staff as

he wrapped his arms around her and pulled her to him. As she began to weep, he rocked her back and forth and assured softly, "You are all right now, child. They're gone. They can't get you."

Ellianta bowed her head and wept more, crying, "Why? Why is this happening?"

"It isn't your fault," he assured.

"I'm not worth the deaths of so many," she sobbed, clinging to him like a frightened little girl. "Papa, they'll never stop until they get me. Why does this have to happen? It isn't fair! I want my old life back!"

He laid his cheek on her head, closing his eyes as he whispered, "I wish I could give it to you."

Shahly approached and looked to the sobbing girl in the wizard's arms. "Is she hurt?"

"No," Leedon replied softly. "She's just frightened."

Her lips tightening, the unicorn's eyes narrowed and she snorted, assuring, "Just let another demon try to get her. I'll be waiting for them!"

"No, Shahly," Vinton corrected angrily as he approached, "you won't be!"

"Uh, oh," the white unicorn mumbled, lowering her head.

Ellianta finally opened her eyes, looking to the little white unicorn and seeing that her head was low and her ears were drooping.

Vinton and the silver unicorn stopped only a couple of paces away, both looking angry as they stared at the little unicorn with narrow eyes.

Shahly timidly turned her head, looking to them like a child would who was expecting a good scolding.

The silver unicorn raised his head and snorted. "Shahly, what have you been told about putting yourself at risk?"

She tried to explain, "But that demon had—"

"You were told specifically to wait in the forest," the bay interrupted. "Shahly, you're carrying our baby and we've been over this a hundred times or more!"

"But it was just a demon!" she defended.

The stallions' eyes widened and they looked to each other, then back to her.

"Just a demon?" Vinton shouted in a whinny. "Shahly, that demon would love nothing better than to kill a unicorn, especially a pregnant unicorn!"

"But..."

"Shahly," the silver cut in, "I told you this is for your own good and the good of your foal. You have a new member of the herd in there that has the favor of the Tyrant himself."

She turned her eyes down and mumbled, "I know."

Heavy footsteps announced the approach of the black dragon, who also looked to the white unicorn with much annoyance as he growled, "What happened to staying in the forest? You do *not* need to jump into the thick of battle like that!"

As the black dragon loomed over her from behind the stallions with his arms folded, Shahly lowered her head more and looked away, her eyes glossy with tears. "I'm sorry. That demon was hurting Ellianta."

"And was going to be attended to!" the dragon roared.

Faelon glared up at him and stood, setting her hands on her hips as she spat, "Before or after that thing killed her?"

Ralligor's eyes narrowed as they turned on the Princess and he snarled, "You'd better stay out of this."

"You were all too busy to see what was going on here," Faelon cried. "We could all have been killed but for her!"

Ellianta reached up and took the Princess' hand, meeting her eyes as she softly said, "They are right. No one should have been put at risk today, not for me."

Leedon held her a little tighter and softly said, "Don't talk like that."

"It's true, Papa," she insisted, bowing her head and closing her eyes again. "How many men died today because of me? How can you expect me to live with that?"

"We all consider you worth defending," the dragon

informed straightly, "and we'll continue to do so."

"She won't stop," Ellianta sobbed. "She'll never stop."

Ralligor growled. "Then we'll stop her before she strikes again! I'll tear her apart myself!"

"Enough, mighty friend," Leedon ordered. "You know why that cannot be allowed."

Growling again, the dragon looked away. "I know, *Magister*, but I don't have to like it."

Faelon folded her arms. "What do we do? We have to figure out some way to protect her." She turned to one of her approaching guards and ordered, "Convene my war advisors. I want—"

"Stop!" Ellianta cried. "Please, no more." She looked to the wizard, tears streaming from her eyes as she raised a hand to his cheek. "I can't do this, Papa. I can't. Please don't let anyone else be risked for me. I am a healer, a Wiccan. I am a woman of peace."

He looked back at her with eyes that beamed both pride and sadness. "You are a rare gem in this world, and you must be protected." He stroked her hair and nodded. "Yet, I understand the demands of your heart."

She nodded. "Thank you, Papa. We should just run away."

"She'll find you again," the black dragon snarled. "You can't run forever."

Leedon closed his eyes tightly. "But she can hide again." He pulled her to him, wrapping his arms around her as tightly as he could. "I will give you your life back, Ellianta, and I will keep you safe. I promise."

CHAPTER 5

The field outside of Castle Caipiervell had been a place of joy, a place where unicorns grazed freely and in safety and people came to admire them.

On this day, as the remnants of the battle were cleaned up and the dead and wounded were attended to, it became a place of heavy hearts.

Ellianta and Leedon led the way, holding each other's hand tightly as they stared at the path before them with blank eyes. Near the tree line, the black dragon sat and watched them approach. Just in front of them, three unicorns also watched. Behind them, the Princess of Caipiervell and her Zondaen bodyguard followed, leading a score of soldiers.

As they reached the dragon and unicorns, they stopped and Ellianta closed her eyes. "I don't want to leave, Papa. I don't want to lose you again."

"Nor I you," he softly replied, slipping his arm around her. "Just know that where you are, my heart will be. I will always be with you, child."

She nodded.

Ralligor reached over the unicorns toward Ellianta, the tip of one claw touching her chest ever so gently, and when it did an emerald light quickly ran around her neck and grew bright right where he touched her. As he withdrew his claw, a golden chain took the light's place, a chain that suspended a golden dragon's talon that held an emerald sphere in its grip.

Ellianta looked down at it and took it gingerly in her fingers. She recognized this as the same kind of amulet the white unicorn wore, and she turned bewildered eyes up to the dragon's, eyes that were mixed with a little sadness at having to leave him behind.

"Always keep it with you," he ordered. "You will know why when it is time."

"It gives you human form," Shahly declared, then she

noticed everyone's eyes slowly turn on her and she looked away, lowering her head as she corrected, "Oh. I suppose it doesn't work that way on humans, does it?"

"It will have an important purpose," the dragon went on. "What that purpose is will be clear in time."

She nodded and wiped a tear from her cheek. "Thank you, Ralligor. I will cherish it always." Looking to the unicorns, she slowly approached, reaching up to scratch Shahly between the ears first and smiling as the little unicorn closed her eyes and lowered her head a little. She turned her attention to Vinton and raised her other hand to stroke his nose, and finally to the old silver at the bay unicorn's side. "I shall miss you all. My greatest dream has been of your kind, and now I will dream of three unicorns who have all touched my heart."

Shahly took a couple of steps toward her and nuzzled her, and Ellianta wrapped her arms around the white unicorn's neck.

"We will miss you, too," Shahly whispered. "Be well. One day we will meet again."

Ellianta nodded and hugged her a little more tightly.

She turned and said her goodbyes to everyone with big hugs and many tears. Faelon held on to her the longest and both young women wept. When they finally parted, Pa'lesh grasped her shoulder and offered her a nod.

"You're going to be okay, healer." She handed her a leather bag, one that was sizeable and filled with things. "Just throw that over your shoulder. There's food, a few supplies you might need, and one of my most trusted daggers, just in case." She half smiled and winked.

Ellianta smiled back, then threw her arms around the big Zondaen, offering in a whisper, "Thank you."

With one arm, Pa'lesh returned her embrace and patted her back as she softly said, "Be well, little healer."

Ellianta's eyes were down as she pulled away and turned back toward the wizard, taking his hand as she reached him.

She cried harder and fell into him as she dropped the leather sack and said, "I'll miss you so, Papa."

Wrapping his arms around her, he fought his own tears as he replied, "I will miss you too, my little Wiccan daughter. Always pursue what your heart sees, and always know that I am proud of you, and that I'll be watching."

She nodded and held him a little tighter, never wanting to let go.

Ralligor looked up, then waved his hand slowly toward the sky.

A translucent emerald dome that sparkled with thousands of yellow stars appeared around them for a hundred paces in every direction and everyone turned astonished eyes up to it.

Looking back to the wizard master, the dragon informed, "She won't be able to see through this, and the girl's destination will be known only to you and I."

Leedon nodded, his cheek resting on his daughter's head as he closed his eyes. Still, he strained to say, "Thank you, mighty friend. Her destination will receive her well?"

"If they know what's good for them," the dragon snarled. "However, it is best for her that she establishes herself on her own."

"Agreed, mighty friend," the wizard said softly.

"That doesn't mean she won't have a little help from time to time," Ralligor added.

Finally looking up from the wizard's chest, Ellianta looked to the people who surrounded her and asked, "How can I ever repay all of your kindness?"

"Live as you have been," Leedon replied, "and keep making me proud of you."

"I will, Papa," she whispered. "I promise."

She embraced him tightly one more time, then she picked up the leather sack and hugged it to her, looking to the ground as she nodded and said, "I am ready. Thank you all, and always know that I will always hold you all to my heart."

Tight lipped, the wizard held his fist up and his staff lanced from it from both sides. He held it up by the end, just over head level, and a thick mist began to fall from it. When it seemed solid, he turned reluctant eyes to his daughter and raised his chin. "I will keep watch over you, child. You shall never truly be alone."

She walked up to the wall of mist, then she looked to him and said, "Thank you for all you've done for me. Thank you for the truth, and for your protection. I love you, Papa." With one last, long look at him, she mercifully turned away and disappeared into the mist.

CHAPTER 6

The road looked well kept and she looked one way, then the other. The trees were different here, fewer pines and more oaks and elms. The smell was a little different and the air felt a little hotter and dryer. Birds sang different songs all around her, beautiful songs. She recognized some but not all of them. Pursing her lips, she answered with a song that she knew, and smiled when a bird replied to her from somewhere.

She pulled the strap from the leather sack over her shoulder and walked in a direction that looked right. She could see what looked like chimney smoke in the distance over the treetops and that seemed like a good start.

Walking for some time, she did not think about the people she already missed horribly. She studied her surroundings as she had done all her life, every plant and flower, every leaf, every mushroom and moss where it grew. She would not pause long at any of them, but she did shift the bag from one shoulder to the next many times as it was rather heavy. The big Zondaen probably did not notice, but a young woman who was not quite so muscular had a much more difficult time with it.

A couple of hours later seemed like a good time to sit under a tree and rest. Settling herself on the ground, and fussing a little about getting her dress dirty, she finally got comfortable and crossed her legs beneath her skirt, dropping the sack in her lap as she loosened the drawstring that kept it closed. Reaching in, she found one reason it was so heavy, and smiled a little as she pulled a full bottle of wine out of it. She set it down beside her and reached in again, finding a water bladder, which she also removed and took a drink from. This was set down beside the wine bottle and she reached in again, finding a tin that rattled a little and no doubt had some kind of crackers in it. She set the tin down and pulled the bag open with both hands, looking inside as she mumbled, "How much stuff did she put in there?"

She took a while to have some lunch as Princess Faelon made sure she had a gourmet meal or two awaiting her in the bottom of the bag. The dagger was very sharp and ideal for cutting cheese, which was very flavorful and coated with wax to keep it fresh. After she finished, she loaded everything back in the sack and just leaned back against the tree for a while, resting her head back against it as she drew her knees to her and wrapped her arms around them. Closing her eyes, she daydreamed a little about people she had left behind only hours before, how she had managed to form close friendships with them, even unicorns and that dragon, and how she would miss them. She pulled her spectacles off and raised her palms to her eyes to stop the tears that already escaped.

It was time to move on, and yet she was reluctant to get up and just sat there with her arm over her knees and her spectacles dangling from her fingers. She stared off into a blurry distance, her eyes blank and her brow arched a little above them. The unknown awaited her. Again. Sooner or later, she would have to face it.

Approaching footsteps that she did not seem to take note of until they were very close, alerted her that she was not alone and her eyes snapped to that side. The forms she saw were blurry, but appeared to be big men and she put her spectacles back on to see them clearly, and her stomach squirmed a little as she realized they had already seen her.

Slowly, she gripped the strap on her bag and stood, now wishing she had taken the time to build another wand.

These were tall and burly men, clearly farmers by the look and build of them. One wore a tattered old shirt with no sleeves and baggy pants with heavy leather boots. The other only wore a leather jerkin and some faded black pants with the same kinds of boots. This one carried a shovel over his shoulder while the other carried a large sack made of burlap. The man with the sack was the larger of the two and had a reddish brown beard while the other's hair and beard were black.

They stopped where they were and just stared at her for a time, then they glanced at each other and slowly approached her.

Ellianta raised her chin a little as they approached her, and she pushed her spectacles a little further up the bridge of her nose.

They stopped within two paces and each looked her up and down, then to each other again.

The larger fellow with the sack looked back to her and placed his free hand on his hip, saying with a strange accent, "Well look at what is here. Got us a new waif, me thinks."

The other one nodded and agreed, "Aye, would say so. What they call ye, Lass?"

She was still very afraid of them, but swallowed it back and answered as politely as possible, "I am Ellianta."

The big fellow pursed his lips and nodded. "Pretty name. Suits ye well, Lass. I be Brogret." He slapped the other man's chest with the back of his hand and continued, "This be me mate, Archem. Be you a traveler, Lass?"

Hesitantly, she replied. "I'm... I am looking for..."

"Ye lost?" Archem asked, something of concern in his words.

She shook her head and turned her eyes down. "No. I suppose I am just looking for a new home. That's what brings me this way."

Brogret dropped the sack he carried and rubbed his arm just above his elbow. "We're a simple people, Lass. Live off what we make and don't do much tradin' with the kingdoms across the desert. Take in the odd traveler from time to time, but much keep to ourselves for the most part."

Ellianta nodded and looked up at him. "Is your village very big? Are there many people there?"

Archem shrugged. "Not knowing what ye mean my many, but a thousand or so souls there give or take. Ye have ye a profession?"

J. R. Knoll

"I am a healer," she replied softly.

Archem laughed and slapped the bigger man with his hand. "Heh, maybe have a look at ol' Brogret's arm. Been a might puny in the fields this last season or so."

The larger man still rubbed that arm as he grumbled back, "Just a touch of the grite, it is."

Dropping her sack, Ellianta took the last strides to him and reached for his arm. She looked closely where he had been rubbing and ran her hand over that spot a few times. She took his hand and glanced hers over his last two thick fingers, asking, "Do you hurt here, too?"

"Nah," he scoffed. "Can't feel a thing there. Just a bit of burnin' in me arm, that's all."

She ran her hand along the outside of his arm and asked, "Here?"

"Aye," he confirmed.

She nodded, then walked behind him and ordered, "Sit down."

He glanced at Archem and both men shrugged, then he sat down as instructed.

Running her fingertips along his temples a few times, she softly said, "Now I want you to just trust me and relax. I've done this many times and relieved many a farmer's pain."

Archem laughed under his breath and nudged the larger man. "You'd best not be lettin' the wife catch you with her doin' that, mate. She'll put ye both in the grave."

Both men laughed, and Ellianta smiled a little.

Positioning her forearms at the sides of his head just under his jaw, she said in a soothing voice, "Now, just relax everything and let me rid you of your pain."

"Pain's in me arm," he reminded.

Ellianta turned his head slightly to the side, then sharply pulled straight up. There were two loud cracks from his neck and he yelled, "Gah, woman!"

As she released him, he raised his hand to the back of his neck and turned an irritated look on her, then he rolled to his feet and faced her. "Woman, what the hell ya doin? Ya could have killed me!"

She folded her arms, raising her chin a little as she asked, "How does your arm feel?"

His eyes narrowed and he reached for it, then looked to it. With a low brow and his features oozing confusion, he looked down to his hand and worked his fingers, then turned astonished eyes to her. "There's a tingling in me fingers, and that burn isn't so bad."

"It should go away completely by morning," she informed straightly. "Problem is all the heavy lifting you do from day to day will bring it back. I can fix it again when it returns."

He looked to the other man and raised his brow, then he looked back to her and nodded. "I'm gonna have to make sure this lass is taken care of." He looked to the sack that was behind her and offered, "Can a gentleman carry that for ye?"

She smiled at him and placed a hand on his shoulder. "No more heavy lifting today, remember?"

Shaking his head, Archem reached down and picked up the sack, then he threw it over his shoulder and looked back to them. "You'll do anything to get out of workin', aye, Brogret?"

"I'll be liftin' some of that ale when we get back," the larger man assured. "Gotta help with the pain." He turned to Ellianta and bowed his head to her. "You have me thanks, Lass."

She nodded back and offered him a little smile.

"Maybe you'll be comin' back to the village with us," Brogret suggested. "Could use a healer like you, says me."

Lowering her eyes, she shrugged and shyly admitted, "I don't know anyone there."

The big man threw his arm around his black bearded companion and informed, "You know Archem and me. We'd be two of the most important men at the village, we are."

"At the pub, you mean," Archem corrected.

The men shared a good laugh, and Brogret said straightly, "I'll see about us putting you up for the night. Archem and me and our families share a big house and there's plenty room for one more tiny lass."

"I wouldn't want to be in the way," Ellianta said softly.

"Nah ta that!" the big man scoffed.

"You're too small to be in the way," Archem added.

She turned her eyes to them, looking to them in turn as she argued, "But I don't have the means to pay you."

Brogret slapped his arms a few times. "Paid in full for a while, says I. Good marks with me. Might bother me again, says you and a healer close to would be a lucky stone."

"Oh, enough of this rabble," Archem growled. He handed the shovel off to the larger man and walked past them to pick up Ellianta's bag. "Come on, Lass. We've a stop at the pub and then we'll be off to the home for a good supper. Come along now, mates."

Ellianta and Brogret looked to each other and shrugged as Archem led the way toward the village, then Brogret offered her his arm and a smile. She returned his smile and slipped her arm around his and they followed.

***

Their village was not so unlike her old village, smaller of course with much less commerce and more bartering than trade with copper or silver. Different foods were carried about by different people who all sought each other. Spices and meats and roots, green things and even some fish hung from crossed poles and were carted about in hand pulled wagons. Villagers greeted each other in friendship rather than suspicion. No one seemed to want to gain an upper hand over anyone else. A man with a cut of lamb sought someone with a wagon of potatoes. A woman with a string of fish sought someone with beans, still others looked for precious salt. Camaraderie was in the air and the whole village was awash with it. There were no defenses here, no fortifications and no weapons that could be used against invaders. This was a community unto itself.

This could be a problem, and that was in Ellianta's thoughts as they went further into the village. She could not know if such a closed community would easily receive an outsider, especially one who studied the Wiccan arts. She had experienced people's suspicions of those who practiced such disciplines, and sometimes their hostility.

She did not get to see much of the village as the two burly men with her led her right to a large shack, one that appeared solid, yet in disrepair. On a wooden shingle that hung on the door was the picture of a mug burned into the wood, and a similar shingle with a mug on both sides hung on a wooden bracket over the door for all to see. This had to be the pub and the two men with her swept her inside.

On the other side of the large, spacious room within was a long, chest high bench, and behind this was another big man who wore a dirty white apron. He was also bearded, but his hair was cut short. Back there with him were three women, each attractive in their own right. They were more colorfully dressed and had very low necklines. These were women who enjoyed showing off for the many patrons who sat on high stools at the bench and a jolly time filled the air. Tables were scattered about with still more patrons, farmers and metal smiths and the like. In one corner was a large instrument that resembled a bellows. A man in a red shirt and red trousers pulled down on a rope that compressed the bellows and forced air into a tube, and as he pushed down on different keys with his other hand, he controlled different notes. A merry tune came from it and set the atmosphere of the entire place. There was nothing but laughter and merriment within.

Ellianta's escorts led her to this long bench where two stools waited. Brogret slapped the shoulder of one of the men already there and ordered, "Dondu, move yourself over one, ya field stump. We've ale to drink."

The man, who was a little grayer, wore a dirty white shirt and had broad shoulders, turned and smiled at the big man. His beard was better kept, but he had clearly been working somewhere and had only recently arrived. Raising his hand to take Brogret's, he greeted, "I thought I smelled a foul odor a moment ago. How goes that harvest to the east of here?"

When Dondu moved over, Brogret sat down beside him and assured, "It goes almost too well, my friend. How about those melons you seeded?"

Archem set the potatoes down beside a stool and put Ellianta's bag beside it, then offered her the stool between them with his hand, waiting for her to sit before he did.

Dondu laughed a little and replied, "Those melons are big and sweet, my friend." He leaned toward the big man and loudly asked, "How are the wife's melons?"

"Bigger and sweeter than any in your field!" Brogret almost yelled, and the two men enjoyed a hearty laugh.

The big man behind the long bench approached and looked to Brogret, resting his forearms on the other side as he asked, "Wantin more of me precious ale, are ye, Brogret?"

"Been a long day it has," the big man informed. "Worked up a thirst."

His eyes narrowing, the pub-keeper shook his head and informed, "You have no more mark here, me friend."

"Heh," was Brogret's reply as she reached around Ellianta's back and slapped his friend's shoulder.

As Archem hoisted the bag of potatoes up onto the bar, the pub-keeper raised his chin as he looked to it, then he nodded and looked to the two men in turn. "You both have a good marks here!"

People not even in the conversation raised their glasses and yelled at the news.

One of the women came along and took the heavy sack as the pup-keeper turned and took two mugs from a shelf behind him, filling them from one of the huge barrels behind the bar. As he turned back with the foaming mugs of ale, his eyes were on Ellianta as he set them down in front of the men, and he asked, "What pretty little lamb is this you bring in here?"

Taking a big gulp from his mug, Brogret put his arm around her and pulled her almost brutally to him. "This, me

A Wiccan's Tale

friend, is Ellianta, a traveling healer and a young lass who has copious marks with me."

The pub-keep nodded, his eyes on her, but not in suspicion as she was used to. "She's too pretty to be some healer, too young. Lass, will ya be staying about or traveling on?"

She shrugged and timidly replied, "I had hoped to find a home here."

"In me pub?" he asked loudly, and everyone around laughed heartily.

Ellianta smiled a shy smile and shook her head. "No, just a home."

Brogret squeezed her to him again and loudly informed, "Took the burn from me arm, she did. Did it with 'er bare hands."

Many of the men sitting close by nodded and mumbled some kind of approval.

All but one man, who rose from a nearby table and turned toward them and folded his arms. "With her bare hands, did she?" He spoke much better, much clearer than the others there, and was clearly a man of education. "Sounds almost like magic."

All of the men at the bar within earshot turned and, hesitantly, so did Ellianta.

The man standing directly behind her had his eyes on her, and his were the only eyes laced with suspicion. They were also dazzling green eyes, very beautiful for a man's eyes. He had a very handsome face that was clean of facial hair, which seemed unusual for this village, as well with a cleft in his broad chin and a powerful jaw that swept back from it. His long black hair was kept groomed and was restrained behind him. He also had very broad shoulders and rather thick arms on his lean frame. Ellianta looked him up and down a couple of times, noticing that his attire, a clean white, sleeveless shirt and a black vest and black trousers, did not look like he took them out in the field to farm or work with metal or build anything. He appeared to have strong hands, but not rough hands like the other men present. Yes, he was a very handsome man, very handsome! But something in his eyes told Ellianta that he did not approve of her presence, in the pub or in the village.

Brogret took another gulp of his ale and regarded the clean, handsome man almost with dismissal as he informed, "You've worked with me arm for six months and haven't taken the pain. She did it in a minute and I'll wager can do it again."

The handsome man nodded slightly, his eyes still on Ellianta, then he raised an eyebrow and asked in a more polite tone, "So, how did this little lamb remove your pain?"

"Turns out it was like the pain me wife gives me," the big man said loudly for all to hear. "In me neck!"

Almost everyone in the pub laughed as loudly as they could, and this roar of laughter continued for a couple of minutes.

The handsome man smiled and nodded, his eyes still on Ellianta. "So, you cured the pain in his arm by going through his neck. Interesting."

"It is something I have done for many seasons," she informed, still feeling a little timid about him, "something I learned a long time ago."

"As a child, I assume," he observed. "So how old are you? Twenty seasons?"

"Twenty-six," she corrected.

He raised his brow. "Just barely out of childhood, and yet you have all of this experience as a healer."

"I have enough," she defended. "I was the healer of my village from a very young age."

"Apparently, and it would seem that your village no longer needed your services for one reason or another. Why did you leave such a successful position, keender?"

Ellianta set her jaw, now feeling less timid and more animosity toward this handsome stranger. *Keender* was a word of an old language, and meant child. He did not look much older than she was, but he clearly regarded her as a threat of some kind. She finally stood and strode over to him, folding her arms as she looked up at him with a challenging stare. He was a head-height taller than she, but with her two big farmers behind her she did not fear him.

With slightly narrowed eyes, she countered, "I could ask the same of you."

"You could," he replied with a nod. "However, this village has a healer, and I have seen many like you who came through here over the seasons looking to make an easy living off of people they claim to wish to help. I have seen much damage done to many of my friends and neighbors, damage that took months in some cases to resolve, damage caused by those looking for an easy living at the expense of others."

"Nothing in my life has ever come easy," she informed with harsh words.

"Except finding your way to the pub here."

She raised a brow slightly. "I had to be shown the way here, but I noticed you found the way here all by yourself."

He smiled ever so slightly again, softly saying, "So I did." Something much more serious took his eyes and he warned, "Be careful about practicing your skills here, keender. Very careful. The village does not look kindly on those who would come looking for that easy living at their expense." He took another half step toward her. "And I would look much less kindly." He looked up and nodded to the now quiet men at the bar and behind it. "Gentlemen." With one more glance down at Ellianta, he turned and strode out of the now quiet pub.

She just watched the door for long seconds after he left. He was sure nice to look at, but had a personality that was lacking in all respects.

Archem took her shoulder from behind. "Don't be worryin over that bloke, Lass. He's the only healer in the village and might see you as competition he doesn't want."

She turned and went with him back to her stool, holding her eyes low as she sat down.

***

The home that Brogret and Archem shared with their
families was a spacious house, perhaps twenty paces across
and almost fifteen deep and was constructed of timbers and
stone. This was a solid house with many windows and two
levels. Right outside, there was a long table beneath an
overhang of the slate roof, and ten simple wooden chairs
surrounded it. A garden was planted right outside the front
for the full span of the house, separated into two parts by a
wide path that led right to the front door. A wooded area was
behind the big house. Located on the edge of town, right
where the wilderness seemed to start, it was big, yet quaint.
Ellianta could hear children playing somewhere, and on the
other side of the table, a woman wiped the table down with
some kind of leather mitt, dripping wax on it from a candle in
her other hand as she did. This was a robust woman, typical
of the people she had seen in this village, and she began to feel
even smaller. With long, dark red hair in two braids behind
her and wearing a white, long skirted dress with a low
neckline and a light blue apron that covered her from the
chest down, she looked just like Ellianta had imagined and
Brogret had described her.

As they approached on a wide path past two large
vegetable gardens, the big man raised a hand to his mouth
and shouted, "Woman! Your prayers be answered and your
living god of a husband has returned to you!"

She looked up from her labors with dark amber eyes, then
stood straight and set a hand on her hip, shouting back, "Me
living god husband's been spending copious time at the pub
again, aye?"

As they approached, he smiled. "Only to drink meself
mortal enough to be worthy of such a ravishing beauty as
you."

The woman's eyes narrowed and she set the candle down
and pulled off the mitt. With her hands set on her hips, she
walked around the table and met Brogret and his party, and

she stopped right in front of them, her eyes on Ellianta as she asked in a harsh voice, "And what waif is this that you bring into me home?"

Brogret put his arm around the young woman and pulled her to him with a mighty grasp, slamming her into his side as he replied, "This be Ellianta, the healer. Took the pain from me arm, she did. Say's I'll be like a young stud by mornin' she did. Me mark be good with this little lass, says I, and hers with me."

Raising her brow, the woman, who towered over Ellianta and stood at or over an average man's height, leaned her head a little. "Cured your arm, says you. Took your pain, she did?"

"Aye, she did. Says she'll do it again if it returns."

"Well then, I'll be settin' another place at me table." She reached to Ellianta and took her arm, pulling her from Brogret as she positioned the young woman before her. With both hands, she squeezed Ellianta's shoulders, then her arms, then she seized her around the chest with her powerful hands.

This tickled horribly and Ellianta giggled a little and twisted away.

"Well, then," the robust woman declared. "You'll be catching no eye of suitor nor husband like that. Need to put some meat on ye, says I." Turning, she bade, "Come along, Little One. Got to get some supper in ye."

Archem gently grasped the healer's neck and pushed her along with him as he strode up to the house. "Aye, me wife Grettslyn and Brogret's Hilliti cook up a feast a couple of times a day. They'll put some meat on ye for sure, they will. No worries, Lass."

***

Archem had not been exaggerating when he had said feast. These people of very little means ate very well. It was no wonder they were all so big!

Archem sat at one end of the table with his wife at his right and Brogret sat at the other end with his wife also at his right. Archem's wife, Grettslyn was also a tall, robust woman who wore her dark blond hair in a bun behind her head. At a look one would think she was an angry woman, but she spoke with a sweet voice and her disposition was polite and friendly, even though she did not smile quite as readily as the others there.

The two couples who shared the house had three children all together. Archem had a son of about ten and a daughter who looked to be four or five. Brogret had a son, one who boasted about being eight seasons old over and over and also boasted because he was the same size as the older boy there. The boys were dressed much as their fathers were while the little girl wore a simple little blue dress and a white apron. Sitting beside her mother, the little girl seemed to be one who was eager to help her and, as Ellianta would discover, she stayed close to her mother and learned all she could. The boys were boys and acted as brothers would, either bickering or laughing or conspiring.

These big people ate big portions and their mannerisms were some strange mix of what one would find at a formal dinner, as they used knives and forks, and what one might expect at a feast with barbarians. Eating daintily as she always did, Ellianta's small portion disappeared slowly, and she felt a little out of place here, but the atmosphere about the table was one that was not unlike the pub. These families laughed often, sometimes sniping at one another but it was mostly the fun of the day or remembering some amusing event from the past.

For the most part, Ellianta was quiet and just enjoyed their company, as she only rarely ate with others. She laughed with them but offered no stories of her own. There was nothing to tell, anyway.

The little girl, who sat almost directly across from Ellianta, looked at her often with a big smile. She was definitely the cutest of the children there with her reddish-brown locks restrained in long braids as her mother wore them. She did not speak at all either until their meal was almost over, when she leaned her head over almost to her shoulder, a big smile on her face that showed the dimples on her cheeks as she told Ellianta, "You're pretty."

Ellianta smiled back at her. "Oh, why thank you, Prenzee. I think you are pretty, too."

Hilliti looked her way and nodded to her. "You'll be needin' to find yourself a husband sooner or later, Little One. A pretty one like you should have a good, hard working man to take care of her."

Looking back to her plate, Ellianta picked at the small piece of meat that was left with her fork as she replied, "I will someday, I think. My work keeps me very busy, though."

"Aye," Grettslyn, who sat beside Ellianta agreed in her dry but pleasant tone. "You just be choosy, little Lass. You find you a big man with strong arms that can work good and give you many children."

"Just get you a looker," Hilliti added. "Get you a man as hard working and pretty as me own Brogret and stay happy."

Grettslyn huffed a laugh. "Me brother's not so pretty, Hilliti. Maybe this healer will fix your eyes."

Everyone enjoyed a good laugh about that, even Brogret himself as he added, "No, don't fix me woman's eyes! She'll never lay with me again!"

Archem looked to their guest with a big smile. "Tell me somethin' Lass. You said you'd be lookin' for a good home. Maybe end your travels and stay at our village."

She raised her brow and looked back down at her plate. "I would love that, but you already have a healer here."

"Fah," Grettslyn scoffed. "He's pretty to look at but I don't think such a healer. Look how long Brogret suffered with that arm."

"I was just glad to help," Ellianta said softly, humbly.

"And help ye did," Brogret announced in his usual loud manner. "Lass, you've a place in my house as long as ye need or want."

His wife turned a look on him and countered, "Or as long

as she can stomach you." Looking to Ellianta, she added, "You'll just be stayin' here, Little One. We'll take care of ye, get ye what ye need for your healin' and find ye a good, strong man."

Ellianta found herself unsure of what to do or say, so she just nodded and offered, "Thank you. I'll try not to be in the way."

"Fah," Grettslyn scoffed again. "Too small to be in the way. Can ye read and write?"

Nodding, Ellianta replied, "Yes. I read and write both Common and Latirus."

"Maybe teach these children about words," Grettslyn suggested. "Maybe about numbers."

Ellianta felt elated at the offer and raised her head, an enthusiastic, "Yes!" bursting from her. "I would love to! I think I can teach them letters and some simple words very quickly and then go on from there."

"I draw pictures," Prenzee announced, speaking with a lisp as some young children would.

Looking to her again, Ellianta said, "And I want to see every one of them."

"After we eat," the little girl said with just as much enthusiasm.

Archem pushed himself away from the table and belched loudly. "Very good as always. I'm going to sit for a spell, then I have to attend to me evening chores before dark." He looked to his wife and smiled a wicked smile. "Got me a woman to violate tonight."

Grettslyn raised her brow and looked back at him, wearing a flirty little smile of her own.

And Ellianta felt herself blush just a little.

Hilliti wiped her mouth on her sleeve and abruptly stood. "Come, keenders. Help your ammi with the dinner wares. I've much sewing to do before we sleep."

Ellianta's eyes lit up and she stood, asking, "May I help?"

"Do ye sew, Little One?"

"I love to sew!"

With a little smile and a nod, Hilliti beckoned her on. "Come along then, me Little One. We'll clear the dinner wares and catch ye up on all the gossip over a shirt or two."

With a broad smile, Ellianta quickly went to task, helping to clear the table.

The evening was delightful. She helped Hilliti and Grettslyn clean up after dinner, then it was off to a corner of the big house, a large family room that had a stone fireplace, for hours of sewing and conversation. Archem and Brogret played with the children most of the night, pretending they were ogres and lumbering about the house and outside occasionally with their arms up and making some horrible growls and grunts. The children fled them with hysterical giggles and would occasionally try to chase back.

Sometime after dark, two little boys and a little girl were tucked into their beds. Soon after, Archem and Grettslyn disappeared up to a partitioned loft where they slept. A wall that separated much of one side of the house was closed by a thick timber door, and that is where Brogret went to await his Hilliti. She did not join him right away. Led by a candle, she took Ellianta to a ladder that led up to the other side of the loft, separated by a timber wall. Once up there, the room was larger than it appeared, though Grettslyn had to crouch a bit as the ceiling was a little low, only a hand width above Ellianta's head.

"Not much," Hilliti sighed, "but the bed's soft, you have a little table there and a basin for water. We keep a pail down in the kitchen near the root basket, so if you want water or linins or anything… Oh, ye know where to find everything, Little One. Just be at home here."

"Thank you," Ellianta offered softly.

Hilliti smiled and grasped the back of the young woman's neck and she almost brutally pulled her to her, giving her a soft kiss on the forehead. "You get good sleep tonight, Little One. Get ye settled in better tomorrow. Maybe make ye a new dress." She set the candle down on the table beside the bed and ordered, "Don't stay up too late, Little One."

As the tall, robust woman turned to mount the ladder and go back to the ground floor, Ellianta quickly bade her, "Good night, Hilliti." She got a little smile in return. Turning to sit on the bed, she looked about her. Last night she had slept in a palace, in a beautiful and huge room on a soft bed with many things about her that a young woman would need or want. Now, she was in a tiny room in the loft of a house shared by two families. A little smile touched her lips as her eyes darted from one part of the little room to another. Her old house at her old village had been a place to sleep and a place to eat and do her work.

This place felt like a home.

CHAPTER 7

The next three weeks would see major changes in Ellianta's lifestyle, even as she worked hard to reclaim her old one.

Her interactions with the families grew. She spent much of her time during the day helping Hilliti and Grettslyn about the house and in the garden. She read to Prenzee when she found books, but the way this town bartered for everything she found herself reading the same stories over and over, as she really had nothing to trade but her services. Deep inside, this made her miss the books she had left behind, many of them written by her own hand, but she would never think of that openly. She did, however, manage to get enough materials together to assemble a couple of new books, in which she resumed keeping notes on her studies in the Wicca, what little she could do. Literature on the Wicca was not to be found anywhere in the village, and any talk of any of the three disciplines that most would consider magic was something that almost provoked hostility, so after a few unpleasant encounters that resulted from just mentioning the Wicca, she stopped her search and tried to just work from memory.

Early mornings were hers. The farmers always rose before the sun and Ellianta rose with them, but she did not go to the fields with them. Following old habits, and to continue her work as a healer and her studies in the Wicca, she would venture into the wooded area behind the house, which went back as far as the eye could see, all the way to the mountains in the distance, sometimes traveling for half a league or more. After a few days of doing this, and realizing that no one else was out there, she felt compelled to free herself as she always had and would pull her dress off when she was well out of sight of the house and wandered naked for hours so that she could connect with the surrounding forest, with nature itself. No one could know of this practice and her study and control of the Wicca was one of many closely guarded secrets that she would not share with the families.

On one such morning, she strayed further to the North than normal, up over a rise in the land on the other side of a fast flowing creek of really cold water. The trees were smaller and fewer here and none grew out of the exposed granite at the top. As she reached the top, she took a moment to look around her. It was almost all exposed rock, worn almost smooth by the weather. There were cracks that had clumps of grass and small woody bushes growing from them, but otherwise it was a clean surface right at the tip, and the mid-morning sun shined brightly here.

Walking slowly to the middle of it, she had a little smile on her lips as she looked about her. The sun felt wonderful against her skin and as she reached the center, she put her bag down, which was already half full with leaves and bark and other stuff she had collected, and she faced the sun. With her feet close together, she lifted her chin to bring her head back. Her hair, which was restrained behind her by several ribbons that Grettslyn had put there for her, dangled behind her in the still air. She breathed in deeply, slowly raising her arms straight out and turning her palms toward the sun as if to capture as much of its warmth and light as she could. Doing this seemed to recharge her and her spirit soared.

After a moment, she slowly lowered her arms and bowed her head, slowly releasing a deep breath as she did. Looking up again, she raised a hand to her mouth, just touching her lips with her fingers as she whispered, "Thank you, Father Sky."

Picking her bag back up, she turned north again and stopped, squinting a little as she saw the turrets of a castle in the distance, and her head tilted a little. None of the villagers had ever mentioned a castle before and she found her curiosity racing. She pushed her spectacles back on her nose a little as she studied the mountainous form in the distance. The stone was dark in places and even at this distance she could tell it had been at the heart of a battle many seasons ago.

It looked like it once had four towers, perhaps five, but only three remained. Those that survived were damaged, and two looked as if they had partly collapsed at the top. All had been burned. The palace itself looked to have been in a horrible fight itself, but newer stone in places told her that it had been repaired, probably within the last seasons or so. In fact, the two towers in better condition had newer stone all over the tops of them, and new conical roofs over them. One of the others appeared to be under repair as well. Still, it looked like it had been uninhabited for many seasons and her curiosity swelled more.

She briefly thought about going out to explore the castle itself, but her dress was not with her, it was at a spot she had chosen to leave it a couple of weeks ago, and exploring the unknown when she was naked just sounded too dangerous. So, this day she would leave the castle in the distance, but she did find some small stones to mark where she had seen it and on her way back to the house she left little markers along the trail she had used. With no clothing to protect her from twigs and thorns, she always made it a point to avoid them.

Later that evening, as the family enjoyed another feast and the merriment of each other's company, Ellianta's mind was still on the mysterious castle, and finally she looked to Brogret and innocently asked, "What do you know about the castle that is to the north of here?"

The whole table was instantly silent and eyes grew wide at the mention of it.

Brogret put his fork down, his eyes on his plate as he picked up a napkin and wiped his mouth. Taking a second to finish chewing, he took a gulp from his mug and finally turned his eyes to her, finally informing, "That castle is not to be spoken of. Ye should'a been told of this before, but we gave it not that thought."

"Why would you not speak of it," she asked with timid words.

"Tis a cursed place," Archem explained. "Keep your

distance from there, Lass. If ye can see the castle, it can see you, and you'll be needin' to head the other direction as quick as ye can."

She just stared at him for long seconds, and her brow lowered a little as she started to feel an uneasy quake in the pit of her stomach. "What is so horrible there? Has anyone gone there?"

"Not and come back," Hilliti said straightly.

"Be keepin' your distance from that place, Lass," Brogret ordered sternly. "Them goblins get you and there's not we can do to save you from them."

Her eyes shifted to him and her brow arched. "Goblins?" When he just stared back, she smiled ever so slightly and guessed, "You are all just teasing me, right? Goblins aren't real."

Grettslyn whimpered and rose from the table, a hand over her mouth as she turned and rushed into the house.

Her lips parted in surprise and concern, Ellianta just watched her disappear behind the door, then she turned to Archem and slowly shook her head.

"Nothing you could know of, Lass," he informed softly. "They took our oldest son a few seasons back. We don't speak of it anymore."

Tightly closing her eyes, Ellianta bowed her head and softly offered, "I'm sorry."

"Not your fault, Lass," Archem repeated. "Just best not to speak of."

"But goblins aren't real," she insisted, looking back to him. "They are just made-up stories."

"Saw them, meself," Archem informed. "You'll not forget the first time you see 'em."

"Are you sure they were goblins and not wolves or something of the like?"

Brogret answered, "Wolves don't carry battle hatchets, Lass. You see them, it's already too late. I'll need ye to stay clear of that place. Go south if ye must wander, but stay clear of that castle."

She nodded to him, then looked to the door. Her lips parted a little as she felt pangs of guilt for having brought back those horrible memories for Grettslyn. Rising from the table, she said, "Excuse me," as she rushed around the table and to the door.

Entering as quietly as she could, she found Grettslyn sitting in her chair by the fireplace, staring into the flames with blank eyes. She approached with the timid movements of a rabbit, and when she was finally less than an arm's reach away, she slipped her hand onto Grettslyn's shoulder and softly offered, "I'm so sorry."

Still staring into the flames, Grettslyn reached up and took Ellianta's hand. "Ya had not a way to know, child. I don't speak of it. No one does. You shouldn't, either."

"I won't," Ellianta assured.

Grettslyn squeezed her hand and nodded. "A good girl, ye are, Little One. Don't dwell." She finally looked to Ellianta and smiled at her. "A good girl, ye are."

Ellianta smiled back.

Hilliti rushed in and shouted, "Dreads! They've attacked our neighbors on the other end!"

Grettslyn stood and wheeled around, rushing to the back of the house as she ordered, "Get your healing bag, Lass."

***

The other side of the village was only a third of a league away, and on a road that led out of the village and into some of the fields, was a three level structure that catered to visitors and those passing through. It was of timber construction with a large pub and restaurant on the lower level. Stables out back kept and cared for visitor's horses. Inside and out, it was one of the best decorated buildings of the village, and was one of only a few businesses that accepted gold and silver as payment, though bartering was not out of the question here, either.

Brogret and Archem were already there when Grettslyn

and Ellianta arrived. Hilliti remained at the house to care for the children.

The scene that Ellianta walked into was not anything she could have expected.

On seven of the dining tables within were four men, two women and a boy of about twelve seasons. They all had been horribly mauled, and one of the men was missing an arm. Blood was everywhere. The rest of the furniture had been moved against the wall on the far side to give those helping the injured room to work. That handsome fellow, the other healer in the village, was already there, much to Ellianta's annoyance. She had managed to avoid him completely after that first confrontation and did not even know his name, she just knew that she did not like him. Something about him just niggled at her and she did not care to associate with him. Now, she found herself thrust in a horrific emergency with him.

Such carnage she had never seen. As a healer in her old village, she did treat injuries, but mostly she treated sickness. This was almost more than she could bear and her stomach churned uneasily within her at the sight of all this blood, all this chaos. One of the women screamed from the pain of her injuries. A man moaned pitifully. Three were unconscious. The other woman and the child wept. Well meaning volunteers from the village worked to apply bandages and stop bleeding.

Looking past the horrific sight, she met the other healer's eyes as he looked up from his patient, the woman who was screaming. When the woman's cries paused, he pointed to the other end and shouted, "Over there! Those three have deep cuts, and the man has a slash to the belly."

Now was not the time for pride or ill feelings. With her bag in hand, she rushed to the man with the deep wounds to his belly. She had never seen such grave injuries and felt a little queasy when she looked upon him for the first time. His shirt had been cut in four neat, side by side lines, and the flesh beneath with it. Two of the wounds had gone through fat and muscle and were open enough for her to see entrails within, and this was the worst she had ever seen.

Ellianta had to close her eyes and roll her head back for a few seconds to collect herself.

The other healer shouted from across the room, "If you aren't up to this then you need to leave. The last thing we need is someone else fainting in here."

Her brow was low over her eyes when she looked back at him, and the glare in her eyes made quite clear her animosity toward him.

Setting her bag down on the table beside the wounded man, she reached to the bottom of it and removed the dagger, pulling it from its metal and leather sheath in a quick motion. Her eyes were still locked on the other healer, but she finally looked down to what she was doing and lifted the man's shirt, inserting the dagger beneath it and cutting it open.

Someone approached from the other side, a man just a little taller than she with sandy hair and a horrified look in his eyes.

Looking to him, Ellianta ordered, "I need a basin of clean water and clean towels or rags. Hurry!"

He turned and ran past everyone on his way toward the kitchen.

She looked behind her, seeing an ashen faced Grettslyn standing behind her and looking down to the bloody mass that had been the man's belly. "Grettslyn!" she summoned. "Grettslyn!" Finally getting her attention, she said as gently as possible, "I need a sewing needle and as much thread as you can find."

Grettslyn nodded and assured, "I'll attend to it. Got some mates who live close by."

As she wheeled around to hurry out, Ellianta turned back to her patient, seeing that his eyes were half open and he was staring at her.

"Just lie still," she ordered as she began to rummage through her bag. "I'll have you fixed up before you know it."

He smiled a little and whispered to her, "You have my trust."

She offered him a strained smile back, and finally removed a small bladder that had once been used for water, and laid it down beside him.

The small man finally returned with the basin and she ordered, "Over here." There was just enough room on the side of the table for it. He had a few towels over his shoulder and she took one and pushed it down into the water. Her eyes were on it in an intense stare as she squeezed the water from it, then she used it to clean the blood from the man's belly, going through two towels before she finally had him clean to her satisfaction. Aware that the little man was still there, she glanced at him and asked, "Can you bring me as much honey as you can find?"

He nodded and hurried back to the kitchen.

Grettslyn returned a moment later, as Ellianta was blotting water and blood from the man's belly, and she reported, "I've her kit. I'll thread the first needle for ye."

"Thank you," Ellianta offered as she continued to work. Pulling the stopper from the bladder, she poured some of the fine beige powder from it into her hand and from there she sprinkled it onto the man's horrible wounds.

He winced and tensed up a little.

"Shh," she commanded gently. "It will sting at first, but then it will take away the pain. Just lie still and I will attend to you."

"How bad?" he rasped.

She shrugged and lied, "Oh, I've seen much worse. You'll be up and around and a horrible thorn in your wife's behind before you know."

He smiled again. "Make good that promise and you'll have copious marks from me."

"I'll give you a few days before I go about collecting them," she said with a smile.

"Could use a cup of ale," he strained to say, "perhaps

something stronger."

"Let me put your belly back together first," she suggested. "I'll buy you that first mug." She took the threaded needle from Grettslyn and went to work sewing up the man's belly, and continued to make small talk with him as she worked. The powder had clearly done its job and he could feel nothing as she worked, but Grettslyn had to look away, raising a hand to her mouth as she stepped outside for some fresh air.

The small man returned with a couple of clay jars and set them down beside the man. "I found these, and there's more in there."

"Will you fetch them for me?" she asked.

"Aye," he confirmed as he hurried off.

The other healer came up behind her and watched her work for a moment, then he looked to the honey and asked, "Do you mean to eat him when you're finished?"

She did not acknowledge him other than to say, "Perhaps someone else in here could use a healer. If you know one, can you send him?"

He turned and went on his way without responding, approaching another table.

Ellianta finished her stitching and opened the first jar of honey, pouring some on the man's wounds before she began to smear it all over his belly, taking great care to work it over and around the wounds.

The other healer returned and looked over her shoulder again, asking, "So… Can you tell me why you're doing that?"

"It will keep his injuries from becoming septic," she answered straightly. "Any actual healer knows that."

"I use a powdered herb mix that does that nicely," he informed, "and it doesn't attract ants."

"Do you have enough of that for everyone in here?" she asked.

"Yes I do," he confirmed. "Would you care for some for your patients?"

"No," she answered curtly.

"Very well, then," he said as he moved on.

Ellianta washed her hands in the basin and looked to the little man, asking him, "Can you throw this out and get me some fresh, please?"

"Aye," he complied, picking the basin up.

Moving to the next table, she found the child laying there with his arm torn almost completely off at the shoulder. He was very pale and his eyes were only about half open, and they were blank and empty. Examining him closer, she realized that he had been horribly mauled about the belly and one leg. The dangling arm was held on to him by very little and would clearly be of no more use to him. A wound to his head had been hastily bandaged, and continued to stubbornly bleed.

Not sure where to even begin, Ellianta started by packing a bandage onto his wounded belly, what was left of it. "I need more water," she announced.

The other healer came up on her again and took her shoulder. "The woman right over there needs you more."

She pulled away from him and continued to work.

"You need to listen," the other healer insisted. "Go over and —"

Turning on him, she glared up at him and spat, "Just go and attend to her! I have my hands full right here."

"He isn't going to survive!" the other healer said just short of a yell.

Everyone grew quiet.

In a calmer voice, he set his jaw and continued, "We need to save those we can, and she needs you now."

As he went to walk around her, she grabbed his arm and tried to respond, but he pulled away and continued on.

"Help her," he insisted, "or kill them both."

She just watched him attend to a man who was groaning in pain, and this was a hesitation she did not need. Looking back down to the boy, her lips tightened and she pushed her spectacles back up her nose.

"Please," the boy whimpered. "It hurts. Help me."

She took the bladder out again and poured some of the powder from it into her hand, then she sprinkled it on the worst of his wounds, those that looked the most painful. He winced and she offered a soothing, "Shh. It will pass quickly and you will feel all better." When she could see that his pain was subsiding, she offered him a strained smile and assured, "I'll be back in a moment. Just lie still."

She moved on and treated the woman's wounds, then was called to another.

When all others were in safety, she returned to the boy, her eyes widening beneath an arched brow as she found him staring at the ceiling. Her lips parted, revealing clenched teeth and a tear rolled down her cheek.

The boy was dead.

Wiping his hands off on a clean towel, the other healer also approached him, looking down on him with eyes that betrayed disinterest. "As I told you. He did not survive."

Her eyes cut to him and she spat, "And you could not make his last moments more comfortable?"

"I had people here I could save," he defended, throwing his towel on the next table. "Perhaps you should think about those you can help first like a healer would."

"Being a healer doesn't mean being heartless," she pointed out spitefully.

He turned to leave, saying back, "Nor does it mean I condemn those I can save to death. Good night, keender."

Ellianta's breath came hard as she watched him close the door behind him, her hands balled into tight fists. She looked back to the boy, and reached to him to tenderly close his eyes with two fingers, then she laid a hand over his forehead and said a silent prayer for him. She did not make it all the way through her prayer when she started to weep, and as she finished, she raised a hand to her eyes and sobbed a little harder, feeling in her heart that she could have saved the boy, but knowing she could not have.

Grettslyn took her shoulders from behind and softly offered, "You did well, Little One. Celebrate the souls you've saved tonight."

The knowledge that the other healer was right stung even more and she turned and hurried out of the inn, crying more with each step.

***

Hours later, she sat on the steps that led to the front door of the house she lived in. Darkness had enveloped the land but for a half moon and her eyes were blank, her heart heavy. She would not know how long she sat there, and was not alerted that the world around her was still there until Grettslyn, Archem and Brogret were standing right in front of her.

As Archem and Grettslyn walked past, each patting her shoulder as they did, Brogret sat down beside her and took her under his arm, pulling her to him.

She laid her head on his shoulder and started weeping anew.

"You never mind what that Malkar has to say," he advised with a fatherly tone. "He's not the healer you be."

"But he was right," she sobbed. "He was right. If I had spent all of that time with a boy who was going to die anyway—"

"You made his last hours less painful," Brogret cut in. "No shame in that, Lass. You heart's you greatest gift."

She nodded slightly. "He knew right away what to do and who to help first."

"But maybe not how to go about it," the big man pointed out. "I be proud of ye, Lass. We all be proud of ye. Don't let jealous spite of ye harden what is the best of ye."

She slipped an arm around his back, feeling loved and protected, a feeling she had longed for over the seasons. "Thank you, Brogret."

CHAPTER 8

After two days, and many visits to the people she had helped after the Dreads had attacked, her curiosity of the dark and mysterious castle was not lessened. She wanted more than ever to go and see what was there, to see if any still lived there. The story of the goblins had to be something that was made up to frighten children, yet something had killed Grettslyn's son, something they were all certain were goblins.

The day arrived and her curiosity would wait no more. Rising early as always, she slipped into the dress her father had given her and padded downstairs to meet Archem and Brogret, who were having an early morning cup of ale before starting their day. To her shock, Grettslyn was also there, and she offered the robust woman a cheerful morning smile.

"Going out again are ye?" Grettslyn asked with her usual dry manner.

Nodding, Ellianta confirmed, "Yes. There is an area near the creek to the west of here that has some berries that I can use to treat some ailments. I am hoping to still find some there."

"Well, that's very good," Grettslyn replied, "but ye keep forgetting something important, Little One."

"What is that?" Ellianta asked with a little nervousness in her voice.

Reaching to the other side of her chair, Grettslyn withdrew her hand with a pair of newly made white slippers. They had fine leather soles and were made of suede all around with straps that would tie them in place around her ankles.

Her eyes widening, Ellianta rushed to her and snatched the slippers from Grettslyn, her mouth hanging open as she asked, "These are for me?" When Grettslyn just smiled, Ellianta threw her arms around her neck and hugged her as tightly as she could, squealing, "Thank you! Thank you!"

That smile curled Grettslyn's mouth more and she hugged

the little healer back, laughing under her breath as one would at an excited child who had just received a fine gift. "Aye, Little One, a man likes a woman with soft feet, and your wanderings will make yours copious rough if ye don't protect them. If ye aim to have a good man, ye take care of them feet."

"Thank you!" Ellianta said again. Pulling away, she dropped to the floor, landing flat on her behind as she worked with the first slipper, pulling it on to her foot. It was a little loose, but as she wrapped the suede strap around her ankle and pulled it tighter, the slipper conformed almost perfectly to her foot, and she smiled broadly again, feeling more like a little girl than a twenty-six season old healer. She quickly tied it off and then put on the second one, then she sprang to her feet and pulled up her skirt as she looked down at them.

Mugs in hand, Archem and Brogret strode into the room, also looking down at the healer's feet, and they both smiled and nodded, Archem commenting, "They do compliment ye, Lass."

She smiled at him, then looked back down and took a few gentle steps.

Watching, Grettslyn asked, "How they feel, Little One?"

"Perfect!" Ellianta declared. "Thank you so much! I want to go walking in them right now!"

"You go on then, keender," Grettslyn ordered. "Be back here by high sun and we will start on meals for the day."

Her eyes snapping to the larger woman, Ellianta asked, "And sewing?"

"Aye, and sewing."

With a broad smile, she spun on her heel and hurried to the door, assuring, "I'll try to be back earlier today."

**

The morning sun was already bathing the bare, granite hilltop when Ellianta got there. She had hurried and was a little out of breath when she arrived, but barely took notice. Her eyes were on the castle in the distance. The words of her adopted family rang in her mind again, warnings of the horrors within, of the goblins that took the lives of men. Legend had it that goblins always hunted in numbers, often ambushing travelers.

And they would eat them.

Feeling a shiver, Ellianta reached across her chest with both arms as if to ward away the horrors of her imagination. She looked behind her, toward a house that was too far away to see, then back to the castle.

"Goblins," she scoffed, trying to dismiss the notion.

A trail seemed to lead that way, one that looked fairly well traveled and she set off down it, curiosity and the need to explore driving her as never before. She would not explore as she usually did, not naked today. There were far too many unknowns out there.

The trail went on for half a league and finally the forest opened somewhat and she stopped.

Ahead of her was the dark castle. There was no mote as she had imagined, no drawbridge and the main gate stood open as it clearly had for many seasons, perhaps decades. Surely it had to be abandoned.

Still, unknown horrors spoke from her imagination and urged caution. Hanging her bag on a tree, she reached into it, down to the bottom, and retrieved the dagger that Pa'lesh had given her. Reaching back in, she found a piece of rope, perhaps the thickness of her little finger that she would carry with her in the event she needed one. It was not quite a height long and was made of wool fibers. Plenty strong, she had never tested her weight against it, but today it would serve a different purpose. Wrapping it around her waist twice, she tied it off as she would a sash at her right side, leaving the two remaining lengths dangling to her hip. The dagger was looped through it on her left, just in case.

Finally mustering her courage, she left her bag where it was and made her way through the tall grass that was between her and the castle ahead. This would be a hundred pace walk, and her imagination was given ample time to run rampant as she trekked toward the main gate.

Not quite there, she encountered a well traveled path through the grass that led from the trees some distance to one side and right to the main gate, and she felt another shiver. Looking the path over from the trees to the castle, she finally realized that someone must live in there. Or, perhaps it was used by travelers on their way to the settlements in the Territhan Mountains. That had to be it. Perhaps some nomads had found the castle and took it as their home.

Slowly reaching down, she placed her hand around the hilt of the dagger.

Inside, the castle was a big, dark place. Ominous dark walls were very high and she could not even see the ceiling. The castle was very dark within, but she was expecting that it would be.

Reaching into her pocket, she removed a crystal she had found weeks before, probably some kind of quartz. Wiccans have a gift with crystals and this one would channel the power within her nicely. It was clear and free of little cracks within, about the length of her thumb and about twice the thickness. She squeezed down on it and channeled some of her power into her hand, into the crystal, and it began to glow brightly. As she opened her hand, it kept its place in her palm, even though she did not hold on to it. It was bright enough to lead the way, and she wisely kept her hand between the crystal and her eyes.

She went deeper into the castle cautiously, her eyes shifting from one side to the other, her head swiveling with her eyes, and that crystal in her hand lighting the way. Another shiver crept slowly up her spine.

A distant, loud moan echoed to her from somewhere and she froze, her eye darting about as if to see what made the noise. As she tried to convince herself that she had imagined the sound, the moan returned, and sounded closer, and louder.

Something moved behind her and she wheeled around, shining her light down the dark corridor. A dragging sound drew closer, but she could see nothing. Turning back around, she fled deeper into the castle, the light from the crystal showing her many old decorations and dilapidated furnishings. She turned down another corridor, turned the other direction into what appeared to be another and turned again as a wall appeared right in front of her. An unknown time later, perhaps only a few moments, she stopped to get her bearings. Whatever was behind her could no longer be heard, but she shined the light that way, anyway. Swallowing hard against a dry throat, she scanned where she was one more time, listening hard in the darkness. As she listened to the thundering of her own heart, she decided it was time to leave.

Looking around her, she realized that, in her panic a few moments before, she had lost her way. She drew a breath in an attempt to calm herself, but was too terrified to close her eyes as she usually did. As she exhaled, the wind left her in broken staggers. She swallowed back some of her fear again, and padded lightly the way she had just come, her eyes still darting about. On one side, old and broken furnishings were lined up against the wall, and fathomless shadows reached back between them to form terrifying caves in the darkness. The other side was very open and as she shined her light that way, she made out a few tables, scatterings of weapons and armor — and bones.

A noise from in front of her caught her ears and she stopped again, her wide eyes trying desperately to pierce the darkness. Somewhere ahead she could see torchlight and she made out a few obscure words, gibberish really. She heard things like *gah* and *urch* and *trok,* very simple sounds that seemed like words, though from a language she had never heard before. Raising her head a little, she realized that whatever was coming was about to appear in the large room she was in, and the strange speaking grew louder, as did the sound of something being dragged.

Looking around her frantically, she found a place between a couple of old wardrobes that was just big enough for her to snugly fit into, and she backed into it as quickly and quietly as she could. Slipping the crystal back into her pocket, her eyes widened as everything grew dark again, and she slowly slid her back down the stone wall and huddled there in the darkness with her knees drawn to her and her arms wrapped tightly around them.

The torchlight drew closer; the speaking became louder.

As the flickering torchlight illuminated the room before her, she realized it was not quite as big as she had first thought. There were a couple of timber tables there, one directly ahead of her. They were lower than tables she was accustomed to, looking like they would only come up to her hips. Something was on the table, but she could not make out what. Perhaps they were implements of some kind, she could not be sure.

Movement caught her attention and her eyes shifted that way, her lips parting in fear at what she saw.

The creature that hobbled into view was just over half a man's height tall, perhaps a height and a half. It walked upright and much of its stocky body was concealed beneath a cloak. Its head looked almost human, but there were no whites to its big, angry looking eyes, just deep blackness. Its arms looked thin, but very powerful and were almost twice the length of its legs, which were stout and also powerful looking, and covered with gray or blue trousers. Bony looking ridges ran over the top of its head, which was flat on top and bulbous at the back with a thick brow over its eyes that sloped sharply down. A broad, flat nose had nostrils that flared as it breathed. Its mouth looked small for its head, but a powerful jaw swept back from a sharp chin. White hair dangled like moss from parts of its head, just over its pointed ears and around the back. This was truly an ugly creature, one that she had heard of and read about.

Clearly, goblins were real.

Others, around a dozen of them, similar in dress, size and appearance, lumbered into view, and they began to gather around the short, two pace long table that was out in the room and only five or so paces away from her. Three of them removed the implements from the table, but others were in the way and she still could not see what they were. The dragging sound grew louder and Ellianta suppressed a gasp as it came into her line of vision and she realized that it was a man. He was being drug by the feet by two of the goblins, and at that point she could not tell if he was alive or dead. The body had no clothing, but was bloody and had clearly been beaten and cut all over, and she could only assume that he had been attacked at some point, probably in the night.

A few others of them grasped the body and hoisted it onto the table, slamming it down without ceremony.

The man moaned as he hit, and Ellianta covered her mouth.

Four torches were put into receivers at the corners of the table and the man was visible in the light that surrounded him. Some of the goblins moved away and she could see what the implements were that three of them had, and her eyes somehow widened further as she realized they were cleavers or axes.

The three that held the axes climbed up onto the table with the man and took their positions over the man, two at his legs and one on the other side of him. They looked down at him as they positioned their axes and the man whimpered pitifully.

One raised his axe and brought it down on the man's leg at the knee, and he yelled with what little strength he had left.

Ellianta gasped loudly this time, her whole body quaking as the goblins began to chop the man's living body apart. She suppressed a scream, barely, but the man they dismembered was unable to. His cries became more desperate, and weaker.

As a leg was severed at the knee, one of the goblins took it from the table and carried it away as another cauterized the wound with its torch. Another took an arm. Still another took an upper leg. Even as they carried parts of his body away, the man still lived, still cried out in agony. Over his cries, Ellianta could still hear the others casually talking amongst themselves. What they were doing, the pain they were inflicting, was completely meaningless to them.

She cringed as one of the goblins looked her direction and the tenseness of her body remained even as it turned and picked up one of the man's arms and hobbled away with it.

This horror went on for some time and the man's screams eventually gave way to pathetic sobbing.

Ellianta was finally able to force her eyes shut, but the image of what they were doing was still burned into her consciousness, and she was unable to rid herself of it.

In a moment the room was silent and she opened her eyes to see the goblins gone and two of the torches remaining at the table. Only the man's torso and head remained, and she prayed he was dead at this point. She rocked forward and peered out of her hiding place, looking left, then right, then left again, her eyes fixed on the corridor where the goblins had disappeared.

Everything was quiet.

Slowly, she planted her hands before her and pushed herself up, standing from her hiding place with cautious movements. Her breaths were deep, and broken both in and out. Terror had a firm hold on her. Still, and for reasons she could not understand, she felt compelled to approach the table where what remained of the man was still laying. Only a couple of paces away, she looked with horrified eyes upon what was left of him, and slowly she shook her head.

His eyes flashed open and fixed on her, his head turning slightly her way.

She barked a scream and backed up a few steps, clamping a hand over her mouth.

"Help me," he rasped.

A breath shrieked all the way into her. Still shaking her head, she backed away more, even as he begged her to help him. The healer inside of her wanted to, but the terrified young woman wanted to flee, and flee she did.

Running blindly into the darkness, she stopped quickly, her hand darting into her pocket and emerging with the crystal that burst into bright light as soon as she had it in her palm. She ran anew, knowing that she was hopelessly lost in this place, and knowing that she had to escape somehow.

She did not know how long she ran, or how far she had gone, but she finally stopped to catch her breath, her wide eyes scanning the area where she was. This appeared to be a junction in the hallway and her mind scrambled over which way to go, and how to best avoid running into any more goblins. Choosing a direction, she started to run again, but stopped only ten paces into her flight as a click and creak came to her from one side, and as a door opened she took a few steps back, balling her hand into a tight fist to douse the light and not be noticed.

A goblin holding a candle emerged from the room, looking almost like it was lost in its thoughts as it turned into the corridor — right into Ellianta!

Woman and goblin were frozen where they were for long seconds as they just stared at each other in the candle light.

Finally, thick lips curled away from many pointed teeth and the goblin made a few gurgled words as it reached to its belt where it had a weapon.

Raising her hand, Ellianta opened it and poured her power into the crystal, and it flashed with the intensity of lightning right into the goblin's eyes.

As it shrieked and covered its eyes, she ran around it and sprinted hard down the corridor. Now they knew she was there, and it was only a matter of time before one of them raised the alarm and they came for her.

She fled into a huge room, seeing light at the other end of it, and she recognized the shape of the doorway. She had finally found the way out! Running as hard as she could, she made for the doorway that was only thirty paces away, catching her foot on something and rolling to the ground. Whatever she tripped over made the most horrible clatter and she balled herself up, covering her ears as she expected the worst.

Long seconds passed and the only sound she could hear was her own frantic breathing. Finally raising her head to look around her, she saw a round shape right ahead of her, and screamed as she looked into the empty eye sockets of a human skull! Scrambling to her feet, she shined the light around her, seeing that the floor was covered with bones, and many skulls from many creatures were there, but most of them were human. Her breath came in short shrieks as she glanced about her, then she finally looked to the light coming through the open doorway and ran toward it again, crying as she prayed she would make it outside in time.

Once out of the castle, she ran down the path in the tall grass, then she veered away from it and followed the little path she had made approaching the castle, sprinting through the grass and to where she knew she had left her bag. Once at the trees, she stopped and clung to one. Her breath would not return easily and she held on to the tree and leaned her forehead against it, closing her eyes to try and dismiss some of the terror that still coursed through her.

Drawing one long, broken breath, she looked toward the castle, seeing a half dozen of the goblins pour out, and one was pointing at her!

A scream exploded from her and she grabbed her bag, turning to run down the trail as fast as she could. Forest and time blurred by and she frequently looked over her shoulder, looking for pursuers.

Her legs ached and her lungs burned for air, but she knew she dare not stop. Horrific images of what would happen to her if they caught her flashed continually through her mind and pushed her on.

She lost her footing and stumbled, scrambling quickly to her feet and running anew, lest the terrible pursuit end in her capture. She could not escape nor bear the thought of what they would do to her if that happened.

Ahead, she saw the incline in the trail that would lead her to the hilltop and a place safe and familiar to her, and she found something within her to run a little harder.

Almost to the top, she had just passed the last big tree when something landed hard on her back, knocking her down. It felt like it was almost her weight and as she struggled to push herself up, hands with long, thin fingers grasped at her wrists. She avoided one, but the other snared her wrist and pulled back on her arm, trying to twist it behind her. Fighting to keep it from getting her arm behind her, she also fought to keep her other hand out of its grasp. Crying, she screamed, "No, please! No, not me! No!"

Another pounced on her and she felt at least one more grab her ankles. Still another appeared before her and grasped at her still free hand, finally seizing her wrist with both of its hands.

She struggled harder. There were four of them, but as small as they were, each of them was at least strong as she was, and they were easily, methodically subduing her. As they got her other arm twisted behind her, she screamed as loudly as she could, struggling to free herself, but their strength was overwhelming, and she could feel them press her wrists together in preparation of tying them there, and she felt that her struggle was almost over.

Managing to kick one ankle free, she quickly drew her leg up and found a foothold, and with all her strength she kicked hard against it, rolling to her side and taking the goblins with her. This little victory was short lived. Even as she thought she would free one of her arms, her ankles were seized again and this time one of them wrapped its arms around her calves, and she felt the first winds of a course rope start around her ankles.

"Please!" she begged, tears streaming from her eyes as she continued to struggle against them. "Don't do this to me! Please let me go! Please! I beg you, let me go!"

"They aren't known for their mercy," a voice boomed from the hilltop.

Everyone froze and the goblins all looked that way.

Ellianta knew that voice and slowly turned her eyes toward it, and her breath froze within her as her gaze was filled with the black dragon.

He was lying on his belly, casually watching them from less than ten paces away. His jaw rested on his fist and his other arm was curled at the elbow in front of him.

Slowly, the goblins backed away, bowing their heads and extending their palms toward him as they chanted in one, gurgling voice, "Ralligor. Ralligor. Ralligor."

To Ellianta's amazement, the dragon spoke to the goblins in their language. He even mimicked the gurgle of their voices.

One of the goblins, the closest to Ellianta and the one that had been right in front of her, dropped to his knees, still holding his palms to the dragon and his head down as he said something in his language.

Ralligor responded, then growled and bared his teeth, finishing with, "*Par gah rut soonter.*"

The goblins backed away more, then turned and fled, noiselessly disappearing into the forest.

The dragon watched them for long seconds before turning his eyes back down to Ellianta. "You are beginning to remind me of a bothersome unicorn I know."

She stared back at him, unsure what to think or feel. When she tried to sit up, she realized that one of the goblins had managed to wind some rope around her wrists and she twisted and struggled to pull herself free of it. There was more rope around her ankles that she worked to kick herself free of. Finally getting a hand free, she pulled her arms back in front of her, looking back up to the dragon as she sat up and unwound her other wrist.

"How did you survive so long on your own?" he asked. "*Magister* must have had an army of people looking out for you."

"My life was not always so complicated," she informed timidly.

"What is so complicated about staying away from creatures that eat your kind?"

She could only offer him a shrug.

He growled a sigh and looked into the forest. "Do you think you can get along on your own for a while?"

Looking down, she nodded, now feeling more like a child than she had for more than ten seasons.

Ralligor's eyes slid back to her and he scolded, "If anything happens to you I'll never hear the end of it. You really should think about others before you imperil your own life."

When her gaze slowly shifted back to him, he almost looked like he was smiling. "How did you know to come for me?" she asked softly.

"Your father told you he would be watching. Everything that happens to you that is outside of your routine he knows about."

"How is he?" she asked, looking away from the dragon.

"As busy as always," was the dragon's answer.

She absently began to roll the rope she still held. "When can I see him again?"

"When it is safe to do so. It might help to stay out trouble long enough for us to figure something out. As long as that witch is looking for you finding a safe place for you both will be almost impossible."

Ellianta bowed her head and gripped the coiled rope tightly. "Then I cannot see him again until she is dead. I just found him, and now…" She shook her head and wiped a tear from her cheek.

"I said *almost* impossible," he corrected.

With a slight nod, she offered a soft, "Thank you." She glanced over her shoulder, then looked back up at the dragon to ask, "Why didn't you… You could have killed all of those creatures easily."

"I know I could. They also know I could. What of it?"

"Do you know what they did to that man in there?"

"Do I care what they did to that man in there?"

"How can you allow that to continue?"

"The goblins have their place the same as you do, and my place is not to wipe out an entire race because they pose a threat to a few of another."

"But they're killing people! Horribly!"

"Your kind hunts what you eat, the same as they do."

She looked away from him, a shiver finding her as she asked, "What if they come for me again?"

He sat up and stretched, his spine popping a few times, then he stood and ordered, "Show them that amulet." He looked aside and opened his wings. "Now if you will excuse me, I have to fly really low over your village and roar at them like it's the end of the world."

"That's mean!" she spat as he turned.

As he took to the air and flew away, he called back, "Just about as mean as putting such a fright into your father. Now stay out of trouble."

Her lips tightened as she watched him fly away. She reached down to pick up her bag, then she walked over the granite hilltop and started the long walk home.

A moment later, she heard the dragon roaring, and she laughed to herself and shook her head.

***

She found herself returning home a little later than she had expected. The walk home had been a slow one as she tried to remember the events of the morning. She knew she had seen something truly horrible, but when she tried to remember, she instead saw a mental image of her father and her thoughts would stray to that first day with him, and their long talk.

Trying again to recall what had happened in the castle, she almost did, but this time her thoughts were pushed toward the unicorns, and that distraction held her attention for some time. No matter how she tried, she could not remember how the goblins had butchered a man alive in their lair. The horrible memory was there somewhere, but something would not allow her to see it.

Approaching the back of the house, she heard a little girl giggling in the bushes and stopped. Her eyes cut that way and she smiled a little and whispered, "Who are you hiding from?"

"My brothers," a tiny voice whispered back.

With a slight nod, Ellianta assured in another whisper, "I sure didn't see you."

Prenzee giggled again from somewhere in the bushes and Ellianta shook her head and continued on inside.

The back door was small, had been seldom used before Ellianta moved in, and it stuck when one tried to open it. She had grown accustomed to this and it had become part of her daily ritual. It led right in to the large family room and faced the door out the front. Past a wall to the left was the kitchen where Hilliti and Grettslyn were already hard at work preparing the evening meal. Ellianta slowly set her bag down beside the ladder that led to her room and padded into the kitchen, her hands folded behind her and a swing in her step that made her skirt bell out as her hips turned back and forth."

"Finally home, are ye?" Hilliti asked, still cutting on some potatoes in front of her.

"Yes," she answered straightly.

Grettslyn was attending a pot that sat on the wood burning stove in the corner and she set the lid back in place, put the spoon down on the counter where Hilliti was working and turned toward Ellianta, wiping her hands clean with her apron as she asked, "Where did we go today, Keender?"

Ellianta shrugged, her eyes on the floor as she skipped one foot back and forth. "Just wandering as I always do, looking for the things I need in healing others."

"And not to some castle?" Grettslyn questioned.

Her foot stopping suddenly, Ellianta felt a little surge of uneasiness, and a familiar squirming in the pit of her stomach.

Hilliti turned, also wiping her hands with her apron as she

eyed the young woman.

Swallowing hard, Ellianta sheepishly turned her eyes to Grettslyn, then to Hilliti. She simply did not have an answer, and in this moment felt that she was a girl of six, not a woman of twenty-six, and these two imposing women were poised to give her the scolding of her life.

Grettslyn folded her arms, her brow lowering slightly as she reminded, "I think you were warned away from that place, weren't ya?"

Ellianta sheepishly nodded.

"And went anyway?" Hilliti asked.

Her eyes shifting to the other woman, Ellianta nodded again.

Closing the couple of paces between them with two long steps, Grettslyn took Ellianta's chin and raised her head, boring into her eyes as she scolded, "Are ye just trying to get yourself killed, Little One? There be reasons we tell ye these things and you'll need to be listening and payin' attention when we're telling you."

Ellianta's eyes glossed with tears.

Grettslyn glared down at her a second longer, then she turned away, back to her labors in the kitchen. "You'll be stayin' in the next few days to think over what ye were told. Tell ye these things for ye own good, Lass."

Her lips tightening, Ellianta defiantly folded her arms and informed, "I am not a child I'm a woman grown, and if I wish to go on my wanderings, then that's…" She stopped as Grettslyn turned on her and for a moment she just stared back. They were both imposing women, but Grettslyn was the more imposing of the two, and intimidation won over pride. Lowering her eyes, she drew a breath and softly asked, "Three days, you say?"

"At least," Grettslyn confirmed. "Be a good girl and ye might wander earlier. Start with the garden and bring me in some of those bean pods. Should be a bucket ready to harvest."

Still staring at the floor, Ellianta nodded, then turned to the door and padded slowly toward it. They were treating her like one of the children. Granted, she was small in comparison and looked young, but she was a grown woman, after all. It had been many seasons since anyone had actually imposed any discipline on her. It was both frustrating and somehow liberating.

Grasping the door handle, she turned back and summoned, "Grettslyn. Hilliti."

They both turned toward her.

She smiled a little and said, "I love you, too."

**

As usual, the evening meal was a feast and everyone treated it like it was a party. Laughter was the order of the evening, as always, and this close family only seemed to get closer. The beginning of the meal was a little awkward for Ellianta and she had a difficult time even making eye contact with Grettslyn and Hilliti, but it was Hilliti and Brogret who warmed her back up and found her smile.

After dark, as the fire in the fireplace began to die down, Ellianta sat cross-legged on the floor in front of it, facing the three children who sat a pace away from her and listened to her tale with wide eyes. Sitting in their respective chairs and also listening, the two farmers and their wives all wore smiles as they watched their adopted daughter weave her tale for the children.

Ellianta's eyes swept from one child to the next, and grew a little wide. "She did not know why the big dragon carried her off or if he would eat her. Had she been saved from one fate only to meet one more horrid?" She glanced from one to the next, giving them a long pause to think about what she had already said.

"Then what happened?" one of the boys asked.

Her eyes narrowed a little. He took her to a land far from her home, and when he finally landed, she found herself in a big field of flowers. He left her alone there and when she had given up hope, she saw a unicorn come to her. He was such a magical unicorn that she wept when she saw him. He saw how sad she was and called to another unicorn, a snow white one who stayed with her and made her feel better. The two unicorns stayed with her and kept her safe until help arrived."

"Who came to help her?" the other boy asked.

Her gaze met his, and a little smile touched her lips. "He was a wise man of the forest. He knew what she needed and where she needed to go. He knew he had to protect her from the horrible person who wanted to hurt her. So, he took her to a castle that was deeper in the forest, a wonderful castle of whitewashed stone and tall towers, and she met a princess there who was friends with the wise man."

Prenzee smiled big and whispered with her usual lisp, "A princess?"

"Yes," Ellianta confirmed, "a princess. She was young and very pretty and helped our heroine to safety and let her sleep in the most beautiful room in the palace. But when morning came, an evil witch sent her demon minions to get her. The Princess' armies fought gallantly, but they were no match for the demons and monsters that the witch had sent."

The older boy's eyes widened and he leaned forward a little. "Did they get her?"

Her eyes narrowing slightly, Ellianta smiled a little and continued, "The wise man of the forest was a wizard and he stood between her and the demons. The dragon was his friend and he and the unicorns also came back to defend her. Together, they all fought the witch's minions off and saved her from them. But, she knew the witch would never stop until she got her, so she had to go to a secret place and start her life over again. So, with the help of the wizard and the dragon, she was whisked away to a far away land that the witch never had heard of where she would be safe from her."

All of the children smiled and the oldest had a little look of relief on his face.

"What happened to her?" the younger boy asked.

Ellianta took long seconds to answer and just stared at him for a time, then she finally smiled a little and replied, "She found a new family. She found people who cared about her as they would one of their own."

"Did she live happily ever after?" Prenzee asked.

With a nod, Ellianta confirmed, "So far, but I'm sure she has many more adventures ahead of her."

"Can we hear more?" the younger boy asked.

With a broad smile, Ellianta assured, "Of course, but I think it's bed time now."

They all moaned their disappointment and reluctantly got to their feet. They took turns giving her a hug and kiss on the cheek, saying their good nights as Archem and Brogret rose from their chairs to see them to bed.

Still sitting cross-legged on the floor, Ellianta was quickly lost in her thoughts. Would she get to live happily ever after? She had a father she would never get to see, but a protective dragon that watched over her, and a new family that was doing the same.

"Quite the tale, Little One," Grettslyn observed.

"Thank you," Ellianta offered softly. "It's just an old story I heard once."

"Hmm," Hilliti started. "Sounds like ye have it quite to memory. Ends like your own life of late. Did ye know the Desert Lord visited today?"

Ellianta turned on her behind, looking to the robust women. "Who?"

"Desert Lord," Hilliti explained. "Big black dragon that lairs east of here in the desert. You didn't see him? Didn't hear him?"

She looked away, nervously answering, "I... I heard something. It was a dragon?"

"Aye," Grettslyn confirmed. "Visits here from time to time."

"Oh," Ellianta said softly. "I suppose it's best to stay out of his way when he comes."

The two women looked to each other, then they stood and

Hilliti announced, "Tis bed time. Much to do tomorrow. Ellianta, you be careful of those demons and witches in there. Have pleasant dreams tonight."

She nodded and assured, "I will."

As they went toward their respective bedrooms, Grettslyn turned and asked, "Going to bed, Little One?"

"Not just yet," she replied, staring into the fireplace. "I have a few things I want to attend to before I do, herbs to dry and crush to powder and all that. I'll retire later."

"Don't be stayin' up too late, Lass. Good night to ya."

"Good night," Ellianta said softly back. There was much to think about, much to work out in her mind, and her conflicting feelings would have to be brought under control.

CHAPTER 9

The man lowered his shirt gingerly, still sore after having the stitches that held him together for many days removed.

Ellianta washed her hands in a water basin and looked back at him as she informed, "You'll be sore for a while longer, but your wounds have healed very nicely."

This was the man's house, a small place with few furnishings and almost no decorations. To make working on him easier, Ellianta had asked him to sit up on his eating table, which he did, and she had removed his stitches as gently as she had put them in, making small talk with him the whole time.

He growled a little and shook his head as he looked to her. "Sore is better than dead, I would reckon. Ye have me thanks again, Lass."

She just smiled at him and dried her hands. "You are most welcome, good sir. Maybe the creatures that attacked you will stay away for a while."

"Gave one a good whack with a shovel," he informed proudly. "That one'll not be back for a spell."

Ellianta laid the towel on his table and joked, "That one will probably be calling on me next."

He laughed. "Well, ye have good marks with me, Lass. You just say what ye need and I'll be makin' it happen. What ya need today?"

She picked her bag up and offered him a big smile. "You just get better. We have time to talk about marks when you are healed and can work again. Is there anything you need? Are you eating okay?"

He nodded. "Me brother and his family are taking care of such things."

"Then tell them thank you for me, and just make sure you heal up all the way before you go out and get crazy anymore, okay?"

He smiled and nodded. "Aye, sure will, Lass. You just keep your marks with me in mind when ye need something."

She nodded to him, then finally left his house.

That was the last of her rounds for the morning and she turned up the village street to return home. There was a cluster of homes here and many people knew her, and many paused to say their hellos. Her warm smile and her charm had won her many friends and her pretty face and the curves of her little body had won her the eye of more than one man of the village.

"Lass," someone summoned from a house behind her.

She turned and smiled at the older gentleman in the blue shirt and brown trousers who approached her, greeting, "Good morning, Roddstek. How is that shoulder?"

Holding a package in one hand, he worked his other arm in a few circles and offered her a satisfied smile. "Doing better, Lass. Doing much better. Glad I ran into you. Before ye get off too far, want ye to have this." He held the package to her, raising his brow.

She set her bag down and took it with both hands. It was very heavy and wrapped in some kind of burlap and she glanced at him as she pulled the top layer off of it, then folded back the second, her eyes widening as she looked down to the marble mortar and pestle she held.

He smiled a little broader. "Heard say that you were lookin' for one of these. Spent the last few days carving and grinding that one."

Ellianta turned her eyes to his, her mouth hanging open as she gasped, "This is for me?"

"Of course," he declared. "Maybe square our marks, aye?"

"Yes!" she squealed, looking back to the tool she held. "This is… Thank you! Thank you so much!"

"A great pleasure, Lass. A great pleasure. You fixed me up, maybe now can fix up me friends and neighbors, aye?"

She bent over and set the mortar and pestle down, then threw herself at him and hugged him around the neck, repeating, "Thank you!"

Laughing a bit as he hugged her back, he simply replied, "You're welcome, Lass."

**

She burst into the house, stopping in the middle of the family room as she called, "Hilliti! Grettslyn! You are not going to believe this!"

They emerged from the kitchen, looking to her with a little curiosity, and Hilliti asked, "What be ye bellowing about, Little One?"

Ellianta held up the mortar and pestle, her teeth showing through the big smile she wore as she showed it to them.

"Well isn't that nice," Hilliti drawled.

Her mouth swinging open, Ellianta looked to them in turn and asked, "Did you two know about this?"

They both shrugged and Hilliti said, "Might have mentioned something to a craftsman in town, one with a bothersome shoulder."

She smiled broadly at them, then she turned and put the mortar down before wheeling back around and throwing herself into the two big women, wrapping her arms as far around them as she could as she loudly said, "Thank you!"

They laughed a little between themselves and hugged her back.

She pulled away and declared, "I have to try it. I've never had one this nice before and I want to use it right now!" Looking around, she loosed a frustrated breath and growled, "I already ground up the herbs I'd collected that were dry. Others aren't dry yet." She turned begging eyes to Grettslyn.

"You should get ye more," she declared. "Got to keep your medicines well at hand for all the healing ye been doing."

Ellianta's teeth showed through her broad smile again. "I can go? Really?"

"Aye, go on, Little One. Get your herbs."

She hugged them both again, then she ran toward the door, snatching her bag from the table beside the mortar as she fled the house.

**

With new purpose and excitement, she set out down one of the trails she had haunted before, knowing she would find the plants there that she could use in her healing agents and the other things she needed for her work. At a safe distance, she pulled her dress off and hung it on a tree that she had used since finding this place weeks ago, and she pulled off her slippers and hung them on the nub of a broken branch beside her dress. Down the path she would find a fast flowing creek that fed into a large pond where many of the plants she would use grew, and when she was unencumbered by her clothing, she felt her connection with the natural world become complete again.

Her journey was not a long one and she found the creek in short order, following it until it widened and slowed. Some of the plants she sought grew in the water while others grew at its edge. Thorny trees would also provide her with some of what she needed, and two of them grew in near a little clearing where the creek emptied into the deep pond. This little clearing in the forest was one that she always looked forward to visiting. With not much light filtering down through the trees that surrounded it, the grass did not grow very tall, but lush blades provided a carpet of green along a relatively flat place where she could lay in the soft grass and just enjoy the day for a while. This was a place she longed for, a place that was very similar to one from her old home.

As she arrived at the clearing, she looked up at the tiny red berries that grew in clumps up in the thorny tree, and she smiled. Another few days and she would be able to harvest some. The seeds would provide a wonderful remedy for several ailments, and she would add them to the list of things to crush with her mortar and pestle. Closer to the creek, she found a bush with broad leaves that she would collect and dry, and they would also be crushed to powder, but only a few select leaves, those that were mature, but not already turning brown. They had to have certain yellow veins in them or they would be of no use to her.

The babbling of the creek upstream of where she was drowned out most of the songbirds around, but the occasional odd splash would briefly catch her attention. Sure it was just big fish she heard, she continued to examine the leaves on the bush, looking for just the right colors, just the right textures. Moving to the other side, she knelt down into the soft, lush grass, looking over the leaves that were a little lower. She pushed her spectacles up the bridge of her nose, realizing she had done this a couple of times. Her skin was glistening with just a little perspiration, but she was barely noticing the late summer heat here in the shade. Once again she found herself completely consumed with what she was doing and everything around her ceased to be for a while. She only found a few leaves that appealed to her on this bush, but she knew she would find others on one that was closer to the pond.

Something else disturbing the water went unnoticed as she looked the bush over once more before she stood. Surely the bush by the pond would yield more than three acceptable leaves. She turned and strode that way, toward the bush that was only about six paces away, then she stopped as she saw the shirt that was spread out over the top of it, a clean, white shirt. On the other side were what appeared to be black trousers. Movement close to the pond drew her eyes and she turned toward it slightly, a gasp shrieking into her as she met the eyes of Malkar, the other healer.

But for the small bucket in his hand, he had nothing else on him, and was dripping wet as he had just come out of the pond. The look in his eyes was similar to what Ellianta knew hers was, and her eyes widened further as she realized she was wearing nothing but her spectacles and that amulet the dragon had given her.

The two stood frozen where they were, just staring at each other. Ellianta's eyes glanced involuntarily over his body, and she was very impressed with what she saw. This was a man who took care of himself. He had a small waist, big legs, big arms, big chest, big… She finally noticed him studying her in the same way, and quickly raised her bag up to her chest, not that it would have mattered at this point.

Malkar finally tore his eyes away from her, turning to approach the bush with his clothes on it. He dropped the bucket and reached for his trousers, and his hands seemed to be shaking as he fumbled with them. The bush seemed to grasp at them as he tried to remove them, and Ellianta was secretly grateful for that.

As he finally liberated his trousers, he kept his eyes from her, on what he was doing as he asked, "Do you mind?"

She shook her head and simply answered, "No." When he set his jaw, she gasped loudly and declared, "Oh! Sorry." Reluctantly, she turned around, still holding her bag to her chest. She could hear him behind her, fumbling with his clothes, and she hoped he felt as awkward as she did. Her eyes darted about as he got himself covered, and she realized that her own clothing was some distance away, and she could never reach it quickly. Her mind scrambled and she did not quite know what to do. After what felt like a very long moment, she cleared her throat as she struggled for something to say, and she did not notice him approach her.

"Here," he offered.

Something was slipped over her head and pulled down over her shoulders and she realized that it was his shirt. Still, she tensed up and shrugged her shoulders up as he pulled it down over her body. She released her bag with one hand and fed her arm through that sleeve, then she reached under the front of the shirt and removed it and shoved her other arm through the other sleeve. Here was the one person in the village she disliked, and here he was actually showing her a little kindness. The shirt was unlaced and the fit was very big, the collar opening halfway down her chest.

"Is that okay?" he asked awkwardly.

She nodded, and finally choked out, "Thank you."

He backed away, his eyes still on her.

Ellianta folded her arms and turned to him, still holding her bag in one hand as she looked up at him. His bare chest was a distraction, but she forced her eyes up to his and pushed her spectacles up the bridge of her nose again. She desperately wanted to appear strong and defiant of his far superior size, but she knew she was not being successful. He was only a pace away, and judging from the size of his arms, he was a very powerful man. Should he want her, she was his, and she was sure they both knew it.

Instead, he looked almost timid, and very nervous.

More long seconds passed between them as neither was able to talk to the other.

Finally, he raised his chin a little and stammered, "So, what brings you this way?"

She glanced down at her bag and replied, "I'm collecting herbs. Still have to build up more healing agents and the like. Um, what are you doing here?"

He motioned with his head toward the bucket behind him and answered, "I'm collecting mussels. Some consider them a delicacy, and… Well, I'm collecting mussels."

She nodded.

"What are you collecting?" he asked, clearly trying to make conversation and avoid the awkwardness that thickened the very air around them.

"Pictel leaves," she replied.

His brow shot up and he folded his arms, that condescending look starting to return to his face. "Pictel leaves. Those are poisonous."

She smiled. "Of course they are—if you eat them! I use them in an ointment and powder that suppresses pain. I thought all healers did that."

He looked away from her. "Huh. A pain killing ointment from a poisonous plant."

"Makes patients more comfortable," she explained, "and

when they are more comfortable they can be attended to much more easily."

Looking back to her, he asked, "You squeeze the juices from them and use the extract?"

"I dry them and powder them and use the whole thing. Using just the juice produces an ointment that is much too weak."

He nodded. "That sounds reasonable. So, um, you do this naked?"

"No, my clothes are invisible today."

Malkar actually chuckled, shaking his head slightly as he admitted, "Okay, I guess I deserved that one."

She looked away, murmuring, "That and more."

"So," he started, "How did you come about doing this?"

"I've wanted to be a healer since I was a little girl," she replied, "and I've always wanted to help others. I've studied since I was eleven."

He nodded again. "I meant your practice of collecting herbs naked."

"Oh." Sharing the truth about her Wiccan studies with him was simply not an option, so she finally looked up at him again and answered, "I don't like the heat and I don't like the feel of wet, sweaty clothes on me. And I didn't expect to encounter anyone else out here."

"I don't much like that feeling, either," he admitted.

"Oh, darn," she drawled, her brow high over her eyes. "Your shirt is so hot and I just can't help sweating like a pig in here. I am so sorry."

He set his jaw. "I'm sure you are. Perhaps you will give it back to me while it is not too terribly sweaty."

Her mouth fell open. "I thought you were a gentleman!"

"As a healer, I need to remain a clean gentleman," he teased.

Nodding, she agreed, "Okay. I'm sure you need a clean shirt." She pulled her spectacles off and slipped them into her bag, then she held her bag to him and asked, "Would you turn around for a moment?"

He hesitantly took the bag and asked, "And then what?"

Ellianta's eyes shifted away. "Oh, you'll see." She had no idea what she was doing, but she felt compelled to get back at him for being such a bastard to her.

He rolled his eyes and turned around. "That isn't necessary. Just wear it as long as you need to. I can clean it when I get home."

"Or," she corrected, "I can clean if for you right now." She ran around him, toward the water.

He dropped her bag and pursued her, barking, "What are you doing?"

She spun around and back-pedaled toward the water, a teasing, mischievous smile on her lips as she replied, "I'm going to clean your shirt."

"Okay," he said, holding his palms toward her. "That's a thin knit wool shirt and we don't need it to get wet. It takes forever to dry and—"

Backing up until the water was up to her knees, she finally stopped and folded her arms. "Oh," she drawled. "You don't want it to get wet. How do you intend to clean it if you don't get it wet?"

He strode into the water as well, reaching toward her as he assured, "Okay, I get your point."

She backed up further and the bottom of the shirt, which barely covered her hips, began to get wet. "Oh, I don't think you do. Now back away."

"Or you'll what?" he challenged.

She raised her chin, then she turned and dove into the deeper water. When she surfaced and turned to face him, she had a big smile on her face as she saw the expression on his, and she swam backward away from him as she called to him, "Now it's going to be all clean. Oh, this water feels wonderful!"

"Okay," he said dryly. "Come back here now and give me my shirt back."

"Oh, no," she countered, continuing to swim backward

toward the other bank. "I think I'm going to repay all your kindness to me and clean it for you. I'll just go over here and beat it against a rock."

"No you don't!" he roared, charging into the water.

She barked a scream and turned to swim away from him, barely making it to shallow water before his arms wrapped around her waist and she was pulled backward, then hurled into the deeper water. Even before she could get her bearings again, he was upon her and she retreated, too slow to avoid his grasp. She screamed again as his big arms wrapped around her, and she finally realized she was laughing.

"Very well," he said loudly over her. "You have my shirt all wet. Thanks a lot!"

"You're welcome!" she spat back as his arms enveloped her. He was pushing her back toward shallower water, and before she realized, he was standing on the bottom, and she was not.

He crushed her to him, even as she pushed against him with her forearms to free herself.

And before she realized, he pressed his lips hard against hers, and she found herself locked in the first passionate kiss of her life. She could not breathe and alien sensations shot along every part of her body

An eternity later he pulled away a little and their eyes met. What had happened seemed to surprise him as much as it did her. She was repulsed by him; what she had felt bordered on hate, and now she raised her hands to his face and struggled to catch her breath.

His arm slid up her back and under her wet hair, up the back of her neck. Now was the time for her to protest his touch, but she could not, instead closing her eyes as he forced his mouth to hers again.

Time passed slowly, and everything around them ceased to be.

When he eventually pulled back again, her eyes were not on his, they were on his mouth. She could not look into his eyes, beautiful as they were. Feelings of contempt for him were still surging forth, but as her hands slid down his bare chest, they were eclipsed by other feelings, and her body began to take full control of her for the first time.

"I'm sorry," he offered softly. "I shouldn't have done that."

She shook her head, unable to respond otherwise as her hands slowly slid around his back and she felt his hand caress down her waist and to her hip. Now was the time to pull away from him and run, to escape what was happening and never even think about it again. He had given her yet another reason to hate him, but that was far from her mind. Nothing seemed simple in this moment but her shortness of breath, her pounding heart, and the tingling all over her.

With her arms no longer between them, his other hand slid all the way around her back and she finally felt the power of his arms as she was crushed to him again, and their faces were drawn closer together. Still, she would not look at him, but all of her senses, including her Wiccan born inner senses, felt his wanting of her, and it was not the animal lust she had felt from others. It was something more pure, something she was sure she felt herself.

"I really hate you," she finally said.

"You want me to stop, then."

"I didn't say that. I just want you to know I think you are a complete, unfeeling bastard and I wish you would fall off of the edge of the world and burn in Hell."

His fingers slowly closed around her long hair and pulled it down, gently forcing her chin up and her open, wanting lips to his a third time.

Here, her inexperience was clear and she acted purely on instinct. He, however, was clearly very experienced. He knew what to do, how and where to touch her, how hard to kiss her, and exactly how to react to everything she did, and she surrendered herself to it all.

When they separated this time, his lips glanced around her cheek and nibbled at her throat and neck, right under her ear.

Not realizing the affect this would have on her, she simply

allowed him there and when he was kissing her in just the right spot, her entire body tensed up and she drew a gasping breath through her wide open mouth. Her eyes were still closed and she rolled her head back as much as she could, sliding one hand to the back of his neck and grasping him there as hard as she dared. She finally did realize that she was surrendering herself to him and grabbed his hair, pulling his head away from her as she looked up at him, and when their eyes met again, she wanted to scold him, slap him, call upon the Wiccan power within her to burn him to ashes.

His breath also came labored, but this time he glared down at her, his teeth clenched as he growled, "You are still an inexperienced little girl. I cringe every time someone tells me how you've treated their ailments."

"I cringe every time you touch someone," she spat back, "especially me. I'm sickened at the thought that these people have suffered through your unfeeling touch as a healer for so long and I'm sickened at how you are trying to violate me now!"

"You don't seem to be suffering at my touch now, Keender."

"My stomach is sour being so close to you," she hissed.

"You still have much to learn, little girl."

"Oh, and you think you can teach me?" Her eyes found his mouth again, her hand stroking through his hair. "Perhaps I have something to teach you."

"Perhaps you do," he countered.

Her eyes snapped back to his and she found herself disarmed. His fingertips slid down her spine and his other hand around her behind, pulling her hips into his. The shirt was still thankfully between her skin and his hands, but at the moment she wished it was not.

He grabbed the back of her hair again and jerked it down, forcing her face up to his. "Do you still think that you have nothing to learn from me? Are you so foolish?"

"Yes I am foolish," she snarled back. "I'm still in your arms, aren't I?"

"Perhaps you are just where you wish to be."

She glanced aside. "Well, I haven't vomited yet, but I still find you repulsive."

"Am I, now?" he growled back, moving his lips closer to hers.

"Very," was her reply as she turned her head and closed her eyes. She whimpered helplessly as he kissed her even harder, but this time she grabbed *his* hair and forced his mouth on hers. Her other arm would not reach all the way around him, but she savagely dug her fingernails into his back.

He pulled back just long enough to say, "Ow."

She laughed as he kissed her again, then she pulled back and stuck her lower lip out at him, saying in a child-like voice, "Oh, did that hurt?"

He smiled back at her and replied, "Yes."

"Good thing I'm a healer," she teased. She winced and flinched a little as his fingers dug into her buttocks. "Oh, but I hate you," she hissed.

"I hate you as well," he growled back.

He kissed her hard again, then pulled her by the hair just enough to separate their mouths, his eyes hard and boring into hers as he asked, "Are you ready for me to teach you about things, Keender?"

She nodded and gasped, "Okay."

"Raise your arms," he ordered.

She complied, replying again, "Okay."

He reached to her hips with both of his hands, sliding his hands under the shirt and slowly drawing them up her body and bringing the shirt with them, and this sent chills and shocks through her all over again. Before she realized, he was balling his soaked shirt up and throwing it to the shore. Ever so slowly, his hands slid down her arms, down her body and she rolled her head back a little as she brought her hands down to grasp his shoulders.

As he drew her to him once again, she pushed back a little, feeling uncertainty and a little fear as she looked into his eyes and said almost in a whimper, "I'm a virgin."

He just stared at her for a long moment, then his fingers combed through her hair near her ear and he assured in a whisper, "I'll be gentle."

**

Ellianta had always fantasized about her first time with a man. Different ways it could happen, different places, different men… She never stuck with one fantasy for very long. How it truly happened was far beyond what she could have even imagined.

Sometime later, perhaps hours, they lay naked in the sunshine on a bed of soft, lush grass. He lay on his back with one arm behind his head, his other around Ellianta. She lay on her side beside him, one leg lying folded at the knee over his hips and one arm lying over his chest. Her head lay on his other arm and she absently ran her fingertips over his chest, her eyes following this motion as she just absorbed the moment, and the caress of his fingers gliding over her soft shoulder.

Finally, after some time of silence between them, she said, "It still rather hurt."

His eyes slid to her and he confessed, "I didn't feel a thing but pure ecstasy."

She smiled. "I may have felt some of that, too."

He loosed a breath, turning his eyes to the clouds again. "Being with you was wonderful, but I feel like I took advantage of you."

She nodded a little, confirming, "You did. Bastard."

Their eyes met and they just stared at each other for a moment more.

"Hilliti is right," she said suddenly. "You are pretty."

He smiled. "And you are nothing short of beautiful."

"I still hate you," she teased.

"And I you," was his answer to her. "Tell me something. When did you discover using poisonous leaves to kill pain?"

"It was something I was taught many seasons ago, when I

really was a keender."

"I see. And your use of honey to keep wounds from becoming septic?"

"I thought everyone knew about that."

"Not everyone does. Still, it seems like very basic knowledge of healing."

"So you know a few things that I don't. Does that make you a better healer?"

"In some ways," he replied. "I sure have seen how people respond to your touch, though."

"Afraid I'll replace you?"

"No, not remotely."

Her eyes narrowed. "You should be, old man."

Malkar laughed a little. "You've got a long way to go before that worries me, little girl."

"You couldn't even treat a simple arm sting," she spat.

"I was not aware that we were competitors," he countered.

"You started that," she reminded.

He released a long breath and nodded. "I've been here a long time. The people here mean a great deal to me and I suppose I've gotten a little protective of them."

"Everyone here?" she asked softly.

Nodding, he softly replied, "Yes, everyone."

She looked back to her hand as she began to massage his chest a little more deeply. "You have those who are fond of you as well. Not many, but there are some."

He smiled. "I see. Any inexperienced young healers among them?"

"I don't know any," she confessed in a sigh. "I still hate you."

Malkar enjoyed a little laugh at that. "I see. I still hate you as well. Perhaps, just to be an unfeeling bastard I'll violate you again the next time I see you wandering naked out here."

She did not respond to that but to smile a little.

Another deep breath escaped him. "I should get those mussels back to the village."

Patting his chest, she asked, "And these?"

"They'll come with me," he replied in a dry tone.

"Oh, okay. I should get back, myself. I'm usually not gone so long."

He got up as Ellianta rolled from him and her eyes were on him as he walked around her and to the bush where his clothes were and his shirt was drying.

As he picked his trousers up, he looked to her and asked, "Do you mind?"

She rolled to her side and propped her cheek in her palm, her eyes on him as she slowly shook her head.

He just stared back for long seconds, then he dressed while she watched. The last thing he reached for was his shirt, and he growled a little as he found it still wet, and turned an irritated look to her.

"Know my wrath," she hissed at him.

Malkar just raised a brow, then he laid the shirt back down and put on his jerkin.

Slowly getting to her feet, she strode over to him and picked the shirt up, slipping into it almost seductively. She turned her eyes up to his and asked, "Would you escort a young and helpless girl through the wilderness and to her clothing?"

"I can," he admitted. "Do you know one who is needing an escort?"

"Oh, never mind," she snarled, striding away from him.

"Forgetting something?" he asked in a teasing voice, and when she turned he held her bag up. "I think your spectacles are still in here, too, or can you see that far without them?"

She folded her arms and confessed, "No."

Picking his bucket up, he strode toward her and took her hand. "Come on, helpless young girl. Let's find your dress."

"I need my spectacles," she informed.

"No," he corrected, "I'll just guide you. I may even steal another kiss."

"That's the only way you'll get one."

They arrived at the tree where she had her dress hung up some time later, and as she reached for it, she looked over her shoulder at him and asked, "Do you mind?"

He set the bucket down and folded his arms, slowly shaking his head.

Staring back at him for long seconds, Ellianta finally murmured, "Letch," as she removed his shirt and took her dress from the tree. Slipping into it, she quickly smoothed it over her before taking her slippers down and turning toward him. Giving him a quick glance, she looked behind her and sat down on a tree root to put her slippers on, which she did with hands that shook a little.

He knelt down in front of her and took the strap from her hands, slowly winding it around her ankle and tying it in place with a perfect little bow. When this was done, he reached to her other foot, taking it by the heel and pulling it closer to him.

Once again Ellianta breathed with some difficulty as he slipped the other slipper into place and slowly wound the strap around her ankle. As he finished tying it, he looked to her, meeting her eyes with his.

She swallowed hard, those feelings of just a few hours ago trying to emerge again.

He stood and offered her his hand, pulling her gently to her feet. "I still dislike you immensely and I still think you are death personified as a healer."

"I hate you even more," she snarled. When he reached past her and took his shirt from the tree where she had hung it, she grabbed onto it and pulled back, her eyes never leaving his.

He pulled his shirt back hard and Ellianta with it. His other hand grasped her neck and his lips took hers yet again, and she barked a little scream behind his kiss.

Their arms slid around each other and they joined one more time.

Finally pulling his shirt free of her grip, he stepped away from her and slipped her spectacles onto her face, then he picked up his bucket and turned to walk away, warning, "Don't let me catch you out here again, Keender."

She folded her arms and challenged, "Or you'll what?"

He looked over his shoulder and smiled at her, then continued on his way.

**

Arriving home, Ellianta slowly closed the door and pressed her back against it, leaning her head back as she closed her eyes to savor recent memories. She was unaware of the little smile she wore, unaware that her hair was still damp, and unaware for some time that Hilliti and Grettslyn were standing right in front of her.

When Hilliti cleared her throat, Ellianta's eyes flashed open and she looked to the two women who stared at her with high eyebrows. Her eyes shifted from one to the other and she nervously smiled, raising her head off of the door as she bade, "Good afternoon."

Grettslyn folded her arms. "Out a bit late today, ye were. Gathered many herbs to use in that new mortar, did ye?"

Nodding, Ellianta confirmed, "Uh, huh." She pulled the bag open and removed the contents, all three leaves. "Most of what I need still needs to ripen," she explained. "I looked and looked but this is all I could find. I should dry them before—"

"You're glowing, Little One," Hilliti observed.

Ellianta raised a hand to her cheek and protested, "No I'm not! I, uh… I just got a lot of sun out there."

The two women looked to each other and shook their heads, and Grettslyn said, "He must not have been so impressive. Probably had small, weak arms."

"He did not!" Ellianta barked before realizing, then she gasped and covered her mouth.

With smug little smiles, Grettslyn and Hilliti looked back to each other, and folded their arms.

Once again Ellianta felt cornered and she shrugged her shoulders up. "You aren't going to tell the men of the house, are you?"

They walked to her, slipping their arms around her and pulling her away from the door and toward the living area.

"That all depends," Hilliti said flatly.

"On what?" Ellianta timidly asked.

Grettslyn smiled a little broader. "On how much ye be willing to tell us."

**

Over a bottle of wine, the three women spent a couple of hours talking about Ellianta's afternoon encounter, Hilliti's first time, and the awkwardness of Archem when he first tried to court Grettslyn. They shared fond memories and laughed with each other until Prenzee got up from her nap and joined them, rubbing the sleep from her eyes as she padded in and crawled into her mother's lap.

"We should get that meal cooking," Hilliti said as she stood up. "Them men folk will be copious hungry as they return from the fields."

"Or from the pub," Ellianta added, provoking laughter from the other two women.

Grettslyn looked to Ellianta and raised her chin. "Still won't tell us a name, eh?"

"Not until I'm sure you won't send Archem and Brogret after him," Ellianta assured.

"He should take you as a wife now," Hilliti said straightly, "make an honest woman of ye."

"I'm not sure I want to be his wife," Ellianta informed.

"You just said how he curled your toes and now you aren't sure about him?"

"Not entirely, but maybe soon." Ellianta's pleading eyes turned to them and she begged, "Please don't tell Archem and Brogret. I will in time, but not now."

"Tis for ye to do yourself," Grettslyn informed. "We'll be keepin' this among the women. Prenzee, be a lamb and go out and find ye brothers. They're in some mischief for sure today."

CHAPTER 10

A day later, a few hours before sundown, Archem and Brogret, Grettslyn and Hilliti thought that their hard working adoptee could use some time at the pub. They did this every now and again and always there was someone there to use his marks to buy her a little glass of wine, as she preferred wine but occasionally she would join them all in a mug of ale or mead and a good time was had by all. She was always the smallest person in there and had the eye of many a single man. How she loved to have fun with the crowd was something that the whole village had come to expect from her.

On this late day, however, she was not having fun. The patrons would see her in yet another heated argument with the town's established healer, as they seemingly went nose-to-nose over some issue involving the proper care of an open wound.

She jabbed a finger into his chest and shouted, "Because you have not an idea how to care for the patient as a whole! A simple wound is only part of the problem!"

Malkar folded his arms and bent down to her, retorting, "Treat the wound, make the patient better and everything falls into place on its own. Why is that so difficult for you to understand?"

"Such an injury does more than just break the flesh, and patients heal much faster with more than bandages and healing agents. If you were any kind of healer you would know that."

"I was a healer when you were still playing with your little dolls, Keender."

"I didn't play with dolls, you butcher."

"No, you probably tried to heal them and ended up killing them."

She took a half step toward him, glaring up at him as she warned, "I've not gotten any complaints from those I've treated. How about you?"

He raised an eyebrow and countered, "I wouldn't have any complaints either if I had breasts like those to show off to every patient."

Before she could respond, Archem took her arm and pulled her away, suggesting, "Perhaps we could continue this later."

A group of men also took Malkar from behind and pulled him toward a nearby table, one saying, "Just let the keender have her day, mate. Not worth all the shouting."

"Let go!" Ellianta protested as she pulled back against Archem's grip. When Brogret stepped in front of her and pushed her back toward the bar, she reached past him to point a finger at Malkar as she shouted, "This isn't over!" In a huff, she turned and allowed them to take her back to her place at the bar, grumbling, "Ignorant bastard," as she sat down.

"Just let it go, Lass," Brogret advised. "You'll win no battles there. Closed ears can't hear ye no matter how loud ye shout."

She picked up her cup of mead and took a couple of gulps, then looked to her other side, right to Hilliti and asked, "If you were hurt, wouldn't you want someone to treat your wound *and* the ill feelings it can give you?"

Hilliti nodded and held her mug to Ellianta and agreed, "Aye to that, Little One."

Ellianta took another gulp and looked behind her, seeing that Malkar was just looking away from her. Her eyes swept over the crowded room and stopped on a really big fellow she had never seen before.

He had long brown hair that dropped just below his shoulders, very broad, muscular shoulders. His arms were huge! He only wore a traveler's jerkin that was made of what appeared to be stag hide. As she was seeing him from the side, she could see that his chest was enormous and his back behind it was just as big. Thick legs filled dirty white trousers and he wore heavy, well worn brown boots that had buckles on the sides.

Sitting with him and facing him from the opposite side of

the table was a much smaller man with straight black hair all the way to his mid-back. This man had bronze skin with deeply chiseled features and steely eyes that looked almost black. He wore a buckskin shirt and similar trousers with lightweight brown boots.

Ellianta had seen strangers in the pub before, but none like these, not a pair like this. One was clearly a man of the forest while the other one looked like a pure warrior, one who seemed like he could hold off an entire army at a time. She could tell that the larger one was a very tall man even though he was sitting, and his size and titanic build would dwarf even the largest of the men from the village.

Turning back to her mug, she tried to forget about the strangers. She had seen many of them in here. These two just stuck in her mind and imagination, even as she tried to dismiss them.

"Ellianta!" a man shouted from the other end of the bar. "Perhaps you will grace us with another melody from that wonderful voice of yours, aye?"

Everyone at the bar erupted in cheers and many at the tables did, too.

Rolling her eyes, she took another gulp from her mug and hopped down from her stool, turning just as the door burst open and five men in black steel and leather armor burst in.

As they fanned out a few paces into the pub, everyone grew silent and all eyes focused on them.

Their helmets were all of the same construction but one. It had a red feather stuck in the brow piece and this man wore more decoration on his tunic than the others. This is the one who strode into the bar with heavy steps. He pulled this helmet off and scanned the pub and everyone in it, then he announced, "We've come a long way in search of someone. She is a young woman who may be in grave danger, and a reward has been offered for anyone who will surrender her to us." He scanned the room again, but this time his eyes locked on Ellianta. "She is an attractive lass, perhaps twenty-five or so seasons old, petite for her age. Dark brown hair, very long." He began to stride toward her, his gaze fixed on her. Two others followed.

Ellianta backed away, stopped by her bar stool.

His dark eyes still locked on hers, the invading soldier stopped about five paces away and folded his arms. "She has weak vision and wears some kind of lenses before her eyes, and she is known as Ellianta."

A deafening hush fell over the pub.

Brogret finally stood and took her side, putting his arm around her as he informed, "I've heard of no such lass here, mate. We'd all know if there would be some fugitive come around."

The soldier's eyes shifted to Brogret. "And who is this you protect?"

He raised his chin. "This be me daughter Prenzee. Hasn't much been out of the village in her twenty seasons, but might be lookin' for a husband."

Ellianta lowered her eyes and softly said, "But not a soldier."

Brogret shrugged. "Well, you're out of luck here, mate. Maybe find another bride in the next village, aye?"

A few people in the pub dared to laugh and the officer actually smiled.

"You know," the soldier finally said, slowly striding forward again, "I think I should just take this lass with me anyway, just in case she is not truly what she appears." He stopped a few paces away and his eyes shifted to Brogret's. "Perhaps my men and I will also kill any and all who stand against us. Now, is this the young woman we seek or not?"

"She isn't," Brogret assured. "Ask anyone. She's me daughter." He looked over the pub and pressed, "Right, mates?"

A collective "Aye!" came from many in the pub.

"I'd best not take the chance." He looked over his shoulder, to the two men behind him and ordered, "Take her."

As they strode forward, Malkar got up and bade, "Excuse me, fair sir."

Ellianta's heart jumped, as did everyone's in the pub.

The officer looked over his shoulder again and asked in an exasperated tone, "Who dares to approach me?"

As the two soldiers took Ellianta's arms, the healer introduced, "My name is Malkar. I am the village healer and this girl assists me. I am apprenticing her as I have been for the last four seasons and I can assure you that this simple girl—"

The officer's fist slammed into Malkar's cheek with such swiftness that he could not see it coming, and so hard that he was spun around and sent stumbling across the room where he crashed into the two visiting men's table. Their ale went everywhere, but for the black haired man's as he removed it from the table as he saw the healer coming, and some went into the big man's lap.

"Malkar!" Ellianta screamed as she tried unsuccessfully to break away from the men holding her.

The healer lifted his head slightly. His cheek was split open just under his eye and bled terribly. In a second his head fell back and he was unconscious.

"Now," the officer said loudly to everyone as he turned to the pub's patrons. "Does anyone else have anything to say about this girl?"

Brogret looked to her and, frightened as she was, she subtly shook her head.

Slapping his hands onto his thighs, the big visitor stood and wheeled around, his brow low over eyes that were locked on the officer.

Raising his chin, the officer glared back at him and gestured to the two men still at the door, who strode forward at his command. Calmly, he stared the stranger down and asked, "Something from you, perhaps?"

The huge man, who was a head height taller than any of the invading men in the pub, closed the distance with three steps, never taking his eyes from the officer's as he growled, "Do you intend to buy me another pitcher of ale?"

"I do not," the officer replied in a matter of fact tone.

As the men behind the big man reached him and reached for their weapons, he swung around to his left and slammed his fist right into the face of the first one, knocking him to his back. Turning fully, he caught the sword arm of the second before the man could get his sword drawn and slammed his fist down onto his elbow, breaking it with a loud snap and horrific screams from his foe. As he turned back, one of the men holding Ellianta abandoned her and rushed forward. This one received a hard blow to his leather armored chest that sent him slamming back first into the bar where he broke two barstools that had been abandoned by patrons and fell to the floor. He raised his head and coughed, then struggled to take a breath, coughed again and spat up blood, then his head fell all the way to the floor and his body went limp.

Three men were down: two remained.

Looking to the last of the officer's soldiers, the huge man raised a brow, and the soldier backed away a step with his prisoner, who broke away from him and ran to the fallen healer, kneeling down beside him. The bronze skinned man, who still had his ale in his hand, just watched her attend to him, and he took another drink.

Now standing alone against the huge barbarian, the officer took a step back himself, reaching for his sword.

The big man stormed forward, growling, "Go ahead and pull it. Let that blade taste air and see how many of your bones I can break before you die."

The officer swallowed hard and let go of his hilt, then raised his hands before him and backed away another step.

Glaring down at the invader, the big man informed, "I'm in the employ of that witch at Ravenhold and I've been sent to find the girl. I intend to collect the bounty on her, and if any little rodents like you get in my way I'll break you into many pieces."

"I have my orders," the officer said shakily, then he backed away further as the huge man advanced on him more.

"Do I look like I care about your orders?" the big man roared. "If I find the girl, the witch gets her and I get my bounty. If you find her you'd better give her over to me or I'll kill my way through your entire army until I find you. Do we understand each other?"

Raising his chin, the officer informed, "I think that might be the girl we're—"

The big man's hand slammed into the officer's throat and he was driven back and slammed into the bar. "Idiot!" the big man shouted. "Don't you think I would have already taken her if that was the one?" He bent down until his nose was only a finger length away from the officer's. "You go on and find her, and when you do you'd best bring her to me or I'll kill you a hundred times before you die, understand?"

The officer swallowed hard and nodded as best he could.

Grabbing the thick leather that covered the soldier's torso, the big man turned and threw him across the pub, toward the door, and as he rolled to a stop, he pointed a finger his way and reminded, "You still owe me a pitcher of ale, and I'll not forget!" He turned to the last of them who still stood by the bar and ordered, "Collect your fallen colleges and get out of here."

In a moment, all of the black armored invaders were gone.

Blotting Malkar's face with a clean bar towel, Ellianta raised her other hand to his healthy cheek as he moaned weakly and she offered him a soothing, "Shh. Just be still." Looking up, she asked, "Can someone bring me my bag?" Heavy boots approached which she assumed were Brogret's, but when she looked up to take her bag, she froze as her eyes met those of the big man, and her mouth fell open as she took the bag from him.

The big man crouched down beside her, looking over the fallen healer as he assured, "He'll be fine. I've taken a blow or two like that myself."

"You're a lot bigger than him," she pointed out, reaching into her bag. She went to work on Malkar's cheek and softly offered, "Thank you for doing that. I don't want to be taken from my village like I've seen so many others taken."

"You are quite welcome. Is there somewhere we should take him?"

Another man informed, "His house is this way."

Ellianta expected several men to carry Malkar out of the pub, but it only took one: The big barbarian fellow.

Laying him down on his bed, the big man stepped away to allow Ellianta to sit down beside him and finish what she was doing. A crowd began to gather in his house and she looked to them and said, "Thank you all for helping, but I really need to treat him without distractions now."

The big man turned and raised his hands, ordering, "Okay, everyone out. Girl's got to work, so give her some room to work."

Everyone complied without complaint and the big man closed the door behind them, then returned to Ellianta and her patient.

"That means everyone," she ordered.

"I think I need to stay with you, Ellianta," he informed.

She froze and her entire spine stiffened. Struggling just to breathe in, she did not look at the big man that she knew she would have no chance in a struggle with, but she did ask, "Please, just let me help him before you take me anywhere. Please."

"Oh, you have all night," he assured. "I'm not taking you anywhere."

She half turned and looked up at him. "And the bounty?"

He smiled at her, a very pleasant smile. "No bounty would be worth what that dragon would do to me if anything happens to you."

She raised her chin, then stood from the bed and faced him fully. "Ralligor sent you?"

"Not quite," he corrected. "You might consider this

repayment of sorts for a great kindness done a long time ago."

"Papa sent you?"

"I volunteered," he corrected again. "Your father may have his enemies, but he has a much greater number of friends."

"And you are?"

He bowed his head to her. "My name is Prince Chail of Enulam, and I am a friend."

"I've heard of you," she breathed.

"Nothing bad, I hope," he joked. The Prince raised his chin to the fallen healer and observed, "He's coming around."

She turned and sat back down on the bed, reaching into her bag again and removing the bladder with her pain suppressing powder in it. "I have to take care of him now, but I would love to speak with you at length later."

"At your convenience," he assured. "Traman and I will be pulling out in the morning, after we have scoured the entire village for you, that is. Got to keep up appearances."

Looking over her shoulder as he turned to leave, she offered, "Thank you, Chail of Enulam. I am in your debt."

He opened the door and looked over his shoulder. "No, little healer, not until mine to your father and that dragon has been paid in full."

She smiled as he left the house, then looked back down to Malkar as he moaned again and rocked his head back and forth. While he was still barely conscious was the time to check for broken bones, which she did. With everything in order there, she sprinkled some of the powder onto his wound, then she reached for her needle and thread.

"Are you all right?" he whispered weakly.

"I'm fine," she assured as she threaded the needle. "It's very kind of you to ask, seeing as how you are lying there with your face bleeding." She drew a breath as she prepared to start stitching his cheek. "That was a very brave thing you did, standing up to them, so."

He smiled a little. "Well if they take you, who will keep me honest here?"

Ellianta could only offer him a little shrug.

"And who will violate you in the wilderness?" he added.

This time he got a glance and she shyly said, "Okay, now. Behave."

He tried to raise a hand to his face and she seized his wrist and pulled it away.

"None of that," she scolded. "You're the patient now, so just lie there and let me work."

"I can't feel my face," he complained.

"That means you can't feel me sewing the wound," she explained. "Now be still."

"Ellianta," he summoned, and when he held her gaze with his, he softly told her, "You have my trust, little healer."

She smiled a little, then she gently ordered, "Shh. Just close your eyes and it will be over before you know."

True to her word, she worked quickly and very precisely, closing his cheek almost exactly as it had been torn open.

"There you go," she whispered. "Now you should rest."

"I'm not tired," he complained, finally opening his eyes.

"Still, you need to sleep. You will heal quicker that way." She removed a jar of honey and a clean, rolled cloth, and she poured some of the honey on his wound, smearing it with some kind of metal spatula as gently as she could. When this was done, she cut the cloth to the right size with her dagger and carefully pressed it into place, forming a neat bandage. "Now don't fidget and don't pull this off or pick at it. It must stay in place until that wound closes."

"What if I want to look at it?" he asked.

"Then you will wait until I take it off, then you can see. Now you need to rest."

He raised his hand to her face and gently stroked her cheek. "I still think about being with you that morning. It's haunted me since we parted ways."

She nodded and looked away from him.

"So you've thought about it, too?" he asked.

Still looking across the room, she finally ordered, "You need to rest." When she tried to get up, he seized her wrist and pulled her back down.

"I need to know," he insisted.

Reluctant to answer, she finally admitted, "I've thought of little else."

"Then why are you so elusive? Why do you act so aggressive toward me?"

"Because I hate you," she replied straightly.

"Or you can't admit that you might have some other feeling for me," he corrected.

She lowered her eyes with a blink, then tried to pull away from his grip. "I have to go. Please let go of me."

"Answer me," he insisted.

"Just let go. You need to rest. Please, Malkar just let me go."

"Why? Give me one good, truthful reason and I will."

"Because if you ever found out what I truly am…" she started. Shaking her head, she pulled against him again and ordered, "I have to go, so let go of me."

"What are you truly?" he asked softly.

She turned her head and stared at the door, her mouth quivering, and she could not answer.

"You're afraid of being judged," he guessed.

"I've been judged," she replied in a tiny voice.

His lips tightened as he stared up at her and watched her try not to cry. "Ellianta." When her head moved slightly toward him at the sound of her name, he offered, "Kiss me one time, like you did before, and I'll let you go."

She considered, then looked down to him and asked, "If I do, will you get some rest?"

He shrugged. "I don't know about that, but I'll let you go."

Her free hand stroked his unhurt cheek, then she bent toward him and kissed him gently at first, and as his hand found the back of her hair again, she fell against him and released all of the passion she had for him.

A moment later she pulled away, and he let her. Good to

his word, he released her hand, kissing it before he did. "Thank you, Ellie," he whispered.

She combed her fingers through his hair and ordered, "You rest now."

"Will you visit me in the night?" he asked directly. When she looked away and indecision took her features, he asked, "Very well. Do you want to visit me in the night and just can't for some reason?"

Ellianta smiled a little and looked down at him. "I'm sure I can find a reason to stay the night, but you need to rest."

"So you've said. We men are very resilient creatures who are well able to take a little combat and shrug it off quickly."

She smiled a little more, reminding, "He knocked you out cold with one blow."

Raising a brow, he asked, "Would you prefer a lover or a fighter?"

"Right now," she replied, "a sleeper." She raised her head, half turning to the door, then she reached into her bag again and rummaged around for a moment before producing a little wooden vial that had a wooden stopper. She rose from the bed and went to his water basin. He had a tin cup there for drinking and she scooped some water out of the basin and set the cup down. Pulling the stopper on the vial, she poured some white powder into it and swirled the water until it dissolved.

"What are you doing?" He asked.

She turned back to him and offered him the cup. "This will help you with the pain tonight. Drink it all."

He sat up and took the cup with a little suspicion in his eyes.

"It's an old tonic my mother taught me to make," she explained. "Really good for pain."

Reluctantly, he drank the contents of the cup, then grimaced and handed it back to her as he lay back down. "That stuff is awful!"

She set the cup down and sat down beside him again. "It

isn't meant to taste good, it's meant to ease your pain."

Folding his hands on his chest, he nodded and said, "I see."

Ellianta watched over the next few moments as his eyes grew heavy and finally, gently closed. He was quickly fast asleep and his head rocked a little to one side. She bent down and gave him a tender little kiss before taking her bag and standing. Turning to the door, it was time to call upon Wiccan senses which she had not used much since coming to the village.

Out there in the darkness of night were others looking for her, others with some wicked intent. They seemed to be searching almost door to door, and there were many of them this time. She knew her only chance to elude them would be to find Prince Chail, or to disappear into the forest for a while. Going home would not be an option as she would not endanger her family, nor would she seek help from the villagers who had been so kind to her.

Slowly opening the door, she peered outside, seeing that no one was out there, then she looked around the door to be sure it was safe to emerge.

Sticking to the shadows and hugging her bag close to her, she headed back toward the pub, hoping to find Prince Chail or his companion there. It was ahead of her, perhaps fifty more paces up the street. The stone wall of a blacksmith's shop was to her right, and it was lined by three torches that fed from oil reservoirs and lit the side of the road she walked for a five pace radius all around them, and they were more than ten paces apart. The next bunch of such torches was on the next building, a smaller wool shop down the street, and it only had two on it.

Someone yelling on one side drew her attention and she stopped and looked that way. Fear began to erupt from within her and showed itself on her face as her eyes darted around in the darkness. Hesitantly, she padded forward again, and seconds later her whole spine grew tense as she heard horses coming up behind her. Veering to one side of the street to give them room, she almost felt relieved when they rode by, then her heart sank a little as the six of them stopped and turned toward her. The garb they wore was more elaborate than the first group that had hunted her. One wore a red cape and an elaborately decorated helmet that covered his entire face. Red colored leather armor, similar to what they all wore, was modeled with intricate designs and was articulated to give maximum flexibility. They all carried swords and other weapons, and that was all Ellianta had to see.

She walked on, subtly pulling her spectacles off and slipping them into her bag, reasoning that if she did not wear them she would not be so recognizable.

"You there," a woman barked from horseback.

Ellianta froze where she was and looked that way, seeing blurry images of mostly black and red.

The soldier with the red cape dismounted and approached. Ellianta had thought this a man, but when the image drew closer she could easily make out the curves of a woman, who stopped less than two paces and looked her over. "I'm looking for a girl," the woman informed harshly. "She would have long dark hair and blue eyes that are weak, so she wears lenses over them to help her see." Looking her up and down again, the woman added, "She's about your size and shape, too, a young woman by the name of Ellianta."

Ellianta shrugged and sheepishly said, "I don't know any Ellianta."

"Your name?" the woman questioned.

"Prenzee," she replied. "My father is a farmer and I am bringing him medicine from the healer. Please may I go? I have to get this to him."

The woman's eyes narrowed and she looked Ellianta up and down again. "So you don't know her. I think you're lying." She strode toward Ellianta and loomed over her, setting her hands on her hips as she growled, "Tell me where to find the girl."

"But I don't know," Ellianta assured. "I don't even—"

The woman slapped her very hard, spinning her around where she crumpled to the road.

Ellianta pushed herself up to her knees, holding a hand over her stinging cheek as she tried to recover from the shock of what had just happened.

"Lie to me again and see what I do," the woman shouted.

She had never been treated so, never been struck like this and she genuinely wept from it. Looking over her shoulder as she still held her cheek, Ellianta whimpered, "But I don't know."

"Get her up," the woman snarled.

Two of the other riders dismounted and approached, taking Ellianta's arms and hoisting her without mercy from the road.

She was turned to face the woman and her hair was grabbed and pulled back, forcing her face up and her wide, terrified eyes to the woman soldier.

Glaring back, the woman's eyes narrowed and she advised, "My patience is growing very thin, girl. You'll tell me what I want to know."

"But I don't know her," Ellianta cried, then she screamed as the woman slapped her again and snapped her head around. "Please!" she begged. "Please stop! I don't... Please don't hit me again!"

The woman grabbed Ellianta's throat and forced her eyes back to her own. "You will tell me what I want to know. In fact, we are going somewhere private where I can get my answers from you."

"Take your hands from her!" a gruff voice ordered, a voice that Ellianta knew was Brogret's. He stormed to the woman from directly behind, Archem and a few other men behind him. "What do you think you're doing with my daughter? Prenzee, have they hurt you?"

She knew what he was doing and wept a little more, some of it more acting than emotion as she begged, "Papa, please take me home! I want to go home!"

The woman turned on Brogret and folded her arms, not remotely intimidated by his superior size.

His brow low over his eyes, he stopped half an arm's reach from the woman and growled, "We welcome visitors to this village, not a bothersome lot as you. Release my daughter and go the way you came."

Her eyes narrowing, the woman nodded slightly and informed, "Oh, I intend to go, just as soon as your little village surrenders a girl named Ellianta to me."

"There is no Ellianta here," he said loudly. "Others have already come and gone."

"Then they were fools," the woman shouted. She pointed at Ellianta and continued, "This little girl knows where she is, and if she does not surrender the girl to me she will die right here in front of you."

One of the men holding her drew his dagger and put it to her throat, and she winced and raised her chin away from the blade, her terrified eyes finding Brogret as she whimpered, "Papa."

His eyes on Ellianta, Brogret set his jaw and finally looked back to the woman. "Do ye kill the chickens because they don't know the lair of the fox? Stop this madness, says me, and be on ye way!"

The woman stared at him for long seconds, then half turned her head and ordered, "Kill her."

"Papa!"

An arrow slammed into the forehead of the man holding the dagger to Ellianta's throat, and he slipped down the wall, falling dead to the ground.

Just as everyone turned to see where the arrow had come from, one of the men still on horseback yelled and arched forward, then fell from his horse with a huge, double bladed battle axe buried in his back.

The remaining soldiers drew their weapons.

Heavy footsteps approached from the darkness and Prince

Chail strode into the torchlight, his eyes on the woman. He paused at the dead guard's body and wrenched his axe from the unfortunate man's back, then he continued on to the woman, who backed away at the approach of this huge man.

A pace away, he stopped and turned his eyes on the soldier who still held Ellianta, and the man released her and raised his hands before him. Looking back to the woman, Chail slid the axe into a ring on the side of his belt, then his hand lanced toward her throat and gripped like a hawk. Baring his teeth, he informed in a low growl, "I am employed by the witch who seeks the girl and I answer directly to her, and I intend to collect the bounty on that girl we seek. Have you found her?"

The woman shook her head.

He squeezed her throat harder, cutting off her air. "Incompetent wretch!" His other hand struck her across the face swiftly and she fell from his grip and crumpled to the ground. When she looked back up at him with wide eyes, she held a hand over the side of her face and blood poured from her nose. Chail turned to her men who were still mounted and shouted, "The girl is not in this village and you are wasting time! Ride on and find her or I'll kill the rest of you! And if you expect to see another day you will bring her to me or I'll hunt down and kill all your lines as well!"

When the woman scrambled to her feet and tried to get to her horse, she winced as the big man grasped her arm and pulled her back to him, but she would not look at him.

"Bring me the girl," he snarled, "or I'll take great pleasures with you before you die."

Her jaw shaking horribly, she nodded, her eyes on her horse.

Traman, the bronze skinned man, stepped into the torchlight with his bow in his hand and an arrow ready to shoot.

Chail turned to him and ordered, "Tell the others we ride in the morning, and kill any of these useless halfwits who remain in this village a moment from now."

Traman nodded.

And mercenaries fled as fast as their horses would go.

By now, Ellianta clung to Brogret, trying not to weep, but unable to stop herself.

Chail approached and stroked her hair. "Word will get out now that you are not here, and that some big, heartless mercenary will stop at nothing to collect the bounty on you."

Brogret looked to him, up at him a little, and asked, "Who would be havin' a bounty on such a lass as this?"

Chail shrugged. "I don't know that there's really a bounty. I just made that part up. I'll tell you what I can about the woman who is looking for her at your convenience, but for now I think she would be safe here."

Daring to grasp the Prince's huge shoulder, Brogret nodded to him and offered, "Thank ye, friend."

Nodding back, Chail smiled slightly. "We'd better get rid of these bodies."

Archem stepped forward and insisted, "First, you're comin' to the pub with us, aye? Got some ale to drink!"

Chail looked to Traman.

Traman pushed his arrow back into his quiver and dryly informed, "I'm not turning down that offer."

Archem patted Ellianta's shoulder and asked, "You comin' to the pub, Lass, or should we just take ye home?"

She shook her head and replied, "I should go and check on Malkar. I gave him some medicine to help him sleep and I want to make certain he is okay." She looked up at Chail and offered, "Thank you again, Chail of Enulam. I shall be in your debt for sure."

He smiled back and reminded, "Already taken care of. I'll see you in the morning before we leave."

She watched him turn and walk with the bronze skinned man, Archem, and many of the villagers toward the pub, and she smiled a little. "I will still repay your kindness someday."

"Sure ye won't come for a pint?" Brogret asked.

Ellianta nodded and looked up at him. She stroked his

bearded face and informed, "I'll be home in the morning, Papa."

He smiled back and kissed her forehead, then he lifted his arm from her and followed the others to the pub.

Turning back toward Malkar's house, Ellianta finally realized that she could not see well, and that everyone had already left.

"Great," she murmured as she squinted in the flickering torchlight of the street and looked around for the bag containing her spectacles.

CHAPTER 11

Malkar's eyes opened slowly. He had always been an early riser, but as he awakened he discovered the sunlight already shining into the two windows of the small sleeping room of his house. This was a simple room and he was used to everything in it. There was only the bed, a night table, a vanity and water basin and a wardrobe on the other side of the room. One door across the room from the bed led directly outside, and beside it was a leather bag that contained his healer's kit. Another door on the wall to the right of this one is where he did his work with powders and potions, much as Ellianta did. This was a secret room and he had never allowed anyone inside, telling them that if the herbs and potions were to become contaminated from the outside that it would take months to recover, and he would not be able to heal all of the ailments that he had. Given this, everyone respected his privacy, and his secret was safe.

Today, he stared at the ceiling for a time. Whatever Ellianta had given him had put him into a deep sleep. She had tricked him, outwitted him in a weak moment, and a little smile touched his lips. As healers went, she had an approach he had never seen before, and her compassion was something he found enviable.

Something felt amiss. Something in the room was different. He looked to the night table, and there, all of his things had been moved aside and a light tan suede sack lay in their place, right beside a pair of copper rimmed spectacles. Looking the other way, he smiled again.

Ellianta was curled up beside him, sleeping soundly with her hands drawn to her chest. Beneath the blanket that covered her she was undressed, her shoulder was bare and one knee was drawn up while the other leg was straight out, and her hips lay at an awkward yet alluring angle. He barely noticed this. Her eyes were closed peacefully, her lips slightly ajar. Her hair was unrestrained behind her head and flailed out on the pillow she laid on, and on the bed behind her.

There was something so precious about her, so pure, something he just could not put his finger on. They got along like oil and water, and yet something about her drew him to her, something very powerful.

As his heart softened for her, it broke a little, too. Something in his past would not let go.

He was still dressed from the night before, still bandaged, and appeared to have been tended a little in the night.

Rolling slightly to his side, he raised a hand and brushed her cheek with the back of his fingers. Her skin was so soft as to remind him of a gentle breeze and the curves of her face would be burned into his memory forever.

Moving slowly so as not to disturb her, he rolled back toward the edge of the bed and got up, finding his boots right beside the bed, but he did not put them on. Something weighed itself heavily on his mind, something very important.

Walking ever so softly, he went to the door that opened into the forbidden room and quietly entered, closing it behind him. His eyes scanned the room that was bathed in morning sunlight by many high windows of white glass. All along the far wall were shelves from floor to ceiling. They were laden with many books, most bound in leather, a few bound in twine and wood. Some of them were rather old, almost ancient. Among them were jars with different organs or plants or preserved animals within. There were many flasks of different powders and extracts, twigs and bark and hundreds of things he used in his work. A long workbench ran along the wall to the left with more shelves full of things above it. To the right was another bench that was covered with many bones. There were a few reconstructed skeletons here as well, glued together with the resin of some tree sap and held together with wire. Lying in the middle was a reconstructed human skeleton and an open book that he had been entering notes in. In the center of the room was a long, cluttered bench with more open books, candles, flasks and all sorts of things he had been working with, experimenting with, and where he dried leaves and herbs to make the powders and potions of his craft.

His eyes found the wood carved symbol that was mounted on the edge of his work bench: A full moon with a waxing moon on the left, a waning moon on the right.

Malkar pressed his back to the door, closing his eyes as he leaned his head back against it. He drew a deep breath, knowing that judgment would come sooner or later, and like a painful thorn, he would rather it was pulled quickly.

He scanned his work room once more and took one more deep breath. It was time.

A moment later he stood by his bed, watching as the object of his affections slumbered peacefully. She was a lovely sight, and his decision would be one of the hardest of his life, and sacrificing her was something that was simply inevitable.

Slowly, he half turned and sat down on the bed, never taking his eyes from her.

The disturbance of the surface of the bed shook her ever so gently and she stirred a little, drawing a breath through her mouth, then she was still again.

He reached to her, stroking her hair just slightly. Hating her would be easy, but the truth beckoned, and he knew he would not be able to avoid it forever.

Ever so slowly, her eyes half opened and she blinked as she drew another deep breath in awakening. She rubbed her eyes and looked up at him, but when she offered him a little smile he could take no more and turned away, resting his elbows on his knees as he stared at the floor in front of him.

Ellianta rose up on her elbow, raising her brow as she said, "I'm sure you would have done the same to me."

He half turned his head and loosed a breath. "I need to tell you something, and it won't be easy for me. Please just hear me out."

She sat up and pulled the blanket to her chest, leaning

against the wall as she gave him her full attention. When he did not speak right away, she slipped a hand onto his shoulder, caressing him in a reassuring way.

"I don't want to give you my heart," he explained. "Hating you was easy and you hating me was easy, but things got complicated the other day."

"How so?" she asked softly.

"You once asked why I would come here from where I was a healer before. That struck a nerve. I was a healer in Troston, mostly getting so-called dragon slayers ready to meet the Tyrant. Most did not live through the day. Many more who came across my care did not live through the night. I tired of that."

"The Tyrant?"

"He is the biggest dragon in the world, and there is such a bounty on him that soldiers of fortune will come from all over to try and collect it. I eventually left, and in my travels I met a beautiful woman. I was so taken with her as to ask her into my life. I wanted her to be my wife and I wanted to be her husband."

A little concern parted her lips.

He continued, "The day finally came when I had to give up my secrets to her. I would not have a marriage based on lies, so I... I told her all about me, what I do and what I am. She left me that very day, and took what was left of my heart with her."

"Wait a moment," she started.

He got up from the bed and turned toward the door to his work room, pausing there with his hand on the handle and his forehead resting against the door.

Wrapping the blanket around her, Ellianta got out of the bed and padded over to him, reaching up to his shoulder again with concern in her eyes. "Malkar, you're scaring me. What is so horrible?"

"I want you with me," he tried to explain, "but I want no secrets between us. If this is to end us, then it needs to end us now."

"End us?" she questioned.

He half turned his head, his voice louder as he informed, "I'm falling for you and I don't want to. As a rival you cannot hurt me as much as you could as a lover."

Folding her arms, she barked, "What makes you think I love you?"

He opened the door. "After you see what's in here, you never will." His head was held low as he led her inside and he stepped to one side to allow her to see everything. He would hide nothing.

Ellianta stopped beside him and scanned the room, her eyes stopping on the blurry Wiccan symbol on the end of his work bench and she drew a gasp, then turned and bolted out of the room.

He clenched his teeth, knowing it was over before it started, but his attention darted back to the door as she rushed back in, this time pulling her spectacles onto her face.

Her full lips remained ajar as she scanned the room again, then she strode over to the work bench and looked at the symbol more closely, the Latirus words scribed around it. Turning to him with wide eyes, she declared, "This is Wiccan!"

Malkar nodded, and looked away from her.

She spun back, striding with quick steps beneath the blanket she wore to his book shelf. Running her fingers along the spines, she finally pulled one off the shelf, a rather old, leather bound copy of Wiccan rituals and she thumbed through the pages. Shaking her head, she mumbled, "Unbelievable."

"Now you know," he said softly. "I will only ask that you tell no one. It is the only secret that I keep from the village."

She raised her eyes, and when she turned to him, those deep blue eyes were glossed by tears. "This is your closely guarded secret? You're a Wiccan?"

He nodded.

Ellianta approached, closing the book and absently setting

it on his work bench. She stopped less than half a pace from him, her eyes on his even as he would not look down to her. She pulled the blanket up her chest a little more, breathing through her mouth and with some difficulty as she softly asked, "And you love me?"

The words stung and he closed his eyes and nodded again.

"Truly?" she pressed.

"Truly," he confirmed in a whisper.

"Then I should tell you *my* secret," she offered softly and when he finally looked to her, she smiled and informed, "I've studied the Wicca most of my life. That's what got me on the path to being a healer!"

He just stared down at her, unsure if he should believe her or not.

She smiled a little broader. "I've never studied with anyone but my mother and... Malkar, we are of one spirit! We just did not see it before!"

"How long," he asked, needing a specific answer from her.

"I was sanctified when I was eleven," she replied. "Since then I've devoted my whole life to the Wicca and the healing disciplines it teaches."

His heart thundered and he took a step back.

"My heart has never been broken," she admitted, "and you must know that I promise never to break yours. I promise. I swear."

He reached to her and took her in his arms, pulling her to him with all his strength. She was lifted nearly from the floor and wrapped her arms around him, and they joined in their first passionate kiss of a new love.

CHAPTER 12

There were a hundred reasons to return home, including unfinished work, an adoptive family that would worry over her...

One thing kept her at Malkar's house until high sun: That was Malkar himself, and her unwillingness to leave the embrace of his thick arms. Lying beneath the blankets on his bed with him, she had managed to forget everything else until someone banged on the door.

They pulled away from the kiss they were engaged in and just stared at each other for long, tense seconds. A second bang on the door had them spring out of the bed and quickly dress, and Malkar was still pulling his shirt on as he reached for the door handle.

"Wait!" Ellianta barked as she clumsily pulled her dress over her head and down her body.

He looked back at her and waited until she had things under control before he turned the lever and pulled the door open.

On the other side were Prince Chail and Traman. They stood there with their arms folded, their brows held high, and the Prince's lips were pursed in an impatient expression.

"Prince Chail," Ellianta greeted, striding up behind Malkar. "We were about to go and find you."

The big Enulam man nodded slightly. "I see. We just wanted to say our farewells before departing. We've a long ride ahead of us."

"I wish you could stay longer," she said.

"We did," he informed. "We were going to pull out this morning, but you were nowhere to be found."

She nervously looked away. "I'm sorry about that. I wanted to be sure Malkar would be okay through the night, so I stayed and nursed him along."

Chail's eyes shifted to him. "He looks well enough now.

You must have nursed him along with great vigor."

"That she did," Malkar confirmed with a little smile.

Clearing her throat, she glanced at the other healer as she walked by and wrapped her arms around Prince Chail, as far as they would go. "Thank you so much. I shall never forget your kindness and I do hope to see you again soon."

"I'll be back sometime," he informed, slipping an arm around her and patting her back.

She pulled away and gave Traman a hug as well, then she watched as they mounted their horses and rode away. A little smile touched her lips and she leaned her head onto Malkar's shoulder, and snuggled against him as he slipped his arm around her shoulders.

"I have many patients awaiting me," he informed softly.

Ellianta nodded and confessed, "So do I. I probably should have already visited half of them."

They looked to each other, then turned back into the house and went for their respective bags, leaving the house as one.

The first patient they visited was in the center of town, an older lady who had displaced a knee. This was one of Malkar's patients and as she looked up at him from her humble wood and straw bed, she offered him a little smile and raised her hand to him, saying, "Bless ye, lad. Was thinkin' you'd forgotten me."

He shook his head and pulled a chair to her bed, looking right at her splinted knee. "How does it feel today?"

"Hurts a might," she complained.

"I told you to keep it elevated," he reminded. "That way it will not hurt so much."

"I try," she whimpered. "Can't keep it up there all night."

Ellianta crouched down beside her and took her hand. "Do you need another pillow to put under it?"

"Where would I get one?" she asked, looking to the young lady beside her.

"I'll find you one," Ellianta assured.

"Nothin' left to trade," the old woman said with despair in

her voice. "Family all gone, too old to work the fields. Can't get around on me leg as it is."

Malkar made an adjustment to the splint and looked to his colleague with his brow held a little high.

"Then we'll just have to check on you more often," she suggested. "I'll come in morning and evening and make sure you have something to eat every day."

"Can't pay," the old woman whimpered, laying her head back down.

"You shouldn't worry over that," Malkar said straightly. "Perhaps someday we will need something sewn or a good meal prepared and then we can call upon you. But, we must get you better first, so I want you to listen to us."

The old woman nodded. "I listen."

"Have you eaten today?" Ellianta asked, her brow arching a little as the old woman shook her head. "Then I'll just have to see to something myself. Have you food in here?"

Pointing to some old cupboards in her cooking area near an old iron stove, she simply said, "There."

Ellianta got to her feet and went to investigate. Opening the doors, she found flour, some dried beans, an unopened paper bag of rice, dried vegetables of some kind and a few wedges of cheese preserved in wax. Looking over her shoulder, she smiled and asked, "Can I cook for you? I can make quite a feast with what you have here."

A little smile found the old woman's lips and she clasped her hands together, saying "Ye must be an angel, Lass."

Malkar closed his kit and stood, turning to Ellianta with a little smile of his own. "I'm going to continue my visits, then I'll check back with you here."

"I'm going to need a little lamb or beef if it's not too much trouble," she said sweetly.

Shaking his head, he turned toward the door. "I'll see to it," he growled back.

Ellianta found a few pots and set them on the stove, then she opened the door and grimaced as it had not been cleaned out for some time. Looking back to the old woman, she set her hands on her hips and complained, "I can't believe no one has come by to care for you!"

**

Good to his word, Malkar returned with a package in his hand wrapped in brown paper and tied with twine. He closed the door behind him and looked right at Ellianta, who was cooking furiously and wearing the old woman's white apron.

Setting a lid back on a pot, she finally turned to him and set her hands on her hips, asking, "What did you bring us?"

He held the package to chest level, dryly answering, "Lamb. It cost me a flask of powdered onion and a bottle of wine, and it's the best cut they had."

Ellianta padded over to him, wiping her hands on the apron she wore, then she took it from him and raised up on her toes to touch her lips to his. She offered him a smile and whispered, "You are a good man, healer."

He raised his brow a little and nodded.

She turned back and walked by the stove, walking to the counter near the water basin where a cutting board waited. Picking the knife up, she cut the string and unwrapped the meat within.

As she went to work cubing the meat, Malkar walked slowly up behind her, softly saying, "We have other patients we need to attend to."

She replied in a low voice, "I can't just leave her with no way to feed herself and no one to help. You should have attended to her needs a long time ago."

"There is only so much one can do," he pointed out.

She paused with the knife, then looked over her shoulder up at him and suggested, "But many can do much more!"

He raised his chin slightly, his eyes narrow as he considered, then he nodded. "I see where you are going, and we have three other such patients who have difficulty caring for themselves. Move them all to one place…"

"And find someone who could help care for them all," she

finished.

A slight smile touched his lips. "This is a relatively large house, too, and she lives all alone."

The old woman shouted, "What be you conspiring in whispers over there?"

"Would you finish this?" she asked, then she turned to the old woman and slowly approached, her hands folded behind her. "What if we could make sure that you aren't all alone here anymore? What if someone was here to help you until you can get around better?"

Her eyes narrowed and she half turned her head. "I be listening, waif, but be careful what ye say about me."

"I… We don't want you to be alone here anymore. You need to eat and keep your strength up, but we have many people who need our help all over the village. Would you consider helping us help others?"

"At what cost to me?" the old woman asked suspiciously.

"None," Ellianta replied straightly, "and that pillow I'm bringing you would be a gift for your generosity, as will your treatments from now on."

Malkar looked over his shoulder as he worked on the meat.

"What would ye want?" the old woman asked, now sounding more interested.

Ellianta answered, "We want to bring you some company, bring in some other people who will be in bed for a spell, and others who can help care for you until you are all better." She shook her head. "You don't have to, but I sure don't want to leave you all alone here and we want to make sure that you have something to eat when you need it."

Looking away, the woman considered, and considered hard.

Ellianta crouched down and took her hand again. "I am going to finish cooking, that has to simmer for a spell, and we have to finish seeing some other people. We will give you time to think about this."

"And if I refuse this?" the old woman asked, her tone one of a challenge.

But Ellianta's response was not. "I'll worry about you all the time."

Patting Ellianta's hand, the woman's face took on a more sympathetic look and she said, "You be a good girl. You think this will help, I try for you."

Ellianta smiled and offered, "Thank you."

"What do I do with this?" Malkar asked, staring down at the meat.

Looking over her shoulder, Ellianta replied, "Into the stew." She looked back to the woman and informed, "It will need to cook for a while, so I will be back soon with something for you to eat before then."

The old woman nodded and said, "Thank ye, child."

**

Ellianta and Malkar had quite the busy day together, and actually managed to enjoy each other's company both as secret lovers and as rival healers. They laughed often at each stop and even managed to learn from one another. During the course of the day they only grew closer and all of the animosity they had felt toward each other before dissolved away and was forgotten.

Good to her word, Ellianta took some bread to the old woman they had seen first, and a few people to keep her company. Her spacious home was ultimately inhabited by three other people, all of whom brought food and the necessary things to live as well as books, sewing and wooden boarded games and cards.

That done, they paused at a fountain with a knee-high wall for a little snack of cheese, some kind of spice biscuits and a bottle of wine. A simply wonderful day seemed far from over and passersby shot them jolly smiles as they saw them, clearly relieved that the two healers of the village were no longer at war with each other. At Malkar's advice, they did not dare show lover's affection toward each other publicly as it was just not proper to do so, and it was best that no one else knew what was between them. Still, such feeling each had for the other beamed from them and would be difficult even for the blind to miss.

They were finally distracted from each other by a nearly human howl from somewhere in the forest north of the village, up in the low mountains there, and they turned that way.

Ellianta was a little fearful at first, but she recognized that sound and the one that followed. It was pain, and her eyes showed a little pity as she heard it a third time. Shifting her gaze to Malkar, she saw a little fear in his eyes as well, and his whole posture was one of uneasiness. She leaned her head a little, then looked back toward the mountains to the North and asked, "What is that?"

"Gronko," he answered straightly, his eyes trying to pierce the distance as if to see the source of the horrible noise.

Her eyes danced about as it howled again, then turned to him. "Gronko? Who is that?"

"You mean *what* is that," he corrected. "He is some kind of troll or ogre that lives in a cave in the mountains. He has been known to raid supplies in the village from time to time, usually at night and always when the moon is full."

"Moon will be full tonight," she reminded nervously, her eyes growing a little wider.

He nodded. "We'll just need to stay indoors tonight, and hope that whatever he finds will placate him. He's killed before when someone got in his way and I'm sure he will again."

That word — placate — was a word that did not settle well with her. Her old village had sought to placate a dragon, eventually using virgin women and girls to do so. Now she saw the pattern starting over. She looked back toward the mountains and raised her chin a little. It was not a threatening call. It was not a warning nor did it even sound angry. That was nothing but pain and despair, and she actually felt for the unseen terror beyond.

Leaning her head a little, she asked, "This Gronko is a troll, you say?"

"Might be an ogre," Malkar replied. "I saw him once a season ago. Don't care to see him again. He's almost two heights tall and built like a tree. Thick arms, rather short legs for his size, gray skin, stringy black hair... Just not a pretty sight."

"And you know something about pretty sights," she teased.

He glanced at her, countering, "I do now."

She looked back toward the mountains, knowing she was blushing.

"Does he always howl like that?" she asked.

"No, that started a couple of months ago. He would send down a warning when he approached, usually right after dusk, but this is new. And the last time he visited the village he made quite a mess. People who saw and heard him said he looked and sounded angry."

She nodded slightly.

A boy, perhaps twelve seasons, ran up to Malkar and tried to catch his breath before he spoke, but pointed back toward the pub and gasped, "Been an accident, Mister Healer. Old Powrenn took a fall and won't wake up!"

Shaking his head, Malkar stood and picked his bag up, then he looked to Ellianta and asked, "Do you want to come? He does this every now and again."

"No," she declined, "I should get back home. They are probably wondering what has happened to me."

He offered her a little smile and a nod, then he looked to the boy and ordered, "Lead on. Let's get this over with."

Ellianta watched them hurry away, then she looked back toward the mountains. Another sad howl sounded and her mouth tightened. That had to be a creature in pain.

Snatching her bag from the wall, she sprang up and hurried toward her house. More supplies would be needed.

She burst in and froze as Hilliti and Grettslyn turned to her from the kitchen.'

"Well, now," Hilliti said as she folded her arms. "Look at who came home in the mornin' as promised."

"Sorry," Ellianta offered as she hurried to the ladder to her room. "Lots of sick and hurt people to attend to today." She climbed up the ladder with her bag over her shoulder and continued, "I have one more patient to attend to and then I'll be home."

"And how is that Malkar?" Grettslyn asked.

"He's just fine," Ellianta replied as she shoved bandages, a clean towel and a metal flask of some kind of powder into her bag. "Got him through the night and now he's just fine, back at work attending to his patients, being a bastard and all that." She hurried back down and the two women confronted her with folded arms.

"And that's just that, eh?" Hilliti asked.

Ellianta shrugged. "That would be that. He's okay and all of the bastard he ever was. I've really got to hurry along, though. Someone is hurt pretty badly and needs my care."

"Be back tonight?" Grettslyn asked with a raised eyebrow.

"Of course!" Ellianta assured as she hurried past. "I have a story to finish for the children."

**

The cave was easy enough to find as a wide, well worn trail led to it right from the village. This meant a lot of walking uphill and Ellianta found herself a little winded when she finally got it in sight. It opened behind a boulder that had rolled down from higher on the mountain, a boulder that was over two heights tall. Striding around the boulder, she saw the entrance to the cave in the gray stone, an entrance that was as high as the boulder and roughly triangular in shape. Only twenty paces behind the boulder, it was partially obscured from view by a few trees and bushes.

As she neared, Ellianta looked around her at all of the bones that littered the ground, and she was unsure if any were human. This gave her a chill as she finally realized that she did not know what she was walking into.

Still, someone there was in pain, and the Wiccan healer she was would not allow that to continue.

That howl erupted from the cave again, very loud, and she froze where she was, just staring inside for a time. There was a flickering orange light in there which told her that this thing was intelligent enough to make fire. Hopefully, he would not cook her over it.

Drawing a breath, she hiked her bag up onto her shoulder and paced on, a little slower this time. Once past the entrance to the cave, she heard something moving and glanced around in the darkness of the cave and the firelight from somewhere that fought to defeat it.

"Hello?" she heard herself call.

Something moved again and a deep, anxious voice barked, "Go away!"

"I heard you from the village," she went on. "You sound like you are in pain."

"Just go away!" it shouted. "Not wantin' you here!"

"I am a healer," she informed as she slowly crept into the cave. "My name is Ellianta. I've just come to help you."

"Needin' not you kind," he shouted.

Entering into what looked like the middle of the room, she saw a fire pit ahead of her that looked about half burned down. Part of the ceiling had come down a long time ago and a slab of stone about four paces long, about two wide at its widest point and about waist high sat a couple of paces from the fire. Beyond all of this was darkness, but she thought she saw the glint of two eyes a height and a half high just beyond the light.

She stopped well inside of the light of the fire so as to be easily seen and stood there with her feet together and her bag held by both hands at hip level, staring back at the moving glints beyond the light. "I'll go if you like," she offered, "but please let me help you first. Let me try."

He strode forward with heavy steps, coming into the light. His eyes were small, his brow hanging way over them. He had a mouth that looked too large for his head and very big teeth within that were bared as his thick lips curled back from them. His nose was flat and his nostrils flaring. Long, thin locks of black hair dangled from his head at the sides. This creature had no neck to speak of, but he had broad shoulders and rather thick, long arms. He had something of a barrel body, a heavy one, and shorter legs than he looked like he should have. He was indeed gray skinned and wore a jerkin of leather and trousers only half way down his thick thighs.

Approaching past the fire and stopping only three paces away, he was an imposing sight, and Ellianta saw immediately why he howled. He was holding his left hand, which looked swollen and had been bleeding. His thumb and two fingers were fisted while his outer fingers were only slightly curled and looked unnaturally rigid.

As he loomed over her, breathing heavily through his nose, Ellianta just stared up at him, right into his eyes. Now she was hoping that her judgment was as good as she had hoped an hour ago. Swallowing hard and trying not to look afraid, she offered, "I will try to cure you if I can. Please let me help you get better."

"Not needin' ye," he growled.

Her eyes shifted to his hand. "It hurts badly, doesn't it?"

His brow arched in the middle and he took a step back, turning a little as if to protect his injured hand from her. "Hurtin' bad. Much pain." He backed away, cradling his hand in the other as he ordered in a pathetic voice, "Goin' away. Leavin' me in peace."

There was pity in her eyes as she stared up at him. He was hurting, and clearly had been for a long time. Another approach might just be what she needed. Looking away, she shook her head and said with as much sympathy as she could muster, "Well, I'm sorry you are so afraid of me. I suppose—"

"Fear nothing!" he roared, storming to her again.

She looked back up at him as he bent down, bringing his nose only a hand width from hers. Still she did not show him any fear, although she was quite near soiling herself.

Raising her brow, she looked back at him and actually smiled a little. "No, I suppose you wouldn't be afraid of little me, would you? You're too big and strong to fear a wee girl like myself who only heals others."

His eyes narrowed and he snarled, "Could crush you."

She nodded. "Like you crushed your hand. May I see?"

He shrank away again and shook his head, cradling his injured hand as he took a couple of steps back.

Ellianta saw what she needed and turned her eyes to the big slab of rock near the fire pit. The surfaced was cleaned and worn smooth and it appeared that he slept on it. Daring to step a little closer to the ogre, she hopped up on the stone and sat neatly on it, then she looked to Gronko and smiled a little, patting the stone beside her with her hand in an invitation to join her.

He just eyed her for a moment, then he hesitantly sat down beside her, still cradling his hand as he stared at the fire pit.

"You sure are big and strong," she observed. "It must have been something of awful power that could hurt you."

He did not respond.

"Surely someone as small and meek as me cannot hurt you," she went on.

Gronko finally cut his eyes to her.

She leaned her head a little and batted her eyelashes at him. "I really only want to help. There is no way I could really hurt you more, is there?"

He drew a deep breath and looked away from her again, then he slowly lifted his injured hand and settled it gingerly in her lap.

Looking down at his hand, she first noticed that it was huge! He could easily wrap his fingers around her entire waist. In form, this hand was much like anyone else's, but for the size, the color, the really thick fingernails, and the fingers that seemed unusually long. Resetting her spectacles, she looked closely and gently stroked the back of his hand. There, behind his pinky, his hand was very swollen and she could smell the foulness of the open wound that had gone septic. It was a long gash and the flesh within was trying to swell through it. The surface was a cracked and fractured crust of dried blood and some foul ooze that erupted from it as she slowly pressed down. It stank of death, and she knew this was very serious.

Looking away, she closed her eyes and breathed some clean air to collect herself, then she looked back to her patient's hand and shook her head. "How long has it been this way?"

"Two moons," he replied. "Hurtin' and can't use."

"You've broken it," she informed straightly, "and the cut here is septic. Why didn't you try to find help sooner?"

"No one to helpin' meh. Livin' alone and..."

She turned her eyes up to his, seeing sadness there now. "I understand. I need to do something. It might hurt, but I need to know how badly you are injured. You won't be mad at me if I make it hurt a little just to see, will you?"

He seemed to become uneasy, but he just looked away and shook his head.

"Okay," she started, "I'm going to lift your fingers and just tell me when it hurts, okay?"

She started with his middle finger and he did not seem to take notice. His ring finger only provoked a slight turn of his head. When she lifted his pinky, his whole body tensed, he sucked air between his teeth and clearly resisted the urge to pull his hand back. She did not lift his finger very far, but she nodded and confirmed, "That is what I thought." She tenderly stroked his arm, placing her other hand protectively over the injury, but only slightly touching it. "I can help, but you must trust me. Some of what I must do might hurt, but it is to make you better and take the pain that you've been enduring away."

His eyes shifted around a little, and finally he asked, "Why wantin' helpin' meh?"

"Because you hurt," she answered straightly, "and I am a healer. And my heart tells me that you are really a nice ogre, and perhaps you would be my friend someday."

"Have no friends," he growled.

"Can I be?" she asked softly.

He glanced at her, then growled and looked away. "No use for your kind. Always your kind torment meh."

"I'm sorry," she offered softly.

Gronko finally looked down to her.

She gently, slowly stroked his arm. "I can see that you really have a good heart, even if no one else does. I won't tell you that making your hand better will be completely painless, but it will ultimately end the pain you've been in for so long. Just promise you won't eat me if I do something that hurts a little." She finished with a wink.

And he finally smiled.

**

Some hours later she had drained the infection and, with the aid of her pain suppressing powder, cut away some of the dead tissue and set the broken bone. Neatly bandaged and splinted, Gronko looked his hand over while Ellianta cleaned her hands and repacked her bag.

"Was that so horrible?" she asked, glancing back at him.

He shook his head.

She turned and looked up at him, and raised her brow sharply. "Okay, now I want you to remember that you should not use that hand at all until the next full moon."

He nodded, then turned his eyes down and said in a sad voice, "Hungry."

"Is that why you raid the village from time to time?"

Gronko nodded again. "Meh hunt for meat, stag and grawrdboar, sometimes bear. Can't hunt well with meh hand bad."

"There is a house at the end of the trail that leads to the village, a big two level house of timber and stone. Just turn right where the trail forks and it will lead you right there. Do you know it?" When he nodded, she continued, "Come there tonight. I will have food for you that will help you heal."

"No likin' meh there," he said softly.

"Someone there does," she said straightly. "I take care of you today, perhaps you take care of me tomorrow, or someday."

He nodded, and a little smile curled his mouth. "Takin' care of Ellianta someday."

She smiled back. "I'll see you tonight." Throwing her bag over her shoulder, she turned and strode from the cave.

As she made her way out and back down the trail, down the mountainside, she could feel his eyes on her, but when she looked back he was not there. She knew he was more than a monster. She knew he was a guardian of the mountains, a thing of legend, something of the strength of the world, and a new friend.

**

This could be a problem. She had heard little about Gronko from those she lived with, and nothing good about him from Malkar or anyone in the village. He was a menace, a mysterious horror from the mountains that would come down to raid supplies, bring terror and havoc to all who lived there, and kill anyone who got in his way. Ellianta had seen another side, one that told her that the rumors and legends were probably not true. Sure Gronko was an ogre and looked the part of a monster. He was huge and powerful. He could also have crushed her at his leisure, and yet he did not. He showed trust and allowed her to treat his injury, and she simply could not see him as a monster.

Arriving home, she knew she would have to tell her adoptive family something. They always reveled about the idea of having guests for their evening meal. These were very open people, very understanding and very giving. Gronko might be just a little too much.

As she walked through the door, she still had not figured out how to tell them about the guest she had invited, and as Hilliti met her at the door with a cup of water, she just smiled and took the cup, savoring a long, slow drink before she greeted, "How was everything today?"

"Just fine," Hilliti confirmed. "How'd ye patient fair?"

"Um," Ellianta stammered, "it went very well. I fixed his hand and he... Is it okay that I invited him to dinner tonight?"

Hilliti smiled and folded her arms. "Got ye a gentleman caller, do ye?"

Ellianta looked away, wringing her hands together as she said, "Well, not really. He wasn't eating right and I want to make certain that he eats well so that he can heal properly." Sheepishly, she turned her eyes up to Hilliti's.

"Ye have a good heart, Little One. I'll see to puttin' on another portion."

"He's kind of big," Ellianta informed. "I'll go out and see to bringing in some more vegetables and perhaps help you with another loaf of bread or two. Or three."

She hurried away to go about her tasks.

To soften the blow, which at some point would have to come, she worked hard and furiously to make certain that her guest would have plenty to eat and that Hilliti and Grettslyn would not have any extra workload to plague them. She kept putting off news of who their guest was, and her stomach squirmed each time she even thought of it.

Setting the table, she was able to briefly clear her mind of what was to come. Archem and Brogret returned home, jolly and half drunk as they were almost every evening and Ellianta was glad to see them. They took their places at the table and listened as the children filled them in on their day and the activities and mischief they got themselves into.

Ellianta felt herself hesitant to go back inside and glanced down the trail often as she expected Gronko any moment and knew she needed to be out there when he arrived. Still, she found herself running in and out to make certain that everything was there, in its place, and as perfect as possible, all this while her adoptive family watched her with growing concern.

Nearly out of breath, Ellianta looked over the table once

more, just to be certain that everything was in order.

Brogret took a gulp from his mug and ordered, "Slow yourself down, Lass. I'm exhausted just watchin' ye."

She nodded, her brow arching a little.

"Who is that coming?" Archem asked, looking to the trail that led into the village.

Ellianta gulped a breath and spun around, expecting to see an ogre lumbering down the road, but instead seeing Malkar striding down the road with his healer's bag in his hand and a nonchalant look about him. She just watched nervously as he approached, then she ran down the steps to the house and met him between the gardens, stopping in front of him with her hands folded behind her. "Well hello there," she greeted. "What brings you this way?"

He glanced aside, appearing to grow a little uneasy, yet he retained his bearing and replied, "Well, I saw how well that pain suppressing powder of yours works and, well, I thought we might do a little trading. I have some other ointments and such here that you could possibly use and—"

"We were just about to have dinner," she interrupted suddenly. "Will you join us?"

"Uh, well…" he stammered. "I really just came to trade and did not want to impose."

"You aren't!" she insisted, taking his hand with both of hers. An ally was called for now, any ally, someone who would be there for her and understand that a healer had to heal no matter who or what the patient was. She turned quickly, her hair flailing as she did and brushing across Malkar's face. "Brogret! Malkar is going to join us for dinner. Is that okay?"

The two big farmers rose from their chairs and strode over to her, their arms folded as they eyed Malkar with suspicion and a little distain.

"So," Archem started. "Ye would come to me house with such words as we heard to our Ellianta."

"We've made peace!" she declared. "We spent the whole day working together and talking of how we can better serve the people of the village. Malkar has had some of the most wonderful ideas!" She spun back to him. "Haven't you? They were just brilliant!"

Turning his eyes to the two big farmers, he shrugged and admitted, "The idea of putting several patients in one place was really Ellianta's idea."

"But…" she tried to add. Finally, she turned back to the farmers. "He and I did really well together today."

Archem and Brogret looked to each other, then back to Ellianta.

Shaking his head, Brogret observed, "Not long ago you two were at each other like forest cats." He shrugged. "I'll not turn away someone in your favor, Lass. Just set another place." He winked. "Maybe show him how to tend an arm sting, aye?"

"I wouldn't mind seeing that done," Malkar admitted.

Archem looked beyond them and raised his chin, and his eyes widened. Brogret followed suit, and their arms dropped to their sides.

Ellianta and Malkar looked behind him, and Malkar whispered, "Oh, sweet Father Sky."

Gronko was lumbering toward them, still cradling his bandaged hand. He may have looked menacing to those he approached, but to Ellianta he looked a little uncomfortable.

She needed to head off hostilities quickly and darted around Malkar and greeted, "Gronko! Thank you for coming. How is your hand?"

He looked down at it and nodded.

Reaching him, she took his healthy hand and pulled him toward the house. "I hope you like lamb. It's been cooking all day and I've helped prepare bread and some vegetables with it."

The ogre's eyes were on the men they approached. He was far bigger, clearly more powerful, but he clearly felt uneasy approaching their home.

Ellianta's eyes darted from one man to the next, then to Hilliti and Grettslyn as they emerged from the house. Smiling

a nervous smile, she suggested, "Shall we eat?"
**

Dinner was not going well. Everyone was seated in their places, Malkar on one side of Ellianta and Gronko on a tree stump on the other. Tension was very high and Ellianta did not know how to fix it. No one really spoke, nor did anyone really make eye contact, especially with their special guest.

Anyone, that is, except Prenzee.

Gronko did not like to be stared at, and stare is what the little girl across from him was doing. Finally, he looked to her, his brow low over his eyes, and he growled deeply.

She giggled back, and finally said, "You're big. How get so big?"

He did not have an answer and just shrugged.

Archem answered, "He eats everything he's given without complaints, even the green things."

The two boys looked to each other, then started shoveling in the squash and cabbage on their plates.

Finally looking to his strange guest, Brogret asked, "So what is it ye do, Gronko?"

Glancing back, Gronko replied, "Meh izt ogre."

Looking to Ellianta, Grettslyn smiled and said, "Never had five ogres at the table before, aye?"

Prenzee laughed and looked to her brother and cousin. "She thinks you are ogres!"

"I want to be an ogre," the older boy said with a mouth full of food.

"Ye ever do any farming?" Archem asked. "Looks like ye could carry a sack of potatoes the size of a horse, aye?"

He shrugged and admitted, "Carried a horse before."

"Sounds like ye be a strong lad," Brogret observed. "Tell me. Ever had a mug or two?"

Her eyes flaring, Ellianta hissed, "Papa, no!"

Protests fell on deaf ears and two hours later two big farmers and an even bigger ogre had drained half of the barrel of ale that Archem had traded from the pub, and Ellianta sat by helplessly as she watched them all laugh at the tops of their lungs and trade insults and jabs and funny stories. She had expected their dinner to be a tense one. She did not expect it to end with her patient drunk with the two men who had adopted her.

Also with a mug in his hand, Malkar sat down beside her, patting her shoulder as he said with a jolly voice, "I'd say everything has just gone swimmingly. Everyone's warmed up to him nicely."

Ever so slowly, she turned her eyes to him, and a look that told him in no uncertain terms that she highly disapproved.

Brogret stood up and threw his arms around the ogre's shoulders, looking to him with eyes that did not appear to be able to focus well. "You know, Lad. I'd always heard what a monster ye be."

"He'd have to be a monster to drink that much ale and still be awake!" Archem shouted.

Brogret looked to him and shouted back, "That makes you a monster too, mate!"

All three of them laughed heartily and Gronko banged his injured hand on the table twice before he realized how much it hurt, and he dropped his mug and threw his head back with a wild howl.

Ellianta buried her forehead in her palms.

"Watch it there, mate," Archem warned. "Ye hand be broke and that can cause copious pain if ye keep it up."

With his brow low, Gronko looked to him for long, tense seconds, then his mouth swung open and he howled in laughter, and Archem and Brogret joined him.

Grettslyn exited the house, wiping her hands on her apron as she watched the drunken threesome enjoy themselves, and she shook her head as she walked around the table to Ellianta. She looked down to Malkar and observed, "Ye aren't drunk yet, Lad."

He took a swallow and said, "I need to keep a clear head about me. Never know when someone will need a healer."

She raised an eyebrow, then turned and strode back into the house.

Gronko threw his arm around Archem and looked at him, rolling his head back a little as he said, "Nacht so different, ogre and you. Just you have better drink."

"And lots of it!" Archem informed loudly. "Lots more, Lad. Let's be fillin' that mug again."

"This is hopeless," Ellianta groaned.

Malkar set his mug down and took her hand, pulling her to her feet as he said, "Come on. I want to show you something."

He led her around the side of the house and to where there were no windows.

Glancing around, she asked, "What is out here that I should see?"

He took her shoulders and pushed her up against the house, and took her mouth with his.

She slipped her arms around him and when he finally pulled away, she smiled and said, "Oh, *that's* what you wanted to show me. Better not let my family see you doing this."

"Well worth the risk," he countered as he bent and kissed her again. As he kissed his way along her cheek and under her ear, he paused long enough to whisper, "When can we be together again?"

"I don't know," she gasped. "Please stop that."

"Or?" he challenged as he continued.

"I can't be with you tonight," she whispered, "and I don't want you getting me worked up so right before you leave."

"Might give you something to dream about," he informed.

"Oh, you sadistic bastard. Please stop."

He did not, and his hands moved slowly down her sides and to her hips, then up again, dangerously close to her chest.

"What if I did this to you?" she whimpered.

Malkar pulled away just enough to look into her eyes. "You do, every time I think of you."

She slowly raised a hand to his face. "We can't tonight.

Hilliti and Grettslyn will know. They always know, but they don't know it's you." When he kissed her again, anyway, she melted into him and slid her hands up his back, wanting him more and more, and knowing they really should not continue.

All the world disappeared for a while and it seemed that nothing was left but the two of them.

"This is very dangerous," she said softly. "If we're caught, there is no telling what they will do to you."

"I know," he confirmed in a deep voice.

She was struggling to breathe again as she ran her hands along his shoulders. The fear and excitement of getting caught was even more arousing and she smiled a little, then she pulled her arms down and pushed back against him. "Wait. I have an idea. Can you stay a while longer, just until everyone's asleep?"

He smiled back at her. "I like the sound of this."

"We'll just talk until everyone goes to bed," she explained, "then the evening can be ours."

"We'd better work on getting more ale into them," he whispered.

She seized his neck and pulled him down to her, kissing him again, then she slipped away from him and rushed back around the house, freezing as Grettslyn looked up at her from her cleaning around the table.

Malkar froze behind her.

Raising her chin, Ellianta looked over her shoulder and said, "I've only found it growing over there, but I'm sure more grows up in the mountains."

"Huh?" he questioned, and when she raised her brow at him, he nodded and went along. "Oh, yes. The mountains. We should go up there and see what we can find some time."

As she reached the front door, Ellianta offered, "Come in and sit down for a while. I can tell you how I mix up some of that pain suppressing herb and between the two of us we could have quite the supply." She froze as she turned and saw Gronko and Archem lying on the planks of the front porch, the ogre on his back and the farmer lying beside him with his head on the ogre's arm. Archem's chair was overturned as he had fallen over with it.

Still seated, Brogret slouched in his chair, looking down at the two, and he raised his chin toward them. "See there? Can't hold their drink." He looked to Ellianta and took another gulp from his mug. "I'll wager this pretty healer behind you can't, either." His eyes rolled back and he tumbled from his own chair, landing close enough to Archem for his head to rest comfortably on his thigh.

Malkar looked to Ellianta and said, "Three down."

**

Ellianta and Malkar talked of healer related things for some time while Hilliti and Grettslyn settled everyone in for the evening. Malkar sat comfortably in Archem's big chair while Ellianta was curled up in Grettslyn's, her legs drawn up and her feet buried in the cushions. She sat like this often, almost as a cat would, and seemed to be comfortable doing so.

Grettslyn had taken blankets outside for the men and ogre, grumbling something about them falling asleep outside and that is where they would stay.

Way after dark, when Grettslyn was in bed, Hilliti came to them and looked in on the fire, which was almost down and flickered only slightly. Her eyes cut to Malkar and narrowed a little, then she turned to Ellianta and folded her arms. "Be sure this fire is down from flame before ye retire, Little One, and be sure the lamp is out."

Nodding, Ellianta assured, "I will. We're just going to talk for a while longer and then Malkar has to go and attend to something."

He nodded and confirmed, "Got to get things together for my visits tomorrow. I'm glad you'll be joining me, Ellianta. I love hearing your input."

"Hmph," Hilliti grunted as she turned toward her room. "Good night, Keenders."

"Good night, Hilliti," Ellianta bade. As soon as Hilliti could no longer be seen or heard, Ellianta looked to Malkar and smiled, biting her lower lip a little, then she whispered, "She falls asleep quickly."

CHAPTER 13

Morning rays sprayed into the windows downstairs. Otherwise, the house was quiet.

Ellianta slipped down her ladder from her loft as quietly as she could, cringing every time the wood creaked a little. She was looking up, where she had just come from and slowly felt her way down. As she reached the bottom, she turned to look around the house and barked a scream as she came face to face with Grettslyn.

Flinching back, Grettslyn's eyes were a little wide as she stared down at the smaller woman.

"Grettslyn," Ellianta gasped. "I didn't see you there."

"I'm thinkin' not," the robust woman replied sharply. "Ye were awfully restless in the night, Lass? Tis no wonder you be up so late."

Ellianta's eyes widened a little. "Late? How late?"

"Sun's been up two hours. The men folk went out before sunup and your little friend Gronko went home when they all woke."

"Where is Hilliti?"

"Went into the village, had tradin' to do."

"Oh. Trading. That's good. So, what do you have planned for this morning?"

Raising her brow, Grettslyn replied, "I have the children put to task in the garden. Thinkin' about joinin'em. Coming with us today?"

"Um, no, I have to go collect some herbs and the like. Many sick people in need of me. Oh, and then I have to visit some of my patients."

"Thought that Malkar was goin' with," Grettslyn said with a little suspicion in her voice.

"Oh, he is. We are going to meet at the fountain at high sun." She glanced about and announced, "Well, I should get my things together and get my day started, late as I am."

Nodding, Grettslyn confirmed, "You just get ye day started, Little One. I'll be in the garden."

Ellianta acted busy until Grettslyn closed the front door behind her, then she sprinted back to her ladder and looked up to her room. "Tsst! The house is clear. Hurry!"

Malkar came down as quickly and quietly as he could, his boots in his hand, then he turned to Ellianta and wrapped his arms around her.

She pushed him away and whispered, "You have to hurry! Grettslyn is right outside."

"She may be busy for a while," he whispered back.

"Or, she could come barging in any second!" She turned him and pushed him toward the back door. "Go on. I'll see you at the fountain at high sun." Opening the door ahead of him, she looked out, then brutally pushed him back into the house as she greeted, "Well good morning, Prenzee. You just go on and pick flowers and I'll join you in a moment." She closed the door and pressed her back against it, her eyes darting about as her mind scrambled over how to get him out without being seen. Finally locking on something, she took his hand and dragged him toward the kitchen. "Climb up on the counter and get out the window, quickly!"

The kitchen window was rather small and he was barely able to fit, but halfway out he paused and looked back at her, whispering with a smile, "I shall look forward to seeing you in a few hours, Ellie. Don't be late."

"I won't," she assured, then she stretched herself across the counter and kissed him one more time. Hearing the door opening, she gasped and pushed him with all her strength, spinning to the door as he tumbled out and slammed onto the ground outside. "Grettslyn! I just thought I'd let some air in so that the house doesn't smell like ale and drunken men."

Looking to the floor, Grettslyn squinted a little and asked, "Where did that come from?"

Following her gaze, a chill washed across Ellianta as she saw one of Malkar's boots lying on the floor. Quick to pick it up, she looked it over and explained, "Oh, it's just an old boot. One of the children must have found it. Ah, it stinks." She tossed it over her shoulder, out the window where it hit Malkar in the face, then she strode forward and announced, "Well, I'd better get those herbs. Patients waiting and all that."

**

Heading north, she eventually slowed her walk as her nerves calmed. This day she was looking for a particular plant with broad leaves and red thorns. The berries from this plant were a bright orange and only a few birds could eat them. They were a little toxic, but when combined with certain other herbs they were a wonderful antiseptic that could actually be used in the mouth or on minor burns and cuts. She had seen them by accident when going to visit Gronko and was sure they were the same berries she had seen in the forest near her old village.

This turned out to be a long hike and was uphill all the way. The summer heat began to penetrate her and she had not thought to bring water, so she paused under a broad oak tree and sat down. Leaning her head back, she rested for a moment, for once missing the sleep she did not get the night before, and a little smile curled her lips.

Something shuffled slightly behind her and her eyes flashed open. It shuffled again and she turned her head slightly. She had been thinking about leaving her dress here while she hiked, but now she felt very uneasy. Her inner senses told her she was not alone. Planting her palms beside her, she slowly pushed herself up, looking one way, then the other. When she heard movement on the other side of the tree, she tensed and took shallow breaths, her eyes now wide with fear.

Lying at her feet was her healer's bag, and the dagger within. She looked down at it for long seconds, too afraid to move, but she finally mustered the courage and slowly, silently began to bend toward it.

Bark was knocked from the tree and hit her on the head

and she froze. Something fell over her head and before she realized it tightened around her throat and pulled her brutally back against the tree. Reaching for it, she realized that it was already too tight to get her fingers between the course rope and her throat, though it was not pulled hard enough to cut off her wind. Whoever it was meant to control her first, and control her they did.

Someone moved behind the tree again, and as she pulled back against the rope, her eyes cut to the left. She pulled against the rope holding her throat harder, but it was tied off and would not budge.

The bushes nearby rustled and a dirty looking man with an unkempt beard and long, ratty hair emerged. He wore a pocketed vest over his chest and mended brown trousers, and his boots looked too big for him and were way too new to suit him. He had a long dagger at his side, worn on an old belt with a rusty buckle. He was very thin, his skin pale and his eyes were dark brown and very wicked.

Ellianta whimpered as he stalked toward her and she fought to free herself of the rope around her throat even harder.

A thin fingered hand grabbed her wrist and pulled her hand from the rope, twisting her arm behind the tree. She started to panic as she felt more rope wind around her wrist and a scream exploded from her.

The man rushed forward and clamped his hand over her mouth. "Shh," he warned, producing the dagger from his belt. She began to cry as he put the point of the dagger against her throat, and his eyes widened with wicked intent. "Don't want to silence ya for good now, do we puppet?" He pushed the point harder against her and she closed her eyes.

That thin hand took her other wrist and this time she did not resist as her arm was twisted behind the tree and bound there.

"You just be a quiet little girl, might live to see nightfall," he sneered.

With her hands bound behind her, all that was left was compliance.

The other one finally strode around the tree to have a look at her. It was a very thin woman with pale skin and long black hair. She wore a disapproving expression and a tattered black dress that was open at the front almost all the way to her navel. Wickedness resided in her eyes as well as she looked Ellianta up and down. Finally, she asked, "What ya think?"

"I like this one," he drawled. "The others far away?"

"Not too far," was her answer. She looked down to Ellianta's bag and reached down to pick it up. She rummaged through the bag for a moment, tossing out what did not interest her, then she got to the dagger and smiled a little. "I like this. Got me a new Zondaen dagger, I do."

"No money on 'er?" the man asked.

"None in here, only leaves and powders and such." The woman looked to Ellianta and demanded, "What else you carrying?"

"Nothing," Ellianta whimpered, tears streaming down her cheeks.

The woman scowled and pulled the dagger from its sheath. "You're lyin' to me, wretch. What else you have?"

"I have nothing!" she cried. "I am a healer and I don't carry much of any value."

The woman looked her up and down again, this time focusing on her feet. "I like those slippers you wear."

"Take them," the man ordered, looking down at her body with a wicked smile. "I see something else I like." He ran his dagger down her throat and into her dress, and she could feel the cold steel right between her breasts.

When he turned his eyes back to hers and pulled the dagger to him, cutting through her dress, panic erupted from her again and she screamed wildly again.

The woman hit her across the face and silenced her, then she put the blade to her throat and warned through bared teeth, "Do that again and I'll gut you right here and now! Get me?"

Ellianta nodded, and she wept as the man slowly cut the dress her father had given her.

Footsteps approached from behind and two more men came into view, one with long brown hair and no beard, and a younger fellow with red hair. Both were rather thin but the one with the red hair was tall and broad shouldered, and looked like a powerful young man. They both smiled as they saw Ellianta and looked at her with hungry eyes.

"Please don't," she whimpered, still trying to shrink away from the man's dagger.

"Quiet!" the woman ordered. She looked to the older man and informed, "If she's a healer then that village'll miss her for sure, and in short order. You blokes get through with her and let's be on our way before anyone comes looking."

"What in hell?" the older one with the dagger declared.

Ellianta had felt him cut her dress all the way to her hips, now she felt the dress closing from her hips up. It was mending itself back together, and this was no doubt her father's influence, a gift within a gift. She knew she could not reason with these bandits, but perhaps she could intimidate them.

Looking to the woman with eyes that still dropped tears, she said, "That's right. I'm a witch. I have powers beyond your imagination and your fears. I do not wish to cause harm to others, but if you do not release me right now I will!"

All four of them took a couple of steps back, looking on her with wide eyes now.

Ellianta was able to calm herself to call upon her inner senses, and she felt someone else coming. Her eyes narrowed and she warned, "Cause me no harm, give me back what is mine and release me now, and I will call off the demons I have summoned."

The woman's lip curled up and she scowled, "You're lying. You have some kind of black magic in that dress but you were far too easy to catch to be some powerful witch."

"Fine," Ellianta countered. "Hold me, or harm me, and see what happens."

Something howled in the distance and the men looked around them, drawing whatever weapons they had.

Glancing at them, the woman barked, "Just relax, you fools. There are no demons coming." She looked back to Ellianta with narrow, angry eyes. "Just gut the wench and let's be on our way."

Ellianta also narrowed her eyes, and informed with hard words, "You were warned."

Gronko slammed into the ground to her right and howled in nightmarish fashion. When the first man turned on him with his dagger in his hand, the ogre grabbed his arm and turned his hand quickly, breaking the man's arm with a loud crack before hurling him into the trees behind him.

The bandits really did not try to defend themselves after that, and only the red haired man looked like he was going to stand his ground, until the ogre charged him, then retreat was too late. Gronko was upon him and Ellianta turned away as the man was crushed under the ogre's vicious attack.

As the woman backpedaled into the forest, she pointed a slender finger at Ellianta and warned, "I will get you for this, wretch. You just mark me words, I will get you!"

Hearing heavy footsteps approach, Ellianta looked up, seeing concern in the ogre's eyes, and she softly assured, "I'm okay."

He nodded, then took the rope that was around her throat and snapped it with one yank.

As he went behind her to free her hands, she looked back and asked, "How did you know to come and help me?"

"Hunting grawrdboar," he replied, "Hearin' scream in your voice and came."

As her hands were freed, she pulled them in front of her, then leaned her shoulder on the tree and offered him a smile as he came back around. "I guess this makes us even."

He shook his head, looking down at his bandaged hand.

Blood had soaked through the bandage and he whimpered in true ogre form, "Hand hurtin' bad."

"Oh, what have you done?" Hers was a scolding voice and she took his hand in both of hers to examine his injury. "Didn't I say not to use this hand for a month?"

"Ya," he admitted grimly, watching as she unwrapped the bandage. "Had to get boar for dinner."

"I told you I would take care of your meals," she reminded.

"Wanted to bringin' something for the family," he said softly. "Family good to meh, want to bein' good to family."

She hesitated, then turned her eyes up to his. "You do have a good heart, even though you killed two men today."

His eyes narrowed and he looked to the one he had flung into the tree. "Would have hurt you. Won't let anyone hurtin' you."

She removed the bandage completely and examined this hand, shaking her head. "Well, I'm glad you came when you did, but you've ripped some stitches out. I'm going to have to do them over again." She turned her eyes to his again and asked, "Are you up to it?"

"Ya," was his simple response.

"Well, let's go back to the house," she ordered, wrapping the bandage back around his hand.

"Gettin' the boar first," he insisted. "Just up the hill there."

As she watched him lumber back up the hill, she saw a glint of light out of the corner of her eye and she looked that way, seeing the dagger that Pa'lesh had given her laying among the leaf litter and grass, and she smiled a little as she bent over to pick it up. She would not look at the men that Gronko had killed, nor would she allow her thoughts to wander that way. She just would not. There were far more important matters at hand in her mind.

**

Ellianta would not linger at the house. News of such bandits stalking the forest so close to the village was not welcome news for Grettslyn and Hilliti, but she would not allow them to dwell. There was a fine hog to be cleaned for dinner, and a kind hearted ogre to help with that.

It was near high sun and time for her visits to start, and someone special would be waiting for her at the fountain in the middle of the village. Her heart thundered in anticipation, and yet she could feel something amiss inside. Something was trying to surface, she just could not allow it. Yet.

In the center of the village, where the market square was and the fountain in the middle of it, she saw him there, sitting on the edge of the fountain wall and talking to a couple of men who seemed to have happened by. She was slow to approach, not wanting these two men, who she did not even know, to suspect that she and this other healer were secretly lovers.

His eyes found her and he raised his chin, loudly saying, "Well here she comes now. Are you still wanting to talk to me about something?"

She paused. He sounded very aggressive toward her again. With narrow eyes, she pushed her spectacles up the bridge of her nose and strode toward him again, closing the ten paces with long strides. "Yes, I do need to talk to you about something. Do you mean to be civil this time, or do I just push you in the water right now?"

"Dream on, little girl," he spat back. Looking to the men with him, he said, "If you could excuse me for a spell, I need to be teacher for this lost little girl."

Her lips tightened in anger and she just glared at him as the two men laughed and strode away. Turning to sit down a pace away from him, she settled her healer's bag in her lap and stared across the market, just watching the activity for a while and trying to ignore him, or seem like she was.

"Remember what happened the last time you got me in the water with you?" he asked with a teasing voice.

A little smile fought its way to her and she ordered, "Oh, shut up."

"I took care of most of our patients already," he informed,

"so now we can finish things quickly and the day will be ours."

"You took care of all the quick and easy things," she accused, still looking across the square.

"Of course," he admitted. "I wouldn't want to be deprived of the pleasure of seeing you work."

She cut her eyes to him.

He was smiling ever so slightly and his unwavering gaze was fixed upon her.

Seeing movement out of the corner of her eye, she looked that way, almost directly ahead of her as about two score of people in white robes, both men and women, began to file into the square, following an older woman with white hair who wore similar robes that were trimmed in blue. She carried a walking stick and walked with purpose to a common area where meetings were often held by groups of farmers or merchants. Each person carried a book that appeared to be bound in black wood of some kind and held together with some kind of course twine.

Raising her chin to the group, Ellianta asked, "Who are they?"

Malkar looked, shaking his head slightly as he grumbled, "Some kind of religious zealots. They come through here from time to time to spread whatever word they are spreading. Theirs is a religion of intolerance and suspicion, and it is people like them that make keeping our identities as Wiccans a closely guarded secret extremely important."

Her brow arched a little. "What would they do?"

"Anything that is outside of their thinking they consider evil and they believe it must be purged from the world, and they can use very brutal means to do so."

"Why does the village tolerate them?"

"They haven't done anything especially malicious, and many in the village have even taken to the message they spread. Some think they could someday rid us of the Desert Lord if they believe hard enough."

She looked to him. "The Desert Lord? I know that name from somewhere. Is he some kind of demon or another misunderstood creature like Gronko?"

"No, he's not misunderstood. He's a dragon of immense power, a huge black beast that is known to visit the village from time to time, much like he did a few days ago."

Then Ellianta remembered Grettslyn telling her about that dragon and felt a little chill. "Black dragon. Oh, yes. Why would he visit the village?"

Malkar shrugged. "Who knows why dragons do what they do? It's been suggested that we start placating him with virgins."

"I don't think that would work," she said straightly.

"I've always heard eating virgins calms a dragon," he informed.

She raised her brow and countered, "I've always heard people who think that are idiots."

He smiled. "You sure are brutal today." He looked back toward the white clad group and shook his head again. "Well, here we go with another rally. I won't be staying for it."

"What do they do at these rallies?"

"Their message is one that denounces all of us who would practice what they call the black arts. If you are born with special abilities then you are evil and deserve to die and burn in Hell."

She grimaced. "Best not to tell them about our abilities then, huh?"

"Best not to tell them anything," he advised. "If you don't agree with them completely, then you are their enemy, and they will go to great lengths to either convert you to their way or turn everyone possible against you. I saw it happen this spring to a young woman who was studying the craft. They made her life so unbearable she finally killed herself."

Ellianta's mouth fell open and she turned bewildered eyes to him.

"Later," he continued, "they said that this Spirit Mother

passed judgment on her and she would be burning in a lake of fire forever." His eyes took on something bordering on rage. "They forced her into a corner, condemned her to a life of misery that she could not bear, and then they ridiculed her even in death." He was silent for a moment, then he finished softly, "How I hate them."

She looked back to the white clad group as they gathered, and many villagers gathered among them. "And yet many of the villagers would follow them."

"They are sadly ignorant, and are being told what they want to hear until they are too deeply tangled to ever free their minds. You and I are being made their enemies, and people will always rally together to fight a common enemy."

"We should do something," she insisted as she set her bag down and got to her feet.

He took her arm, and when he had her attention, he shook his head. "Don't stand against them. They have ways of turning friends against you and bringing an end to the life you know now. I truly don't know how far they would go if they found out about you."

"But we have to do something!" she insisted.

"Like?" he countered. "What would you do? What would you say to sway them? They are too set in what they believe to listen to a lovely young woman who they would consider too ignorant for her own good. Believe me, Ellie, they will go to great lengths to convert you or destroy you, including seeking their goals with your family."

That thought sent a chill through her and she looked away from the group. "What they are bringing here is more dangerous than anyone realizes."

"I know it is," he admitted softly. "They'll have their rallies, then they'll be gone for a few weeks, perhaps months. Hopefully months."

She turned her eyes down and nodded.

Malkar stood and took her hand. "Come along, Ellie. We have people to help."

She picked up her bag and looked to the group again as the old woman raised her hands and began to speak.

"Hear me!" the old woman shouted. "They are among us! They are bringing evil to your lives and they labor day and night to bring you and your families to the very gates of Hell! Seek them out in your village and in your heart. Accept the Spirit Mother into your heart and she will protect you from them. Let her give you shelter against the evil that would see your babies stricken blind and eaten alive by their heathen rituals!"

This made Ellianta's blood feel as if it was going to boil, but she took Malkar's advice and said nothing. As they left the town square, she looked away from them and tried to tune them out even as more people gathered to hear what the old woman had to say.

**

They checked in as promised to the last remaining patients and found themselves walking back toward the fountain to enjoy a snack of some bartered cheese, some salt crackers of some kind and some dried meat discs bartered from someone else. Ellianta wanted her hand in his, to feel his grip holding onto her, but she knew such affection publicly would not be wise, especially with these zealots running amok. She had managed to wash her mind of them and found herself enjoying Malkar's company, laughing with him and occasionally bumping him with her shoulder. Light and discreet flirting was the order of the afternoon as they slowly strolled toward the fountain they loved.

Sooner or later, they would be discovered, but how bad could it truly be?

Much to their displeasure, the zealots had not left the market square, and the woman had started a new speech to a new crowd of villagers. No matter. They simply had to ignore them.

A loud crash was heard from within one of the shops and they turned that way to see what had happened. Their eyes darted about as a few people fled from a bakery there and the healers both stood, grabbing their bags as they turned toward the commotion. Making their way that direction, they only had forty or so paces to travel, and halfway there fire belched from the roof and Malkar seemed to know what would happen next. He took Ellianta's shoulders and threw her to the ground, then his body fell on top of hers and he covered his head with his arm. A second later an explosion ripped the bakery apart and damaged the two shops around it. Flying debris was on fire and smoked as it cascaded all around.

Malkar finally got off of her and offered her his hand, pulling her to her feet as his eyes were locked on the smoldering wreck of a building that had been the bakery.

Together, they ran toward it as people limped and hobbled away. Someone was screaming in there. There were survivors in the shop next to it as well.

A crowd began to assemble to help and Malkar pointed to the shop on the right, shouting over the commotion, "Check for injured there. I'll be in the bakery."

She nodded and headed that way. When she tried to pull the door open, it came off completely and she backpedaled as it fell from its hinges. A few things fell from the ceiling within, but she was not to be deterred and stormed in anyway, finding three people lying on the floor. Now, Malkar's words came to her again, but this time they did not sting. She quickly checked the bodies as she came to them, looking for severity of wound and likelihood she could save them. Her feelings, for the moment, were completely suppressed as her work totally consumed her.

Others entered to help and she looked back at them, ordering, "Clear off those tables and help me get these people up on them.

Three people set about the task of clearing three of the tables while another two helped pick the injured up and onto the tables. One was a man who appeared to be in his forties, another a middle aged woman, and the third was a girl of about thirteen or fourteen seasons.

And the girl was the one who distracted Ellianta. The woman was horribly burned and her battered body was limp. She barely breathed. The girl, who was cut all over, burned a little and was pale with shock, had her eyes on the woman, and she extended a hand toward her, whimpering, "Ammi. Ammi, wake up."

Something from Ellianta's past surged forth and she hesitated. Looking back to the woman, she knew her injuries were too severe and that she would not survive, but her heart would not accept that. She had lost her own mother and would not allow this girl to go through the same.

Looking to a woman who had come in to help, she took her shoulder and said, "Go to the pub and bring me clean towels and clean water. Hurry, please!" As the woman fled, Ellianta tore open her patient's shirt, gasping a little as she saw the grisly wounds on the side of her chest. Closing her eyes for a second to collect herself, she ground her teeth and went back to work, saying loudly, "I need some clean cloth over here!"

Someone complied, bringing her what appeared to be a new shirt, and she used it to start cleaning the woman's wounds. Looking up from her work, she looked to the man who lay on the other side of the girl and asked, "How does he look?"

Another woman across the room was already attending to him and looked to Ellianta, nodding to her as she assured, "He's stunned but lookin' not too worse for wear. Bruised and cut a bit."

Going back to work on the mother, Ellianta looked to the daughter and asked, "How are you doing over there?"

"Please save my Ammi!" the girl cried.

"Someone attend to this girl!" Ellianta barked. She met the girl's eyes again and offered her a reassuring nod. "I'll give her my best care, so don't you worry."

The woman sent on the mission for towels and water returned with another woman behind her, one who worked at the pub. She set the bucket down and turned to the other woman, taking a towel from her, then she offered it to Ellianta, who quickly took it and dipped it into the water and began to clean the mother's injuries. Her side was open and shattered pieces of ribs came away with the blood and soot that Ellianta cleaned away. Bubbles boiled up from the big wound and she knew this was the worst of it. The heat within mixed with the settling dust and Ellianta found sweat trying to trickle into her eyes. She turned to the woman beside her and ordered, "Blot my face," closing her eyes as this happened, then it was back to work. Her pain suppressing powder would be of little use here as the woman was unconscious and was unlikely to feel anything, so she began to clean deeper, and something within the wound began to snag the towel she was using.

Malkar hurried in, reporting, "They are under control over there. Nearly everyone made it out, but for one poor chap and a woman who was hysterical but not badly hurt."

She nodded and kept working.

He gently moved the woman helper aside and stood behind Ellianta, raising his chin as he saw the horrid wound. Setting his jaw, he suggested, "Perhaps you should go and attend the girl over there."

"I can handle this," she insisted.

"Ellie, go attend to the girl."

She turned on him and screamed, "I won't let her die!"

He stared back for long seconds, then he reached down to the mother's wounded side, into the wound, and grabbed onto something, pulling out a jagged chunk of blood soaked wood almost the length of his forearm. Setting it down on the table, he softly said, "She's dead already. Go attend to the girl."

Tears overtook her eyes and she looked down at the mother, finally realizing that the woman was lifeless. Her mouth was a little ajar and she shook her head slightly. Turning away from him, she softly said, "I'll take care of the man over there."

She could not look at the girl as she walked past and her heart broke a little as the girl began to scream, "No! Ammi! Help her, please help her!"

**

In less than an hour the patients were treated for their injuries and were taken home by other villagers. The dead were placed onto carts and taken away to be tended as the dead would be.

Ellianta wandered from the wreckage of the shop, her eyes blank and her spectacles low on her nose. Blood covered the front of her dress and her hands up to her elbows. Slowly, she made her way to the fountain and sat down on the wall, staring blankly ahead of her. Her mouth was still ajar; her brow arched over her eyes and held a little high.

Not quite a half hour later, Malkar approached with a bucket and both their bags, and a couple of clean towels over his shoulder. He sat down beside her and put their bags down, then he turned and dipped the bucket into the water, setting it between them. Ever so gently, he took her wrist and lifted her arm out of her lap, dipping the end of her hand into the bucket. As he slowly began to wash her hand and arm, he looked to her and softly asked, "Are you okay, Ellie?" When she did not respond, he just continued to wash her arm, finally getting it clean. Pulling a towel from his shoulder, he dried her arm and her hand, then he reached around her and took the other one, and as he began to wash it, he looked to her again, this time to say, "You did well in there, and two more people will live thanks to you."

Slowly shaking her head, Ellianta whispered, "She'll have to grow up without her mother."

"Her father is going to be fine," he pointed out. "It was lucky that you found the injury to his neck and those broken ribs."

"I couldn't save her mother," she whimpered.

"No one could," he pointed out.

She turned eyes to him that he had never seen before, eyes

that were pools of distress, sadness, failure. "I couldn't save her, just like I couldn't save Mama."

Malkar's gaze locked on hers and he raised his brow, and he finally understood.

Slowly getting to his feet, he offered her his hand, and she took it. He pulled her up, then reached to the wall and took their bags. He slipped his other arm around her shoulders, pulling her to him as he led her from the fountain, even as others still approached the scene of the explosions with shovels and wheel barrows.

Malkar closed the door to his house behind him and watched Ellianta wander to the middle of the room.

She just stared blankly ahead of her for a moment. Slowly, her gaze drifted down the wall across the room and to the floor before her. Her head bowed and her body began to quake as she took quick breaths through her mouth. Raising a hand to her lips, the pain within her surged forth and she suddenly found herself crying harder than she had ever cried. Her other hand found her belly and she dropped to her knees and doubled over as sorrow and pain poured from her in an unstoppable surge.

Malkar was at her side and enveloped her in his arms before she realized, and as he pulled her to him, she leaned toward the warmth of his body, almost wanting to crawl inside of the protectiveness of his embrace. The tighter he held her, the harder she wept. He sat down beside her and pulled her as close to him as he could as he wrapped his arms around her and squeezed her to him, holding her head to his shoulder as he soothed, "Shh. It's going to be okay. Just let it out. It's okay."

Slowly, she slid her arms around him and held him as tightly as she could. Not since the death of the woman she had always known as her mother did she allow her fragile heart be held by someone like this.

They could not know how long they sat on the floor as she wept, nor how long after she stopped. He held her the entire time, slowly rocking her back and forth, slowly stroking her hair. He said nothing, not knowing what he could say, but he wished to be there for her, and she let him.

Finally, she lifted her head and looked to him, as deeply into his eyes as she ever had. When he slowly pulled her spectacles from her face, she let him, and she just stared at him after.

"Do you want to talk?" he asked softly

"I couldn't help her," she whimpered. "I was only fifteen seasons old. I was only a girl, and she was so sick. Why didn't I study harder? Why didn't I learn more before she got sick? Why did I have to be such a difficult daughter?"

He kissed her gently on the lips and combed her hair back on one side. "Ellie, we cannot stop death. When it comes it comes, and it doesn't matter how much you know or how gifted a healer you are. When Father Sky and Mother Land call us home, we must go."

Slowly, she laid her head on his shoulder as she tried to make sense of what he said.

"Do you know about the horizon? Do you know why we never get there?"

Hesitantly, she shook her head, staring blankly across the room.

"It is where Father Sky and Mother Land meet," he explained. "It is where they can be together, where they speak of the important matters of the world. It is where they make love, where they can finally touch each other. And it is where they wait for us when we are finally called home."

A new tear rolled from her eye.

"That is where your mother awaits you, at the horizon. Our bodies, our vessels will never arrive there. We can travel for a hundred seasons and never reach the horizon, that place where Father Sky and Mother Land touch. Only after we our true selves are freed can we connect with them again, and that is where those who have passed await us."

She snuggled against him. "No one has ever explained that

to me before."

"Most Wiccans learn that when we come of age, when we are truly old enough to understand that death is really only change."

Ellianta smiled a little. "She is waiting for me?"

"She was called home, Ellie. You could not go with her, but she will always be with you, always in your heart. And I know she is very proud of what you have become."

Her eyes closed and she shook her head. "She can't be that proud of me, not..." She pulled back and looked into his eyes again. "You where completely honest with me, Malkar, and now I must be completely honest with you." She drew a deep breath to prepare herself. "You once asked why I would leave the village I lived in, why their only healer would just leave. I didn't just leave. They wanted me to rid them of a dragon they had been sacrificing girls to. The Mayor came to me and said that the lottery had lost favor and... I told him what to do, but he wouldn't listen. They wanted me to kill the dragon but I couldn't. I'm a healer. He just wouldn't listen so he tried to have me arrested and I fought back." She looked away, distress on her features as she recalled, "Then he mentioned the baby."

Malkar raised his chin a little. "The baby?"

Closing her eyes, she went on. "A family in the village had a sick newborn. I wanted to treat him but they... They wanted to leave his fate up to something else. They wanted night gods to cure him, so they left him outside of their house in the cold. I heard him crying early one morning and went... I took him, and they thought he had been carried away by some beast or had been abducted by someone else. He had gold coins inside the blanket he was wrapped in as an offering to the gods, and that made everyone in the village suspicious of everyone else. I tried to help him, really I did, but he was so sick." She wept anew and leaned into him again. "I did all I could, all I knew how to do, but he died the next night."

"And there was nothing you could do," he finished for her.

Her eyes opened again, and were fixed on the floor. "I had to know. I did not want him to die in vain. Malkar, I opened him. I thought I could find what went wrong, thought I could… He became just something to study. I took out his heart, his lungs… I needed to know what killed him. I preserved his organs in jars and his body with wax and salt. I learned so much from him. And then the Mayor accused me of taking him in the night for some kind of sacrifice. He accused me of horrible things, but had no idea. There is no way he could have known, he just wanted something to accuse me of. But the little boy's body was right there in my house, right there among all of the other things I've used to study healing.

"After they took me, they ransacked my house and… They found him, and then my trial was not all about making up stories about me anymore. They had the evidence they needed to condemn me to death, and I hadn't a way to defend myself." She sniffed hard and raised a hand to her eyes. "They brought his little body to the trial. They made me out to be a monster! They said I killed him and ate his heart."

When she started to weep again, he held her close to him, rocking her back and forth. "The ignorant will believe what they want to."

"But I opened him," she cried. "I desecrated his body!"

"And from that, you learned to heal others. I have a body in the next room that I learned from. You saw it there."

She looked away from him. "Did you steal it in the night?"

"He asked me to learn from him before he died, and his family was kind enough to respect his wishes. I offered to return him to his family, but they wished that he remain with me. They want me to advance my art as a healer and keep learning from him all I can. I'm certain that the little fellow you opened would not condemn you for wanting to learn from him to help others. I'm sure he is as proud of you as I am."

"How can you be proud of me?" she asked grimly.

He drew a breath and stroked her shoulder. "You heal more than the body, Ellie. You heal the heart and the mind. You put down fears and give people such confidence in you that I find myself envying you."

She pulled away and turned bewildered eyes to him, her mouth agape as she could barely believe what she was hearing.

He raised his brow. "That surprises you?"

"Yes," she breathed.

Smiling slightly, he informed, "You have a lot to learn from me, Ellie, and I have a lot to learn from you, especially in matters of the heart. People look at you and feel trust, and they feel compassion from you. Just a glance at you can defeat most of their fears."

She stroked his cheek with her fingers, her eyes locked on his as she said, "To think we wasted so much time at each other's throat."

"I suppose you can blame me for that," he admitted.

"Oh, I do," she confirmed.

He smiled a little more and nodded. "We have now, though, right now and into the future. Thank you for confiding in me."

She smiled back a little.

He took on a more serious look. "Ellie, I want to tell you something. I've not felt this way about anyone for a long time, and I pray to Mother Land and Father Sky every day that you feel the same. Just know that I promise that I shall never abandon you, no matter what. When you are in your greatest need, I shall be there. When your heart hurts, I shall mend it. When you weep I shall brush away your tears and find your smile. I shall never leave you, and as long as there is breath in my body I will be yours to have."

She smiled ever so slightly, her eyes sparkling. "That sounded almost like a marriage vow."

"It is what it is," he said softly. "It is my pledge to you."

"And it shall be mine to you," she whispered.

They gazed lovingly at each other in silence for a moment, and then he finally informed, "I still hate you."

She broke out into uncontrollable laughter and fell into him, wrapping her arms around his neck and held him as tightly as she could.

Hugging her back, he observed, "You seem to be feeling a bit better."

"Thanks to you," she confirmed. "Thank you, Malkar, thank you. I can finally feel her in my heart again. I don't feel alone anymore."

"You won't be ever again," he assured. "As long as there is breath in my body or light in my spirit, I will always be with you."

Ellianta buried her face in his neck and whispered, "I love you, Malkar."

So long had it been without those words told to him that he wept a little as he heard them, and he embraced her tighter as he whispered back, "I love you, Ellianta."

**

Their affections could not be bridled this time as they strode through town and back toward her home. He held her hand tightly and they smiled and laughed with each other, walking close together as one. Ellianta could never remember being so happy, but Malkar did. This time for him he knew it was real, no secrets, no lies, just two hearts that had been joined forever.

Rounding the last curve in the road, her eyes were on him as he spoke, and he had her absolute attention.

"A few times a season," he went on, "I will get a letter letting me know how things in Trostan are faring, and once in a while they will take the nine day journey here with a trading caravan or a group of travelers to come see me."

"That sounds delightful," she said wistfully, "your family coming to visit."

"It is for the first couple of days," he admitted grimly, "but then the questioning begins. When are you going to start collecting money for what you do? When are you coming back to Trostan? Have you heard from your sister? When are you going to find a woman and start a family? It goes on and on."

"Still sounds delightful," she insisted. "And at least you have that last question answered, don't you?"

Raising his brow, he smiled a little and confirmed, "That I do. Of course, that's just going to lead to questions about grandchildren, how many, what to name them, how many sons you'll give me, and on, and on, and on."

She raised a brow slightly and wrapped her arm around his. "Children, huh? Already thinking ahead?"

"I wouldn't mind having a son," he admitted.

"What if I give you a daughter?"

He shrugged. "We'll just have to keep trying then, won't we?"

"Try all you like, good sir."

"We should practice all we can before we commit to a family," he suggested.

She laughed and fell into him, then looked forward and stopped, her eyes growing a little wide as she mumbled, "Oh, no."

And there they were, Brogret, Archem, Hilliti and Grettslyn, all on the front porch and in front of the dining table, all with their arms folded, and all staring at Malkar with narrow eyes.

Ellianta and Malkar had not realized they were so close to the house and had stopped only about ten paces away. They were already between the gardens, and the four most likely had been watching them hang on each other for some time. The secret was out and denying it further would be a futile gesture at best.

Brogret raised his chin a little, and beckoned them forward.

They were hesitant, but complied, slowly walking forward until they were two paces from the bottom of the steps that would take them onto the porch. Quietly, nervously, they watched the four people there, mostly the biggest of the farmers.

His eyes shifting to Ellianta, Brogret ordered in his usual, gruff voice, "Little One, go into the house."

She swallowed hard and looked to Malkar, still clinging to him as she argued, "You don't understand. We... We were just—"

"Little One!" Grettslyn barked. "Do as ye Papa said!"

Ellianta lowered her gaze and nodded, feeling much more like a girl of ten seasons than the grown woman who was a healer. She strode slowly forward, up the steps and then around Hilliti and Grettslyn, turning fear filled eyes back to Malkar as the two farmer's wives took her arms and escorted her inside.

Once the door closed behind them, Ellianta rushed to the window that looked out onto the porch, terrified that the men might do something to her handsome and charming healer.

They both took the steps down to the garden path and strode right up to Malkar, who held his ground gallantly as they approached. She whimpered as they loomed over him, and she listened hard to what was said out there.

"How old are ye, Lad?" Brogret asked, his voice reminding one of the calm before a fierce storm.

"Thirty-two seasons," was Malkar's reply.

"Hmm." Brogret nodded. "She's only twenty-six, a might young for ye, wouldn't ye say?"

"Our hearts think otherwise," the healer countered.

"Do they, now?" Archem cut in. "It would truly be a shame if that lass were to get her heart broken. Brogret and me might just have to do some breaking of our own if that happens, says I."

"I would sooner die than break her heart," Malkar said straightly. "She is the breath in my chest, and all that sustains me."

The two farmers looked to each other, then back to Malkar, and Brogret observed, "Pretty words, healer. Pretty words. If ye mean to court me daughter, you'll do it proper. Come tonight for dinner and ale and we'll discuss the particulars."

Without waiting for a response, the two farmers turned toward the house and strode away, and Malkar seemed to know that it was time for him to leave, which he did with much haste.

As they entered, Ellianta rushed to them, her hands clasped together as she asked with nervous words, "What was that about? What do you intend to do this evening?"

They just smiled and Archem roughed her hair as they strode by her.

She looked desperately to Grettslyn, fear still in her eyes as she begged with a look for an answer.

"Come along, Little One," Grettslyn said as she turned toward the kitchen. "Time to get a meal prepared. You'll need to be washin' those three pewter mugs that be waitin' in the cupboard, then…" She paused and looked back to Ellianta. "Goodness sakes, Little One. Ye be covered with blood!"

Looking down at her dress, Ellianta lifted her skirt with her hands and shook her head, then she looked back to Grettslyn with an arched brow and said, "We had a little incident in the village this afternoon."

"Need to clean it good for tonight," Grettslyn insisted. "Haven't finished that other for ye. Hop up to ye room and get out of it, bathe good and stay up there until I'm done with it."

Looking down at her dress again, she agreed, "Yes, it will have to be cleaned. Are you sure I can't help?"

Grettslyn bent to her and whispered, "You'll be naked."

"Oh," Ellianta realized. "I will be, won't I?"

"Hurry along, Little One. Much ado tonight."

**

This was more anxiety than Ellianta had felt for a long time. With a blanket wrapped around her, she rushed around the house to make certain everything was perfect, helped with the meal, helped outside with preparing the table and even collected a few vegetables from the garden. The three special mugs were kept in a safe place in the kitchen until the time.

She rushed outside and looked toward the sun. Time was growing short, and yet it seemed to pass very slowly, and she found herself growing more and more anxious by the moment. Her eyes darted about and she barely noticed Hilliti stride up behind her. "When will he be here?" she asked, frustration finding its way into her voice.

"In short order," Hilliti assured. "You'd best hope he takes his time, Little One. Might get the wrong idea with you wearin' nothing but that blanket."

Ellianta looked down at herself, then folded her arms close to her and nodded. "How is my dress coming? Grettslyn won't let me help with it and she's been working on it for a long time."

"Just leave it to us, Little One." Hilliti had three plates in her hand and she began setting them in their places on the table. One was put in Brogret's place, one in Archem's place, and the last one was put in the middle chair usually occupied by one of the children.

Slowly raising her brow, Ellianta hesitantly asked, "Only three place settings?"

Offering her a little smile, Hilliti explained, "Tonight is an affair of men, Little One. The children'll eat out back with your ogre friend, Grettslyn and me will eat in the kitchen and you… Well, you'll be too unnerved to eat anything, anyway."

Ellianta loosed a hard breath and looked back toward the road, then she turned and rushed back into the house, through it, and out the back door where Grettslyn was working on her dress. Seeing her standing at the drying line, she asked frantically, "Did the stains come out? Are you done? He's going to be here any minute!"

Grettslyn looked over her shoulder as she hung something up. "You need a nip, I think. Ye nerves are a mess, Lass."

"What are they going to do to him?" Ellianta whimpered.

"They'll talk the business of men, Little One. Your suitor

will have to ask for permission to court ye proper like, and he'll have to impress the men folk of the house to boot. Got to make certain he can care for ye."

"He's a healer!" she barked.

"Ye also called 'im a letch not too long ago," Grettslyn reminded.

Ellianta folded her arms again and looked away. "I remember. So, what do we do while they talk about me. And don't I get a say? What if I really like him?"

Coming out from the house, Hilliti informed, "The men folk must like him. Ye have to be patient and follow customs, Little One."

Her brow arching, Ellianta reluctantly asked, "What if they *don't* like him?"

With a little shrug, Grettslyn replied, "Oh, the worst would be they kill him and toss his body in the woods."

Ellianta's eyes were wide with horror as she turned to Hilliti, her mouth agape as she cried, "No they won't! That isn't funny! Please tell me they won't do that!"

She also shrugged. "Men be men, Little One. Of course, they may just castrate 'im, or maybe break a bone or two and send him on his way as a reminder to others."

Raising a hand to her head, Ellianta grasped a handful of hair and tried to reassure herself that Brogret and Archem would like her suitor. They had to!

"Ellianta," Grettslyn called from behind, and when Ellianta turned, she held up a white dress with a low neckline trimmed in lace, full sleeves with wide cuffs, also trimmed in lace. It had full skirts that looked just long enough to brush the ground as she walked and ribbons of the same lace layered the skirts. It was also very small about the middle. Blue flowers were embroidered around the waist and along the cuffs of the sleeves, almost the same blue as her eyes. The dress was clearly made to show off her shape, and perhaps to exaggerate it a little. It was beautiful.

Raising a hand to her mouth, Ellianta smiled behind her

fingers as she saw it and she looked it up and down many times, slowly shaking her head as she softly said, "It's so lovely."

Hilliti took her shoulders from behind and bent close to her ear. "Ye must look a stunning sight to catch the eye and heart of ye suitor, Little One."

"Thank you so much," Ellianta breathed.

Grettslyn looked beyond Ellianta, to Hilliti, and said with narrow eyes, "Let's get her dressed."

**

Two things were to happen that evening. First, this would be the first and only time in her life that a suitor would come to formally ask to court her. Second, this was the first time she had seen the inside of Brogret and Hilliti's bed chamber.

The place seemed bigger than one would think. It was simple inside, only their bed, a couple of wardrobes that looked like they were homemade. Against the far wall was a vanity, not so unlike the one at Caipiervell Castle. The dress fit her even better than she had imagined, though a little tight around the middle. Her chest was almost too large for it and she was feeling a little modest looking at her reflection, and yet she smiled. She felt pretty and alluring and watched in the mirror as Grettslyn slowly brushed her long hair.

"You are truly of the angels, Little One," Grettslyn said proudly as she stood beside Hilliti. "A prettier sight I've not seen." She produced a little barrette that was made of gold and blue glass and was in the shape of a flower. This she fixed into Ellianta's hair, right above her ear, and when it was in place, she smiled. "Wore this when Archem came to call. Hilliti wore it before that when me brother came to call. You wear it now, Little One. Bring you good fortune, like with Hilliti and me."

Ellianta stared dumbly at her reflection for a time. That did not quite look like the same woman she had been. With a fine pink powder dusted onto her cheeks and a darker pink powder darkening her eyelids, she gazed at a woman she had never seen before. Her already long, thick eyelashes were enhanced more by a mixture of coal and some kind of oil that Hilliti had in a little jar. This she had applied with her fingers and Ellianta's eyelashes curled upward a little.

"Thank you both so much," she finally breathed.

In turn, they each bent down to kiss Ellianta's head, then they stared at the reflection with her, proud smiles on their faces, smiles like very proud mothers.

A meek knock at the door and a click of the handle drew their attention.

Prenzee peeked in and smiled as she saw Ellianta, declaring in a soft voice, "You are really pretty. He's here and he and Appi and Uncle Brogret are sitting there drinking ale."

All of Ellianta's body tensed up and her eyes widened. She drew a breath to calm herself, but still grabbed the other women's hands.

"Very good, Prenzee," Grettslyn said. "Now go on into the kitchen and fetch that pot that's near the basin. Got spiced apples cooked in it for ye and those boys."

The little girl's face lit up and she darted out, slamming the door behind her.

"I think I'm going to be sick," Ellianta whimpered.

"You'll be fine," Hilliti assured, rubbing her back. "Just relax yeself and let the men do as they do, and we'll be with you to help along the way."

Nodding, Ellianta tried to respond, but she was barely getting breath and words could not be made. Swallowing hard, she slowly got to her feet, feeling her knees shaking as she stood.

They emerged from the room to find the front door open and the men outside talking casually about the day, the explosion at the bakery, and the things men will speak of.

Entering the kitchen, they still found everything in its place and ready to take outside to be served to the men. A big pot of pulled pork had been simmering in some kind of spicy red sauce most of the day, and this was picked up by Grettslyn to be taken out. A large metal tray of assorted cut vegetables and apples also waited, as did a metal pitcher of very dark honey ale, clearly a drink preferred by the men of the house.

As Hilliti picked up the tray and looked her way, Ellianta went for the pitcher, pouring some in a small cup before she set the heavy pitcher back down. She picked up the cup and gulped it all down before slamming it back onto the counter. Picking up the pitcher again, she looked to Hilliti and drew another deep breath.

"Better?" Hilliti asked.

Ellianta nodded, and she held the pitcher with both hands as she followed Hilliti to the front door.

Outside, Archem and Brogret sat in their places while Malkar sat toward the center of the table, his back facing the door. He had changed his attire and wore a very clean, very bright white shirt and a sky blue jerkin. His black trousers looked perfectly pressed and he had clearly spent some time working on his hair. The man was as perfectly groomed as he could be.

Ellianta felt her anxiousness surging up again and looked down to the pitcher, and she thought about taking another drink from it.

Hilliti set the vegetable tray down near the center of the table, then turned and strode to her husband's end of the table, patting his shoulder as she got there. Grettslyn already stood by Archem, her hand on his shoulder and her eyes on Ellianta.

The conversation ended abruptly and Malkar looked over his shoulder to see the woman he loved standing behind him and to the left, hugging the pitcher to her as she stared back with a little fear in her eyes and an uneasy little smile on her glossy lips. Slowly standing, Malkar turned to face her, his eyes wide and glancing over every part of her as he softly complimented, "Ellianta, you are absolutely stunning!"

She shyly looked down, hugging the pitcher to her a little closer as a smile pulled her lips back from her teeth a little.

Malkar reached to her and stroked her hair, just over her ear, but before he could speak again Brogret pounded his hand on the table over and over and the startled healer backed away from her and turned to the big farmer.

Pointing a finger at him, Brogret growled, "You'll be watchin' where ye put those hands, healer. Sit yeself down and let's talk of matters." As Malkar took his seat, the farmer looked to Ellianta and barked, "Don't just stand there with that ale, Little One. You've three thirsty men to quench."

Grettslyn had gone over this with her, and Hilliti had as well. She turned gracefully and strode to Brogret first, carefully filling his pewter mug almost to the top. Walking around him, she strode down the table to fill Archem's, being sure to walk on the opposite side of the table so that Malkar could have a good look at her. She did not return his gaze, but she did fight to keep that little smile at bay as she felt his eyes on her.

As Archem's mug was filled, Brogret took his and looked down into it for a time, leaning back in his chair as he said, "Healer, I've no daughter of me own, none from me own loins. Ellianta came to me sent from Heaven itself and she is as much me own daughter as she would be if I'd made her. Been a little over a month since she came here, it has, and you'll be knowing it feels like she grew up in this very house." He finally turned his eyes to Malkar's. "She's not me flesh, boy, but she's me family. She's me daughter as if I'd made her and I'll always consider her so. You just be keepin' that in mind."

Nodding, Malkar assured, "I will."

Archem took a gulp from his mug and announced, "That makes her me niece, boy, so you've two men in this house to contend with, two men who would have quite an irritation if she gets hurt in any way. She feels pain, we'll make sure whoever causes it feels even more, says me, and she'll always be welcome in this house be she runnin' or widowed."

Nodding to him, Malkar swallowed hard and softly said, "I understand."

"So ye would court me daughter, would ye?" Brogret asked. "Ye can provide for her, I trust? Give her good care and handle her heart as your most prized possession?"

"That will be my vow to you," the healer assured.

Brogret stared into his ale as he seemed to consider, then he looked across the table to Archem and raised a brow slightly, and Archem responded with a subtle nod. "Very well, boy," Brogret finally said, "Ye may court me daughter." His eyes narrowed as they turned on him. "But you'll be watchin' ye step, boy, and so will I." He raised his mug and declared, "Now we drink to ye good fortune!"

The men raised their mugs and took long gulps from them, and even before Malkar could put his down, Ellianta set the pitcher down and wrapped her arms around his neck, hugging him as tightly as she could.

He tried to return her embrace, but Brogret slammed his hand onto the table again and barked, "You be watchin' them hands, boy!"

Ellianta retrieved the pitcher and backed away, and as Grettslyn gestured to her to follow her back into the house, she did, but she was bouncing a little as she walked.

As they got back into the kitchen, Ellianta set the pitcher down and anxiously asked, "You don't think Brogret and Archem know about… Well, they don't know, do they?"

Grettslyn leaned back against the counter and folded her arms, raising her brow as she replied, "Well, the boy ain't bleedin, so I'm thinkin' no. Might be waitin' for ye to go to sleep so they can have at him."

"Grettslyn!" she cried. When a smile broke its way through the robust woman's features, Ellianta relaxed ever so slightly. "They wouldn't really hurt him. They aren't those kinds of men, not violent at all."

Hilliti entered and took the little healer's shoulders, softly saying in her ear, "You've never seen'em protectin' their family, have ye?"

Ellianta's eyes widened a little more.

**

A half moon was more than enough light to see the road by and Ellianta walked stride for stride with Malkar, her eyes on the road and her hands folded behind her as they were both lost in their thoughts.

"Wasn't so bad," he finally said, his eyes on the road.

She smiled and agreed, "No, it wasn't. And to think you were afraid to come here."

"I came back, didn't I?"

Ellianta nodded. "Are you glad you did?"

He cut his eyes to her. "Are you?"

Her gaze shifted to him and she raised a brow to him and offered a little shrug.

Malkar finally stopped and seized her arm at the elbow, spinning her toward him and pulling her to him with his other arm. "Now we're out of sight of the house."

She laughed under her breath, offering him a seductive smile as she said, "So we are. You don't intend to take your pleasure of me, do you?"

"Oh, I might. Or I might just want to steal another kiss."

"Steal a kiss? Well, good sir, I don't think I could ensure your safety if you do."

Wrapping his arms around her fully, he grasped her wrists to keep them behind her and he squeezed her to him even tighter. "For you, I am willing to take my chances."

She squirmed a little, working her shoulders back and forth in a feeble-hearted effort to escape from his grasp, but she never took her eyes from him. "Good sir, you should let me go before you get caught trying to defile me."

"I will never let you go," he insisted. "As long as I live, I shall hold you. And I will keep you. And I will never let you go."

His words were very pretty words that touched and captured her heart and she smiled a little before closing her eyes and offering her mouth to his, which he took like a ravenous animal. She whimpered a little, still acting like she wanted to escape him, but very soon giving herself to him completely.

He pulled back a little and informed, "Your keepers are going to make life very difficult for us. We need to figure out how to respond to that."

She smiled. "You mean being together. Perhaps you shouldn't have me until marriage."

"I'm not willing to wait, woman. I've had you and I'll never get enough of you." He glanced aside. "You know, I am running low on an extract that I get from a specific cactus, and I'll need to go for more soon."

"And you would like for me to come with you?"

"If you wish. There is part of the country out there that is too beautiful for me not to show you. It's always been so lonely collecting this extract, as it is in a remote area, and I've always wanted to share it with someone."

"I think this is another excuse to bed me again."

"Well, there is that, but there is also the extract I need."

She leaned her head. "So, we're going out there to work and that is all anyone needs to know?"

"Exactly."

Nodding, Ellianta conceded, "I'll see what I can do, but I can't promise they'll let me go with you. They are all very protective of me."

"I would be, too," Malkar confessed. He released her wrists and slid his hands up her arms, over her shoulders and to her neck, stopping his fingers just beneath her ears as his thumbs slowly caressed across her lips. "Meet me by the pond where we first made love and I'll show you a place so beautiful you will dream about it for the rest of your life."

Just as slowly, she slid her hands around his waist and closed her eyes as she offered her mouth to his again. This time, he touched his lips to hers ever so gently and a wistful breath escaped her at a kiss so pure.

He pulled away and paused long enough to see her eyes in the moonlight, and finally he turned and started the long walk home.

As he disappeared down the road, she slowly raised a hand to her lips, touching where his had so gently kissed her that last time. A little smile returned to her as she spun around to return home, herself.

CHAPTER 14

Somehow, Hilliti had managed to clean all of the blood from her dress and it sparkled as it did the first day she saw it. Hanging the dress Grettslyn and Hilliti had made for her on a hook in her room, she got dressed and pulled her slippers on before she descended downstairs to start her day. Her heart raced as thoughts of seeing her suitor danced through her mind. Brogret and Archem were just about to leave when she grabbed an apple from a basket in the kitchen and her bag from a table near the door and left with them.

"Off early again, ye are," Archem observed.

"Yep. Running low on much needed elixirs," she replied in an exasperated tone. "This is what it was like in my old village. Almost every morning I had to go and collect the things I need for powders and potions to help the sick, and I find myself just as busy here."

Brogret's eyes narrowed and he pointed a thick finger at her, warning, "Ye just keep a distance from that boy this morning, aye?"

She set her hands on her hips and countered, "He's thirty-two seasons old!"

"All the more reason ye keep your distance," he said straightly. "He wants to see ye, he'll come here for it where we can keep our eyes on him."

"He's doing the same thing I am," she laughed, "and he's doing it on the other side of the village. I was thinking about inviting him to dinner again tonight if I may, Papa."

He growled, and looked to Archem, only getting a shrug from him, but he finally conceded, "Very well, Lass. If ye see him, talk to him only long enough to ask him here this evening."

"Thank you!" she squealed in a girlish voice as she bounded up to him. After giving him a kiss on the cheek, she turned and hurried around the house in the early morning glow, making her way to the path that would lead her into the forest, and to the path that followed the creek that fed that pond.

Anticipation was surging through every part of her.

The journey there seemed to take forever and she found herself trotting for much of it, but she finally arrived and darted to the center of the clearing, glancing about as she searched for him. Drawing her breath, she clamped her mouth shut and blew it out through her nose, and much irritation with it.

"Figures he'd be late," she grumbled.

"I'm not late," he informed from behind her.

She swung around and smiled, dropping her bag as she sprinted the four paces to him. With arms open wide, she slammed into him chest first and wrapped her arms around him as he enveloped her with his. Staring up into his eyes, she said softly, "I missed you last night."

"And I you," he replied.

She only knew to do one thing at this moment, and that was to close her eyes and surrender her mouth to him. They would not know how long they stood there and kissed, but they finally pulled apart just enough to look into each other's eyes again.

"We have work to do," he whispered.

"I don't care," she whispered back.

He smiled at her and stroked her hair. "You'll want to wait. Just trust me on that."

"No I don't," she whined, her lips pouting and her brow arched over her blue eyes.

Malkar pulled away from her grasp and took her hand, ordering, "Come on. I want to show you this place. It isn't far from here, perhaps three hundred paces."

"Okay," she conceded, following and pausing just long enough to pick her bag up.

As he led her toward the swift running creek upstream from the pond, she stopped and pulled back on his hand, saying, "Wait a moment."

He turned and watched her sit down and untie the ankle bands of her slippers and he folded his arms as she pulled them off and stood. A big tree was nearby and she approached it and hung her slippers on the broken stump of a branch that was about at eye level for her. When she reached over her head and started pulling her dress off, he finally raised his brow and stammered, "Uh... Um... What are you doing?"

She looked over her shoulder at him and smiled. "I always forage naked. Don't you remember?"

He tried to turn his eyes away from her as she hung her dress by the straps where her slippers were hung, but he just couldn't.

"I suppose I forgot," he admitted as she turned and picked up her bag.

A pace away from him, she took her bag from him and hugged it to her chest, really more to tease him than anything, and she lowered her head a little, raising her brow as she locked her eyes on his. "You'll remember from now on, won't you?"

"And I won't forage without you," he added.

She took his hand and he led the way again, this time through denser growth, which he moved for her as best he could. As they walked, he looked at her frequently, and when she looked back she had a teasing little smile on her lips.

He cleared his throat, then informed with authority, "You realize that once we're married I'm going to make you sleep naked."

She laughed. "I already do."

"Well, then. Problem solved."

Ellianta rolled her eyes and laughed again, then asked, "So where is this place again?"

"Not much further," he assured as he turned his back to a bush and backed into it, pushing it out of the way so that she could pass. A smile touched his lips and he added, "Not much further at all."

She walked by him, watching him as she did, then she looked forward again and stopped where she was. Her mouth was agape and her eyes were very wide as she looked ahead of her. She had not noticed that they had been traveling mostly downhill and what opened ahead of her was a sight that simply took her breath away.

Ahead was a cliff side of white stone, and overhanging it was harder stone of gray and black. A layer of crystals was between the layers and glistened as she slowly moved her gaze from one side to the other. It was a hundred paces away, perhaps five heights tall and was solid forest at the top. It stretched on until it wound out of sight and gave way to the water of a very blue lake that seemed to be carved right out of the forest itself, and seemed to go on for more than a league. A similar white cliff was on the other side of the lake and was topped with forest. Ferns, fruit bearing trees and flowering bushes were all around them. But for the wind and the birds, it was quiet here, peaceful.

Ellianta finally noticed that she was standing on an ankle deep carpet of grass, grazed down by deer and other animals. Her eyes sparkled as her gaze swept from one side of this enchanting scene to the next, and finally she breathed, "This is beautiful!"

He slipped his arm around her shoulders and drew her to him, nodding as he said, "My thoughts the first time I saw it. Sadly, I had to spend all of those seasons visiting it alone with no one to share it with."

Still looking out over the lake, she slipped her arms around him and leaned her head against his shoulder. "It's the most beautiful place I've ever seen."

Malkar nodded again, and for a time they just stood there and enjoyed it.

Ellianta finally glanced up at him and smiled, then looked to the water that was just beyond some white bleached rocks that were speckled with gray, and only about ten paces away from them. "You know, I think this is a perfect time for a swim." She pulled off her spectacles and dropped them onto her waiting bag, then she broke away from him and sprinted toward the lake, seeing that it was a short, half height jump into water that was clear and deep blue.

"Ellianta!" he shouted, chasing her. "Wait!"

She jumped onto the rocks and then into the water which was just less than a man's height deep here and about as cold as winter ice. As the chill sliced through her, she crossed her arms over her chest and screamed. Breathing in was difficult and she found herself in a mad struggle toward the rocks and the warmth and safety of the shore.

Malkar offered her his hand and, as he pulled her from the lake, he informed, "This water comes from snow that melts off of the mountains to the north of here. It doesn't really get any warmer than that."

Shivering, she huddled up against him with her arms drawn to her chest and said, "I see. I am going to die of cold soon."

With a smile, Malkar reached to her legs and swept her from the ground, turning to carry her back to the grass. "No, you won't die of anything today." He knelt and laid her down in the sunshine, then lay on his side beside her and propped his cheek in his hand as he stared down at this shivering, naked young woman for a time. Her eyes were closed and her arms were still drawn to her chest as she tried to warm herself. Sitting up, he pulled his shirt off and she finally opened her eyes and looked to him as he held the shirt in his hand.

"Thank you," she offered with trembling words, then she watched him throw the shirt into a pile on the other side of her.

"Cold?" he asked with a smile.

"Yes," she replied in a girlish, shaking voice.

He laid his body over hers, stroking back some of her wet hair as he whispered, "Let me warm you."

She closed her eyes as he lowered his lips to hers, and slowly slid her arms around his back.

**

Ellianta was not cold anymore, and as the sweat dried from both their bodies, they remained in each other's arms, kissing affectionately and caressing each other's skin. Lovemaking was still new to Ellianta, but she found these times with Malkar to be her favorites and never wanted them to end.

He finally drew back a little and looked into her eyes, informing, "We should get some work done at some point today."

She offered a reluctant nod and looked away from him. "I wish we could just stay here like this forever."

"Even when I'm a wrinkled old man?" he asked teasingly.

"Well," she replied, "I'll be a wrinkled old woman, so sure."

He laughed and shook his head. "Sounds lovely. Come on, let's get dressed and show some progress, otherwise your keepers will string me up by my entrails."

"They won't mind once we're married," she pointed out as she watched him stand and reach for his trousers. "In fact, they'll probably expect you to take me at your whim." She smiled. "That actually sounds very nice."

"Yes it does," he confirmed as he pulled his trousers on. "Let's get dressed and… Oh, wait, you don't have your clothing with you. How unfortunate."

"You prefer me naked, I think," she laughed.

"What man wouldn't?" he countered.

Helping her to her feet once his shirt was on, they made their way along the shore, toward this place where a rare cactus grew. The going was a little treacherous in places, but neither seemed to mind.

They arrived at a rocky clearing and Ellianta first noticed that almost nothing grew here as far away from the water as a hundred paces, and twice that along the lake. A few rugged trees struggled to grow from the dark stone and a few grasses sprouted from cracks and crevices. The most prominent plants were bulbous cacti with long thorns and bright red orbs that grew from the tops of them by the hundreds, each half the size of a man's fist. As they approached one, Ellianta finally realized that the bulbs were flat and not only covered in long needles, but shorter ones at the bases of the long ones. This was a plant that belonged in the desert, but here it had a foothold and thrived. There were thousands of them out here, each with bright red orbs atop them.

"Just watch your step, little healer," Malkar warned. "Many of those needles have fallen over the seasons and if you get one in your foot it's very painful to try and get out." He set his black bag down and crouched down to it. Rummaging through for a moment, he produced some long metal tongs and a wooden box almost the size of his head, and the box looked like it took up most of the room in his bag.

She watched as he approached the first cluster of cacti and she folded her arms as he began to use the tongs to pick some of the fruit from it. "Um," she started, "what do you use this for?"

He carefully plucked another one and replied, "It's an ingredient that I use in a tonic that helps people recover from sickness. It also makes one hell of a good wine."

Nodding, Ellianta said, "You'll have to let me try some."

"Traded most of it," he informed, "but I still have a bottle or two around the house somewhere."

"I like sweet wines," she informed.

"Then you'll like what I've made." He paused and looked beyond the cactus he was working on, and slowly stood. "Ellianta, I need you back away, very slowly."

Seeing movement in the cactus field, her eyes widened a little and she crossed her arms over her chest as she began to back away.

Also collecting some of the cactus fruit were a half dozen goblins, and all of them were looking right at the pair of healers.

"This isn't good," he mumbled, dropping the box and tongs.

All of the goblins were armed and wore hoods over their head that shaded them from the sun. They also dropped what they had and drew their weapons, four with axes, one with a short halberd and the sixth with what appeared to be a sickle.

Ellianta could still not remember the horrid event in the castle short of her frightening escape, but she did know fear of these creatures that were only half her size, lots of fear. Her wide eyes darting from one to the next and her arched brow high over them, she whimpered, "Malkar," as the goblins advanced through the cacti.

With a low hand, he motioned her back, his eyes locked on the closest of the advancing goblins. He retreated with her, trying to stay as close as he could, trying to keep himself between the goblins and his Ellianta.

The goblin in the lead waved his hand and the others fanned out, trying to outflank the two humans who were in their sights.

Hearing movement toward the trees, Ellianta looked and screamed, "Malkar!" as she saw two more trying to get behind them.

Malkar responded quickly, half spinning and directing two fingers toward the closest of them. Yellow lightning lanced from his fingers with a sharp crack and the goblin shrieked as he was knocked to his back.

The rest of them hesitated.

Ellianta's eyes widened as she saw this, but her heart sank a little as the goblin staggered back to his feet.

"I can stun them," Malkar informed, "but that's about all. Just stay behind me. Perhaps I can drive them off."

She started to remember stories from many seasons past, how goblins ate men and women, how their victims would sometimes die quite horribly, and sometimes over many days. Sometimes the goblins would eat their victims alive, as they watched...

Those thoughts drove her fear and she raised her hands toward her neck – and felt the chain. Looking down, she saw the amulet the dragon had given her. "Use the amulet," he had told her, or as close as she could remember, and perhaps that was what was called upon now.

As Malkar stunned another, and then another, she grasped the amulet and pulled the chain over her head and pulled her long hair through it, then she took the end of the chain and allowed the amulet to dangle. Holding it in front of her, she took Malkar's shoulder and pulled him back, showing the goblins the amulet as she shouted, "Ralligor!"

The goblins stopped and raised their heads, and lowered their weapons. The closest of them took a few more steps forward, closing to within three paces or so as he looked closely at the amulet, and he leaned his head a little.

Covering her chest with her free arm, Ellianta raised her chin a little as she stood her ground, her heart thundering. She tried not to tremble, but this was beyond her control. She repeated, "Ralligor," in a calmer voice, seeing that she had their attention.

The goblin took another tentative step toward her, having a good close look at the amulet. Unexpectedly, he put his weapon away, then turned and mumbled a few unintelligible words to his fellow goblins, who also put their weapons away. Looking back at her, he raised his palms toward her and backed away, and the others did as well, and they began to chant in one voice, "Ralligor. Ralligor. Ralligor."

In a moment, they had retreated into the forest and were gone.

Slowly, she lowered her arm, her eyes glancing around to make certain they had all gone.

Malkar took her shoulders from behind and pulled her into him, and as she released a soothing breath, he asked, "How did you do that? And what was that name you said?"

"I want to go," she whimpered, leaning back into him. "I want to leave before they come back. Please take me home."

**

Their journey back to the village was one made almost

entirely in silence, and Ellianta kept her hand in Malkar's as much as she could. The amulet and the dragon's influence had worked, but still in her mind was what could have been, and her growing fear of the little gray skinned creatures that were dangerously close to home.

Just as they entered the village, Malkar slipped his arm around her shoulders and observed, "You've been awfully quiet, Ellie."

She shrugged and softly replied, "Just thinking."

"About something that bothers you," he guessed.

She nodded.

"The goblins?"

Ellianta turned her eyes away and her lips parted slightly. Fear was in her eyes. When he took her chin and turned her toward him, she could not look at him.

"Many are afraid of them," he informed softly. "It is nothing to be ashamed of."

"I'm not ashamed," she said in a whispery voice. Stopping and pulling away from him, she folded her arms over her chest and turned her eyes down. "In my other village there were no such things to be afraid of. Here, where the people are so pleasant and life seems perfect most of the time, well there is so much… Ogres and goblins and…" She released the rest of her breath and closed her eyes.

He closed the distance between them with two steps and wrapped his arms around her, settling his chin on the top of her head as he reminded, "You befriended that ogre. You are the first one of the village he's ever had contact with, the first one he didn't try to kill."

She nodded. "What do you know of goblins? I never knew they built castles. I grew up thinking they were just made up stories that were told to frighten children."

"As did I until a few seasons ago," he said grimly. Pulling away from her, he took her hand and they resumed their slow walk toward the village. "They didn't build that castle. It was built over two hundred seasons ago by our kind. I'm told that more than sixty seasons ago it was a thriving kingdom that prospered off of the backs of the villagers here."

"Sounds familiar," she mumbled.

"Well, then came the Desert Lord," Malkar went on. "He apparently established a territory somewhere in the desert and hunted here, and had an appetite for the sheep and goats that were raised by farmers who were employed by the castle. They tired of him raiding their herds, and one day they were ready to receive him."

She turned her eyes up to him. "Uh, oh."

"Yes, uh oh. They hired dragonslayers to kill him and on the day he returned to feed the castle was bristling with huge crossbows called ballistas. Apparently these dragonslayers had killed dragons with them before, but they were not counting on him being as powerful as he was. One of the huge arrows they shoot actually penetrated him, his leg, I think, and he regarded that as an act of war. Long story short, the castle lost after a two day siege. When the royal family tried to flee, he caught them in the open along with most of their army."

Ellianta's eyes widened a little. "He killed them all, didn't he?"

Malkar nodded. "Yes, with terrible purpose. After, he returned to the castle and fired it again, and it is said he laired there for some time before moving on. The sheep herds were decimated and everything within was burned. At one point, I guess about forty seasons ago or so, someone else tried to inhabit the castle and he returned to drive them out or kill them."

"So why won't he drive away the goblins?" she asked.

"I don't know," was his simple answer. "It is said that he has a pact of some kind with them, but no one knows for sure."

"So he destroyed the castle and killed the royal family and everyone who lived there, but he did not attack the village?"

Malkar raised his brow. "You know, he's never actually

attacked the village. It is said that when he finished with the castle and the royal family, he landed in the village square where the fountain is now. People fled into shops and houses, but if a stone fortress could not stand against him then no wooden house could. It was a very tense time. He just sat there and looked around. At the time there was a village leader and he dared to come out and confront the dragon. It is said that he spoke to the Desert Lord and they struck a deal. All of the gold and silver in the village was collected, and people collected what they could find from the ruins of the castle. All of it was taken in wagons into the desert and given to him in exchange for sparing the village, and he left with a promise that he would demand no more tributes."

She raised her chin, her mouth and eyes widening as she declared, "I understand now. That's why everyone barters here and no one really uses money."

"That would be why. For some reason, he won't allow it, nor will he allow a standing army here."

"But what if someone attacks the village?"

He glanced at her. "From what I've read, that's happened twice. The last time was the best recorded incident of that happening. A huge force of over a thousand men came across the desert and tried to take over. They were met with no resistance, but only an hour after they arrived the dragon returned and they had to face him."

"And it didn't go well for the invaders," she guessed.

"Not remotely," Malkar confirmed. "He wiped out the bulk of them and ordered that the village remove the rest. Quarter was offered to the survivors and they wisely took it and most left here forever."

"Most?"

He smiled slightly. "It seems that a few elected to remain and settle down here, and the dragon did not seem to mind."

She laughed under her breath. "It sounds like we're his pets."

"And I think we are," he said straightly, raising his brow.

"Not that anyone really minds. We've had more than fifty seasons of peace here, and a simple prosperity. He returns from time to time, often just flying overhead and roaring to announce that he is still with us. Most flee when he does that, but the older people who know him simply cheer and wave." He looked down to her. "He was here only a number of days ago. Didn't you see him?"

Looking away, Ellianta smiled a little and confirmed, "Oh, I saw him. He's quite magnificent."

"And among the biggest dragons in the land," Malkar went on. "I wouldn't want to see him angry, that's for sure."

"No, you wouldn't," she mumbled.

As they got into the village and approached the market square, he looked to her and asked, "Would you like to go to the inn for something to eat?"

She offered him a smile and a shrug, and her eyes told him she was willing to go anywhere with him.

Once in the square itself he stopped and she stopped at his side. Looking toward the fountain, they found the zealots still there and they were still trying to rally support for their cause. Disturbingly, many of the villagers seemed to be going along with them and a crowd of two score surrounded the old woman who stood atop a broken wagon to be seen by all.

Her eyes scanned the crowd and she held up a staff that was topped by a brass emblem the size of her head, an emblem that was a four point star with a crescent moon within.

"Hear me!" she shouted. "Among you are agents of evil! Spirit Mother has sent us to cleanse your people, to spread her word of joy and oneness. Only through acceptance of Spirit Mother can you truly find salvation in the afterlife. Only through rebirth through Spirit Mother will your spirit live on in you and beyond. Death is the end for non-believers and rebirth for those who are cleansed and reborn through Spirit Mother."

"And people believe this?" Ellianta asked, a slight snarl on her lips.

Malkar nodded.

"Your simple lives here are not fulfilled," the old woman went on. "When you find Spirit Mother in your heart you will discover riches beyond your wildest dreams. You can find joy and happiness that you never imagined, but only through rebirth." She lowered her staff, her eyes narrowing as they swept the crowd again. "But beware those who are not at one with her. Beware those who would reign over you with unnatural power. They are the ones who call themselves sorcerers, witches, wizards… They would come in the night and steal the light from your soul. They would cause your crops to wither, your cow to give blood and not milk, your water to sour. They may look like us, they talk like us, but they are great deceivers. Guard yourselves and your children from them."

Malkar folded his arms, leaned toward Ellianta and mumbled to her, "Now you know why anonymity is called for."

She raised her brow and nodded.

"You must seek them out!" the woman shouted. "Find them where they lurk and burn the evil from their souls and their bodies."

"That seems a little extreme," Ellianta murmured. Her spine stiffened as the old woman looked over the crowd, past them, and seemed to look right at her. "Can we go?"

"I think we should," he agreed as he took her arm and started to lead her away.

A black haired woman in the white robes of one of the zealots noticed them, then she turned and pointed at Ellianta as she cried, "Witch!"

Everyone looked that way and Ellianta froze and looked back. Fear crept up inside of her belly as she found herself the object of attention for over eighty people.

The black haired woman stalked toward her, hate in her eyes as she repeated, "Witch! I remember you from the forest.

Two of me mates died because of you!" She turned back toward the crowd and shouted, "This witch found us lost in the forest. We only wanted food and a place to rest, the hospitality of your village." She swung around and faced Ellianta again, pointing at her as before. "She summoned fire and demons and two of me mates were killed! She brought down death on innocent men and would walk among you in daylight. How long until this demon she commands comes for you all?"

Slowly shaking her head, Ellianta defended, "That isn't what happened at all!"

Another of the white robed people pointed at her and shouted, "Witch!"

Ellianta swallowed hard and clung to Malkar's arm, shaking her head still as she protested, "That isn't true! I'm no witch, I'm a healer!"

Malkar pulled her along and urged, "Come along. Let's get out of here."

The old woman pointed their direction and cried, "The evil must be purged. Hear me people, she must be cleansed by fire!"

Ellianta cringed and forced her eyes from the crowd, whimpering, "Malkar."

He slipped his arm around her and pulled her to him. "Let's get you home."

**

They got back to her house at a hurried pace, glancing behind them from time to time to make certain that no one followed.

"Who was that woman with the black hair?" he asked as they saw the house just down the road.

Shaking her head yet again, Ellianta replied, "She was part of a band of thieves who caught me in the forest. The meant to rob me and I think rape and kill me, and Gronko intervened and…" She looked away. "I felt him coming and warned them to release me or there would be dire consequences. I might have claimed to be a powerful witch, too."

Malkar groaned and raised a hand to his head. "Ellie, you didn't."

"I didn't know what else to do!" she cried. "They were going to kill me!"

"A witch? You told them you were a witch?"

She had no answer for him and turned her eyes down.

"We'll figure something out, Love," he assured.

A stone flew by her head, barely missing her and rolling to a stop down the road from them.

They looked over their shoulders to see a sizeable mob in pursuit of them, a mix of white robed zealots and villagers that were at least two score in number.

"Run," Malkar ordered in a low voice.

They darted toward the house, now only sixty paces away, but the mob behind them gave chase, shouting and throwing whatever they could pick up quickly. Finally reaching the front door, they burst through and Malkar turned and quickly closed it, slamming the bolt into place before he turned and pressed his back to the door.

Ellianta bent over and grasped her thighs, struggling to catch her breath. Turning fearful eyes to Malkar, she gasped, "What do we do?"

Brogret and Archem, who had been sitting near the fireplace, entered the room, looking a little startled as they saw the pair gasping for breath. Grettslyn came out of the kitchen and Hilliti from the back of the house.

Malkar pointed behind Hilliti and ordered, "Bar the back door. They are coming for Ellianta."

Something slammed into the door Malkar had his back to, and then something else and the angry crowd could be heard shouting from outside. One voice shouted over the rest, "You be harboring a witch in there! Send her out and we'll protect ye from her!"

Grettslyn glanced about, a fearful look in her eyes as she cried, "Witch?"

Looking to her, Malkar's brow was low over his eyes as he reported, "They think Ellianta is a witch. Someone accused her of summoning demons and casting spells or some nonsense of the like."

"Damn," Brogret swore. "Well, I've an old battle axe from many seasons ago. Hilliti, fetch me that axe."

"And me sword," Archem added. He looked to Ellianta and growled, "They come in here for ya, they'll surely pay for it in blood, says I."

Standing fully, Ellianta looked around her and gasped, "Where are the children?"

"Playing in the forest," Grettslyn said straightly. "Said somethin' about going to see that ogre. Had something to show them, he did."

Nodding, Ellianta confirmed, "So they're safe, until they come home." She raised a hand to her forehead, desperately looking around her. "What do we do? Oh, Father Sky, what do we do? They are going to come for me no matter what!"

Hilliti returned with a rusty old double bit battle axe in one hand and an almost antique sheathed sword in the other.

Seeing this, Ellianta shook her head and cried, "No. No! There are too many."

"We'll defend ye to the last, Little One," Brogret assured. "They'll not take ye."

"And then what?" she asked desperately. "They'll just keep coming. People like them will never, ever stop."

"Perhaps they can be reasoned with," Malkar suggested.

She covered her eyes, shaking her head. "You heard them, Malkar! They won't listen. Oh, Mother Land, what have I done? What have I done?"

Malkar rushed to her, wrapping his arms around her and holding her as tightly as he could. "This isn't your fault, Love. It isn't your fault. We'll figure something out."

She wept, and finally shook her head again, insisting, "No. My family has been good to me, as have you. I will not bring this misery to you. I won't!"

"Can we get her out the back?" Malkar asked of Brogret.

Ellianta countered, "What would they do to you for helping me? I... I couldn't live with that. I just couldn't." She pushed away from Malkar, backing away from him with eyes that were pools of hopelessness boring right through him. "I won't visit this on you, on any of you." She turned and looked to Brogret, insisting, "Give me to them. Just give me to them."

"Not a chance!" the big farmer roared. "They'll get ye over me dead corpse!"

She strode to him and took his big hands with hers. "Please, you have to. I won't visit this upon your family."

"And I won't surrender you to them," he growled.

"What of your children?" she cried. "What of Hilliti? What of Grettslyn?"

"And what of you?" Archem countered.

"Burn the house!" someone outside shouted. "When they flee we have them all!"

An angry roar of agreement sounded outside.

Ellianta reached up and grabbed his shirt, begging, "Please! Please give me to them! Don't make me have to live with what they would do to you all!"

"And how would we live with what they will do to you?" he countered.

"They mean to burn your home and hurt or kill your entire family!" she insisted. She could not stop herself from crying at this point and pulled herself to him. "I love you all too much to let anything like that happen to you. If you won't give me up, then I will have to go on my own. If you do, they will leave you alone." She buried her face in his shirt and wrapped her arms around him as far as they would go. "Please, please give me to them! Please! Don't let them hurt your children."

Brogret turned eyes to Archem that no one had ever seen before, and both men knew the little healer was right. She was not begging for her own life, she was begging for theirs.

As Archem, Hilliti and Grettslyn slowly approached her she turned and hugged them all as tightly as she could.

Malkar was the last to approach her and she turned to him almost reluctantly. As she stared down at the floor between them, he gently stroked her hair and whispered, "You can't do this."

"I have to," she insisted. Reaching to her neck, she removed the dragon's amulet and finally looked to his eyes, slipping the chain over his head, and when she did, she grasped his neck with both her hands and whispered, "This will keep you safe. I wish I could make you forget me."

"I never will," he insisted.

Tears streamed from her eyes. "I love you, Malkar. Please understand why I have to do this. Please always remember that I love you, and find another."

He looked away from her, tears dropping from his eyes as well.

Their eyes finally met one more time and they joined in one last, passionate lover's kiss.

She pulled away, staring at him with those hopeless eyes, and mercifully she looked away, but not at anyone as she said, "You will have to take me out. Make them think you want rid of me. It is the only way I can repay the kindness you have all shown me." When they were reluctant, she implored, "Please. You have to. Don't let them hurt your families, I beg you."

Archem strode to her with purpose and took her arm, looking down at her with blank eyes as he asked, "Be ya sure ye can't be talked out of this?"

"I'm sure," she replied. "I don't think they'll really hurt me, but I shudder to think what they'll do to you and your families if you protect me." She looked back to Brogret and raised her brow, and she offered him her other arm.

He turned his eyes down, his mouth tightening to a tight slit, then he stormed to her and took her arm, and drug her toward the door.

They stopped there near the door and he stared ahead at it for a moment, and as he spoke he did not look at her. "Ellianta, I love you as ye were me own, and I always will."

"Thank you for doing this," she offered softly. "I love you, too." She looked over her shoulder. "I love you all." When she turned away from them, she stared at the door and said, "You will need to look angry, like you are anxious to be rid of me. If they think that, they will never bother you again. Now promise me you will close the door and not watch what happens. Promise! Both of you!"

"We love ya, Lass," Archem said abruptly. "Always will."

Brogret slid the bolt back and opened the door and the two men escorted her past the threshold by the arms, and once she was outside, they returned inside and closed the door behind her, and when the bolt slid locked into place, she knew she was all alone, and facing more than forty people who despised her.

Her eyes darted about as the crowd closed in on her and she backed up against the door. As many of them climbed onto the porch all around and slowly closed on her, she raised her hands to her chest, and her gaze locked on the old woman who slowly stalked forward, leaning on her staff as she did. She shrank away from the old woman, looking into eyes that held contempt for her, eyes that scrutinized her with cruel intent.

Holding a glare on Ellianta, the old woman's lips curled back from yellow and missing teeth and she hissed, "Witch."

Shaking her head, Ellianta whimpered, "But I'm not. I'm not what you think, I promise. I'm just a simple healer."

The old woman's eyes narrowed and she took a step closer, coming well within arm's reach. "Healer, are you? A perfect place for you to work your sinister purpose with these people."

"I don't do that," Ellianta defended. "Please, I am not what you think." When the old woman turned to walk away, Ellianta reached for her shoulder. "Please, Miss. Please listen to me. I am not as she —" A stone the size of an apple struck the left side of her head, right between her eye and temple. Her spectacles broke into pieces as her head was spun around and she collapsed, falling to her knees as she reached for her head. She caught herself on her free hand, barely clinging to consciousness as she tried to force her wits back about her. Someone seized her arm and someone else took the other. She heard her spectacles crunch under someone's boot as she was hoisted brutally to her feet and slammed back against the door. Blood ran freely from the wound left by the stone and she found herself unable to hold her head up. Forcing her eyes open, she tried to focus on the form that stood in front of her, and finally realized the blurry image was the old woman.

"You shall be judged," the old woman sneered. Spinning away, the old woman barked, "Bring her!" as she beckoned for the rest to follow.

**

Her wits returned to her slowly as she was taken to the market square. Still she could not hold her head up easily and she could feel where the blood had dripped off of her cheek and chin and onto her dress. More had streamed down her neck and much of it was already dried on the side of her head and her neck and throat.

The white clad zealots and many of the villagers gathered around her as she was pushed up against a pillar that held up the roof of one of the shops. Her hands were pulled behind her and ropes were wound around her wrists. More rope was pulled along her chest and around the post behind her and still another around her belly and her arms. Several people were very interested in being sure that she did not pose a threat, though she barely had her wits about her enough to even think about it. As she was finally able to organize her thoughts, she looked around her, squinting so see clearly. Her head was hurting terribly but she had no time to notice it, and fear crept along every particle of her being as the unknowns of what they meant to do to her fueled that fear.

The old woman stepped in front of her, turning to the crowd as she raised her arms and the staff above her head. "Hear me!" she shouted, silencing the crowd around them.

"The time has come to cleanse the village. The time has come for the judgment of this witch. How find ye?"

Someone approached, a small, thin form. As the form drew closer, Ellianta recognized her as the girl she had tried to help when the bakery had exploded, the same girl who had lost her mother that day.

Half an arm's reach away, the girl stopped and stared at her, and even without her spectacles she could see the rage in the girl's eyes.

The girl breathed with deep, angry breaths as she glared at the bound healer before her, and she clenched her teeth and hissed, "You just let her die."

Ellianta's brow arched and tears filled her eyes. "I swear I did everything I could. I just couldn't… She was too badly injured."

The girl glared at her a moment longer, then slapped her as hard as she could.

Her head snapping around, Ellianta closed her eyes against the pain, and she wept. "Please," she implored. "I could not help her. I tried, I really did!" As she cried, the girl grabbed her hair and forced her head back up, but Ellianta could not look at her.

A man came and took the girl by the shoulders, pulling her away and leading her back into the crowd.

Another woman came forward, one wearing the white robe of the zealots, but this one took Ellianta's chin in her hand and gently turned her head, and she bent to her ear and whispered, "I told you I'd get you, didn't I puppet?"

Recognizing that voice, Ellianta looked to her, and knew this to be the woman with the bandits.

The woman smiled, then she turned back to the crowd and shouted, "This witch called down a demon to kill me mates. They died horrible deaths, and she'll call this demon again to deliver her wrath to the next poor soul that displeases her!"

"That isn't true!" Ellianta cried.

The black haired woman glanced back at her, then

continued, "She wanted intimate favors from me and she killed the poor men she thought to be in her way. She called forth a horrible monster from Hell itself to do her bidding."

"You are lying," Ellianta screamed.

Pointing toward the mountains to the north, the black haired woman shouted, "Go to the hills and find their broken bodies! They were crushed by this monster demon she summoned. I barely escaped with my life!" She turned to Ellianta and folded her arms. "What will we find if we go up there, witch? What will we find?"

Ellianta closed her eyes and turned away from her.

The old woman approached and took her by the throat, forcing her eyes up as she offered, "Confess, witch. Confess so that you can be properly cleansed. Confess and we'll spare you the pain of the evil you have brought to these people."

Tears dropped from her eyes anew as Ellianta pitifully said, "But I'm not a witch."

"You are a lying demon!" the woman shouted. Turning back to the crowd, she raised her hands and staff again and said to them, "She must be cleansed. She must be purified. Don't be taken by her words and her pleas and lies. She is here to bring death and misery to you all!"

"That isn't true!" Ellianta sobbed.

"Cut her loose," the old woman ordered. "Bring her to the holy place to be cleansed."

"To the holy place!" someone else shouted.

Shouts of agreement were brought and those behind started untying her.

"What are you going to do to me?" Ellianta cried. No one seemed to hear her. Her arms were seized again as she was freed of the ropes and two big men escorted her forcibly through the crowd, across the market square and toward the edge of town. The whole crowd followed and a bloodlust followed with them. Angry shouts and curses surrounded Ellianta, but she knew resisting them would be futile. She still found herself dizzy from that blow to the head, but the fear within her gave her a strange alertness. "Please," she implored desperately over their angry shouts. "What are you going to do to me?"

When they left the market square and eventually the village itself, Ellianta saw ahead of them a straight, blurry image, something gray and tall like the stripped trunk of a tree, a pole or pillar, and another chill ran through her. From seemingly everywhere, villagers and zealots alike labored away at something. They were building something around that pole ahead, but she could not see past the people in front of her. Somehow, an excitement grew as they got closer. Only fifty paces away, Ellianta felt a familiar dread, one she had felt when she had been sacrificed to the dragon in the old village, when the goblins had her...

The crowd finally parted and she could see clearly ahead of her. The forest had been cut back over the seasons and a broad, empty area opened up, and the pole was sunk into the ground right in the middle of it, and put there recently. A log that looked just over half a man's height long was stood on its end at the base of the pole and the two were tied together with some coarse, grass rope of some kind. People in white darted about the clearing and in the forest, and all were collecting sticks and twigs and taking them with purpose to the pole in the center. Others tied clumps of them together and the assembled faggots were being pushed against the base of the pole on end. Many were already there and many more were being placed, all around except for a trail leading to the log bound to the pole.

Cleansed. The old woman said cleansed, purified.

Ellianta raised her chin, her eyes widening in terror as the realization of what they had planned drove home, and as the villagers and zealots lined up to form a pathway of angry people that led to the pole, she resisted out of sheer terror, her breaths coming in shrieks. With her eyes locked on the pole before her, she frantically shook her head as she tried to stop her forced advance toward it, and finally she screamed, "No!

Please, don't do this to me! I... I haven't done anything wrong, please!"

Ahead of them, the crowd began to form a circle around the assembling pyre, and the old woman who apparently led them stepped from the crowd directly in front of her, leaning on her staff as her eyes were locked on the day's victim.

Somehow, Ellianta tore away from the men and ran toward the old woman, dropping to her knees right in front of her and grasping at her robe as she cried, "Please stop them! Please! I beg you, don't do this to me! I beg you!" She buried her face in the priestess' robes, sobbing as she wrapped her arms around the woman's waist. "Please help me, please! Don't let them burn me!"

Someone struck the back of her head and she collapsed as the priestess backed away from her.

Forced back to her feet, she was made to face the old woman, and two big men appeared at her sides.

One of the men stepped forward and shouted, "You are not to touch the priestess, witch!" and he slammed his fist into her belly.

Breath exploded from her and the pain was too much for her to stand, and consciousness abandoned her as she doubled over.

She did not know how much time had passed when she finally raised her head. Opening her eyes was a struggle but she finally managed it. Everything around her was still blurry and sounds reached her as if they were coming through a tunnel. Something jerked her backward and she realized her back was pressed tightly against a pole, and this realization brought her fully awake. She shrieked a breath as she realized her hands were already bound behind her, behind the pole. She was bound about the chest, the waist, her hips, knees, ankles. She could not move! The last of the ropes were wound around her throat and around the pole, alarmingly tight, though it was not choking her.

All around her, the crowd began to chant, "Burn the witch!

Burn the witch! Burn the witch!" There seemed to be more of them. Other villagers had actually joined this madness.

Several women in white who carried large clay jars approached from the village and passed through the parting crowd.

The old woman, the priestess stood before their victim, contempt still in her eyes as she stared unblinking at her. The priestess seemed to hate her the most, and only through the priestess could this madness possibly be stopped. As the women with the clay jars reached her, the priestess raised her hands and staff and the crowd about them fell silent.

Ellianta stared back at her with desperate, fearful eyes, and she felt herself begin to cry anew.

Slowly lowering her arms, the priestess finally shouted, "The time is at hand, and the village will be cleansed this day." Her eyes never left Ellianta, but her brow lowered slightly as she finally spoke directly to her. "You have been found to be a witch, one who controls demons and who would feed upon the life of the people of the village. We know your kind. You would kill infants to consume their hearts and their living essence and you would drain the living for your own wicked intent. You are a taker of life and a deceiver, a bringer of suffering and an agent of great evil. For this you will be cleansed by fire."

"Please don't," Ellianta whimpered, tears rolling down her cheeks.

"Mercy may be granted," the priestess continued, "but only if you confess your sins to the people you meant to bring evil upon and to the Spirit Mother."

Ellianta leaned her head back against the pole and closed her eyes, praying in a whisper, "Father Sky, Mother Land, what do I do? Please help me. Please guide me."

"Do you confess, witch?" the priestess demanded.

A moment of clarity washed through Ellianta, a moment of truth. She opened her eyes and looked down to the priestess, slowly shaking her head as she said for all to hear, "If I don't confess, you will burn me to purify me. If I do, you will burn me anyway. Yours is about rumors and innuendo, not truth, and you would murder the innocent to advance your cause." She looked past the old woman, into the crowd and shouted, "You know the truth, and still you allow them to do this. You haven't considered that any of you may be next." New tears dropped from her eyes. "Please, my friends, my neighbors, those I have helped and those who have helped me. Please don't let them do this to me. I beg you, don't let them kill me like this!"

Those who did not stare back blankly looked away from her.

Her fate was sealed.

In one last appeal, Ellianta looked to the priestess and begged, "Please don't do this to me. I'm not a witch, really I'm not." She was crying shamelessly by the time she said in the voice of a little girl, "Please don't burn me."

The crowd remained silent for a long moment after, and the priestess just glared back at her with narrow eyes.

One man pushed his way through the crowd, one wearing a bright white shirt and a black vest, and his long black hair flowed behind him. To Ellianta, he was just a blurry image of a man, but she knew who he was even before he jumped upon the tightly formed faggots of sticks and wood around her. Green eyes pierced into hers for only a second before he turned to the crowd with careful steps on the uneven surface of sticks around him. His hand found the pole behind Ellianta and he made his stand beside her.

"Hear me," Malkar shouted, "and remember my words. This girl came to our village a friend. She came here a healer. She came here to help us with injury and sickness, the same as I did many seasons ago. No, I did not want her here for that first month, but then I got to know her. I saw the compassion about her, the gentle touch and caring way about her. Many of you out there have felt that healer's touch from a young woman who has asked nothing back. And now you would stand idly by while she is burned alive by these people who come to our village to spread fear and mistrust, and for some reason you trust that their word is the truth and you trust them over your own judgment. If you are to burn one healer of this village, then you will burn us both, and live without a healer at all."

Ellianta softly scolded, "What are you doing?"

He glanced at her and reminded in a low voice, "I told you I would never leave you."

Mumbles of doubt finally rippled through the crowd.

Pointing up at him, the priestess ordered, "Get him down from there. He's been bewitched by this demon."

Two men climbed onto the pyre and reached for him and he pointed two fingers at one and zapped him with a burst of that lightning he had used against the goblins, knocking the man backward and to the ground. The other man froze, his wide eyes on Malkar's then he backed away and jumped down, retreating into the crowd.

Malkar's eyes swept along the crowd and narrowed. "None of you knew I could do that, did you? I've been a student of the Wicca my whole life, and I've been the only healer here for almost seven seasons. I had your trust before when I helped you all. Do I not have it now?"

Silence ruled the crowd for a moment, and then someone in a white robe shouted, "They are both witches! Burn them both!"

A wave of agreement radiated out from there and hostility took the people once again.

Malkar looked about him as the chants of, "Burn the witches," began, and he raised his brow. "You know, I really thought that would work."

She turned her eyes to him and said softly, "You can still get away. You can still leave here and start a new life. Please go. Please."

Still staring out at the crowd, he shook his head, then he turned fully to her, his arms slipping around her and around the pole she was bound to as he insisted, "Ellianta, marry me."

Her breath caught and she breathed, "What?"

"Marry me," he repeated, a slight smile on his lips.

"Malkar, they mean to burn me to death in a moment."

"Then give me that moment to be the happiest man in the world." He pulled back slightly and took the chain from around his neck, the chain that suspended the dragon's amulet. Slowly, he slipped it over her head, putting it back where it belonged. His gaze pierced into hers and he combed his fingers through her hair, finally grasping her neck as he insisted, "I mean to spend the rest of my life with you, whether it is a moment or a hundred seasons. I have Brogret's blessing. I have your whole family's blessing. Please be my wife. Please marry me."

"I don't want you to die with me like this," she whimpered.

He reached into his vest and produced two glass vials. "We won't. These contain a tonic that I use to suppress pain in my patients. It is a very powerful tonic and there is far too much of it in each vial for only one person. Marry me, Ellianta, and let's deprive them of our horrible deaths and meet at the horizon as husband and wife."

She squeezed her eyes shut and her body shuddered as she sobbed, then she looked to his eyes and smiled, saying in a breath, "Yes! I'll marry you!"

As always, she surrendered her mouth to his and they joined in what could only be their last kiss, and he kissed her with all of the passion he had. Everything around them disappeared, melting away outside of the love and passion they felt for each other.

The women with the clay jars began to pour a liquid that smelled like lamp oil onto the pyre all around them, but they barely took notice. Men and women with torches made their way through the crowd, holding the torches high over them, and the crowd went into macabre cheers and backed away from the pyre.

Malkar pulled the stopper from the first vial and pulled

away from her slightly, raising the vial to her mouth, and as her uneasy eyes met his, he nodded to her and assured, "You'll quickly just fall asleep, and after that you'll feel nothing at all."

She drank the clear liquid within, then blinked and her brow lowered over her eyes as she absently said, "It is water."

"What?" he cried, the alarm on his face feeding new fear into her. He dropped the vial and pulled the stopper on the second, taking but a sip, and he glanced about as he shook his head. "I don't understand. It should be very bitter, almost unpalatable. Oh, Father Sky, this *is* just water!" He glanced about as the torches surrounded them, and he clenched his teeth together and closed his eyes. "I'm sorry, my Love. I don't know what happened. I'm so sorry."

"Don't fret," she whispered. "I still love you, and I always will."

As the torches were lowered in one motion to the pyre, Malkar pressed his body to hers and wrapped his arms around her as tightly as he could, closing his eyes as he buried his face in her neck and whispered, "I love you with all my heart, Ellianta, with all that I am."

"And I love you," she replied in a whisper.

"Why won't this light?" someone shouted.

"Witchcraft!" someone else yelled. "They've bewitched the fire!"

"The lamp oil!" a woman said with alarm. "It's turned to water!"

Malkar jerked his head up and looked over his shoulder. Ellianta looked where he did.

A few of the torch bearers had backed away, bewildered eyes on the oil soaked wood. Many of them kept jabbing the pyre with their torches, but to no avail. The wood simply would not ignite.

When Malkar looked to her with confusion in his eyes, she shrugged and defended, "It isn't me."

Thunder rolled from the sky all around, and clouds began to gather with unnatural speed, and the crowd began to slowly back away from the pyre. Lightning flashed from cloud to cloud and ear splitting claps of thunder boomed all around. Wind picked up, blowing from everywhere and to everywhere.

The priestess pointed to her two victims on the pyre and shouted over the noise of wind and thunder, "Stone them! They've called upon the powers of evil and must be stopped! Stone them!"

People all around picked up whatever they could and hurled it at the two Wiccans, and Malkar shielded Ellianta with his body. Most of the objects missed, but a few found their mark, hitting Malkar's back, and he groaned in pain as they did.

Fire finally erupted from the base of the pyre, but it did not consume the wood. As it grew in strength, it began to shoot outward, toward the crowd of people, who all retreated from it as fast as they could, and in an instant it was gone.

Ellianta saw something before her, right over the thickest part of the crowd and she looked around Malkar as another stone struck him, her eyes widening as lightning converged over one spot and the very air exploded into a ball of flames.

The villagers and zealots fled from under the sphere of fire as it expanded in all directions, and they screamed in terror. Only the priestess would not run as she watched the ball of fire grow larger, and she slowly retreated toward the pyre, her eyes on the horror above her.

With a deafening clap of thunder, the ball of fire collapsed on itself and exploded and a ring of flames burst forth, growing ever larger to consume the sky over the clearing, and a black shadow dropped from the middle of it.

Slamming onto the ground only ten paces from the pyre, the black dragon dropped to all fours, his red glowing eyes locked on Ellianta as he lowered his head to the level that hers was. A soft growl rolled from his throat and his brow was held low over his eyes as he held her in a menacing, predator's gaze. His nose was only three paces away from her and she could feel his breath as he exhaled.

The clouds above slowed and the fire and lightning were suddenly gone. An eerily silent moment followed.

Malkar turned toward the black dragon and pressed his back to Ellianta as if to shield her from his wrath, his terror-filled eyes locked on the massive predator.

Looking to the puny human who dared stand before him, the dragon raised a brow ever so slightly.

"It's all right, Malkar," Ellianta said softly. "Move aside. Let him see me."

Hesitantly, he did, but never took his eyes from the dragon.

The crowd was silent and no one dared to move, lest they draw his attention and his wrath.

As the red glow faded from his eyes to reveal pale blue, the black dragon glared at her for a long, horrifying moment, then he slowly he shook his head and boomed, "Unbelievable. Simply unbelievable. I had hoped to go another month before having to return here to get you out of some kind of trouble yet again, but you didn't even make it halfway."

Her brow arched and she timidly offered, "I'm sorry."

"You're sorry," he snarled. "We've had this talk already and you need to realize that I might have a life outside of rushing to your aid every few days. I'm a busy dragon, little Wiccan, and I find myself very annoyed at such interruptions all of the time."

Finding her courage, the priestess thrust her staff at him and shouted, "Down, unholy beast!"

Ralligor's eyes cut to her and narrowed.

"Feel the power of Spirit Mother," she ordered, "and return to the depths of Hell from whence you came!"

He raised a brow again.

"Burn, you hideous demon of evil!" she roared as loud as she could. "Feel the wrath of Spirit Mother and be cleansed from this place!"

The dragon's eyes flashed green and the top half of her staff exploded in fire and fleeing sparks.

She dropped what was left and backed away, falling to her back in her retreat.

Ralligor looked back to Ellianta and ordered, "Stay put. I'll handle this." He stood to his towering five men's heights and swung around, facing the huddled crowd whose slow retreat toward the village stopped as they came under his attention. Folding his arms, he roared over them, "I thought when I spared this village so many seasons ago that I was sparing humans who were of higher intelligence than those I destroyed. I thought you were worthy of my favor." He raised his head a little higher, his eyes narrowing. "Who is the village leader here?"

An older man approached from the crowd with hesitant steps, then he fell to his knees and raised his palms to the dragon, declaring, "You are, Desert Lord."

Ralligor bared his teeth and growled, "I thought we were beyond this kind of behavior."

"They are witches," the man timidly informed.

The black dragon bent toward him, his scaly lips drawing further away from his sword sized teeth as he roared, "And I am a wizard! Do you mean for these white robed idiots to convince you to turn against me as well?"

Everyone cringed, and the dragon stood fully again.

His eyes slid to the priestess and he growled, "So righteous and pure are you that you would burn to death anyone who would not conform to your beliefs. Perhaps you would like to have a taste of the impurity that you accuse others of." A bright emerald fire overtook his eyes.

All of the zealots, everyone in a white robe burst into flames and they screamed in agony. Many of them fell to the ground while others tried to run from the flames that slowly burned them to death. The villagers backed away from them in horror, many of them screaming in fear as they looked upon the horrible scene before them. This continued for a moment and the screams of agony grew louder and more gruesome. Robes were burned from them, flesh was burned from them and all that remained were writhing, burning skeletons.

Ellianta closed her eyes and turned away as best she could, cringing at what was happening, what might have been her.

The Emerald glow in the dragon's eyes was suddenly gone, and just as suddenly the fires that consumed the zealots were gone, leaving them unburned and as they had been. Many screamed on for long seconds more as the memory of such pain clung to them.

Ralligor looked to the huddled and weeping priestess and leaned his head. "Well, now. That's not so fulfilling when it happens to you now is it?"

She looked up at him, tears streaming from her eyes as she begged, "No more, demon. I beg you, no more."

"There are some things worse than death," the dragon informed coldly, "like living with the memory that you have been burned alive. And that is what I leave you with for as long as you pursue this foolish crusade of yours. You and your people will remember when you see flames and that will be your dreams for the rest of your lives." He raised a finger. "Unless, of course, you are willing to denounce this madness you've been spreading. When your heart and mind agree on that, then your curse will be over. Until then, enjoy." He bared his teeth. "Now leave my territory forever."

Slowly, they got to their feet and began to humbly back away. One woman, who appeared to be in her forties, strode to the dragon and stripped her robes off, leaving them heaped behind her as she approached him. She dropped to her knees, weeping as she pled, "Please, great dragon. I am yours."

Others slowly approached and stripped their robes off. Those who did not gathered behind the villagers and waited for the priestess.

She finally got to her feet and staggered away. Defiantly, she pointed a finger at the dragon as she backed away from him, warning, "Spirit Mother will have her way with you, demon. She will bring you down and cleanse you from this world forever."

Ralligor smiled ever so slightly and bade, "Enjoy your dreams, old human." His brow lowered over his eyes as he finished, "And be out of smelling distance before my patience runs out and those flames return to you all."

As they fled, the dragon turned back to Ellianta and watched as Malkar tried frantically to untie her. He grunted, drawing Malkar's attention, then he asked, "What are you doing? If you leave her there then she can't get herself into trouble again."

Raising his brow, the healer admitted, "You bring a good point."

Her mouth agape, Ellianta looked back at him.

"I took care of that poison you meant to kill yourselves with," Ralligor informed, "as well as the oil they meant to burn you with, since you two can't seem to take care of yourselves."

"And you have my thanks, Desert Lord," Malkar offered.

The black dragon made a simple gesture as he had before and the ropes crumbled away from her and she was free from them. He took two strides toward her and shook his head yet again. "It's going to take this whole village to look after you, I think." Holding a hand over her, an emerald light sprayed down from his fingers and showered her in its warm glow.

She raised her chin as she was covered with little emerald sparkles and she closed her eyes as she felt every part of her enveloped in an unnatural warmth. When the dragon withdrew his hand, all of her wounds were gone, all of the pain from the day, and all of the blood she had lost was back in its place. Offering him a warm smile, Ellianta softly offered, "Thank you."

The black dragon grunted back, rolling his eyes as he turned away from her, toward the crowd of nervous villagers.

Before he could speak, a familiar howl came from the forest and everyone looked to see Gronko burst from the cover of the trees and run toward the pyre. About twenty paces away he stopped, a little shock and confusion in his eyes as he saw the black dragon standing there.

Ralligor returned his gaze with exasperation and he observed, "You're late."

Raising his head, Gronko dumbly stared back.

"And," the black dragon added, "you don't want to be caught in the open when Agarxus comes this way. He's not as tolerant of your kind as I am."

Gronko looked to Ellianta as Malkar helped her down from the pyre and he rushed to her and pushed the black haired healer aside as he grasped her and hoisted her easily from the ground, hugging her as tightly as he dared.

She smiled and wrapped her arms around his thick neck and hugged him back as tightly as she could. She looked up at the dragon, squinting to see him clearly. "Thank you so much. I am further into your debt."

"Yes you are," he snarled. "You may start repaying me by staying out of trouble from now on. Gronko, you are to help with that."

The ogre looked up at him and nodded.

Turning to the villagers again, the black dragon opened his wings and announced, "This woman is in my favor. She is the daughter of someone who is most important to me and will have the protection of this village for the rest of her life. She is my direct liaison to you and I shall speak through her. If those white robed idiots return for her I will expect you to unite and rid my territory of them."

A mumbling of agreement swept through the terrified crowd of villagers.

He looked down to the zealots who had stripped off their robes and knelt humbly before him. "And you may as well take these in, too." He sighed and turned back around, striding toward the forest.

Ellianta jumped down from Gronko and ran toward the dragon, shouting, "Wait!"

He stopped and looked over his shoulder, raising his brow. She really did not know how to ask, but she raised her hands to her face and informed, "I can't see well."

"Nothing I can do about that," the dragon snarled.

"But a man in my old village can," she said with a pleading voice.

The black dragon's eyes narrowed slightly and he looked away, then he nodded slightly and informed, "Yes, I believe he can." Looking back to her, he said, "A mist will rise in the morning, one isolated to one part of the forest where you live. Walk into it and make certain you have that amulet with you and it will take you to where you want to go."

"How will I get back?" she asked with a little desperation in her voice.

"That will be attended to," he replied. Looking past her, his eyes narrowed, then his jaws gaped and he belched flames toward the pyre, igniting it in an explosion of fire. He turned his eyes back to her and said, "Just in case anyone gets any more foolish ideas." With a wink, the black dragon turned again and swept himself into the sky.

As Malkar took her under his arm, she grasped his hand and leaned her head into him, smiling a little as she softly said, "I should have known. By now, I should have known."

CHAPTER 15

Her old village was much as she had left it, and this day it was bustling with activity as it always was. It was familiar, and still Ellianta felt a little unnerved about being back and for the first time in her life she felt out of place here. She was a fugitive in this village now and knew that any word of her return would not be welcome news.

She was, however, not alone this day. Malkar would simply not allow her to go alone.

They both wore hooded traveler's cloaks of green wool and avoided much contact with anyone that she thought she might know.

Walking down one of the main streets with slow purpose, her mind kept wandering from the task at hand and her eyes wandered frequently to the man at her side, meeting his just as frequently. He smiled at her often, and eventually took her hand in his.

"This seems like a pleasant enough village," he observed.

She nodded, confirming, "It is, until they decide to sacrifice you to a dragon."

"I wish we had the day to explore this place," he said in a low voice. "I'd love to see some of these shops and see what they have to offer, perhaps visit an eatery or two."

"As do I," she said softly. Raising her chin, she looked ahead of them and announced, "There it is. I think the man who runs it might still hold me in his favor. I hope so, anyway."

"Are you sure that's it? You can't see very well, after all."

"I'm sure enough. It is a craftsman's shop with a hammer and tongs on the shingle above the door, right?"

"Sure is," he confirmed. "I'm a little nervous about approaching anyone who knows you here. If you get caught—"

"I know," she hissed. "Just try to think about something

else."

A smile touched his lips. "Like what I intend to do to you on our wedding night?"

And a smile overpowered her mouth, too. "Yes, like that." Turning her eyes up to his, she asked, "So you really intend to marry me, do you? It wasn't all about the moment of losing me?"

"I see it as an opportunity," he informed straightly. "Brogret could have made me wait months or seasons before giving me his blessing. Now, we are engaged and you'll be mine forever soon."

"We aren't married yet, good sir," she reminded, "and I think you should not have me again until we are."

"Oh, you are sadistic," he grumbled.

"It just means we'll have to marry very soon," she informed, then her brow arched and she finished, "like tomorrow."

He laughed under his breath and agreed, "That sounds good. And it's really nice to know that you are as anxious as I am."

The place they approached was not the largest shop in the run but it was well decorated, well trimmed and the woodwork around the door was very extravagant. This was the shop of a craftsman, someone well suited to creating what people needed.

The covered porch was only a couple of steps off of the street and Ellianta drew a nervous breath as she strode up them, her eyes squinting and locked on the door.

As they entered and a small bell rang. Looking about them, they saw that high shelves lined both walls to the sides, and more shelves were behind them, and they were laden with gadgets of every description, tools, and simple curiosities. Across from the door was a bar and workbench where the man awaited his next customers as he tinkered with some other half finished gadget. There was a door behind him that stood open and led into a room at the back of the little shop.

The man behind the counter was a bigger fellow than one

would expect a tinkerer to be. He had a bald head, a short red beard and he wore a leather apron over a dirty tan shirt. Before his eyes were goggles with thick lenses that made his eyes seem rather large as he focused on the little gadget he worked on.

Ellianta strode slowly up to him, finally pulling the hood from her head as she greeted, "Hello, Braiton."

He looked up from his work and abruptly pulled the goggles from his face, his eyes finding her quickly and he declared, "Ellianta!"

She offered him a little smile and asked, "How have you been?"

"I've been very well," he replied, bewilderment still on his face. Glancing at the door, he said in a lower, softer voice, "You should not be here! Do you know what they'll do if they catch you?"

Ellianta nodded. "I know. I just need..." She raised a hand to where her spectacles once were, and meekly raised her brow.

"Oh, child," he said softly. "You can't see to the other side of the room without those. What happened?"

"Something hit me and, well, they were broken."

He shook his head. "Told you to be more careful, child. Wait here."

As the craftsman hurried into the back room, Malkar took her side and whispered, "Do you think we can trust him?"

She nodded, just watching after the big tinkerer.

Braiton emerged a moment later with a hinged wooden box in his hands, one that was a hand length and a half square, but only a finger length high. He set it down and opened it, revealing red velvet within and two pairs of spectacles, very similar to what she'd had before.

Gingerly picking one up, she looked them over closely, then smiled a little as she settled them onto the bridge of her nose and hooked them behind her ears.

"Polished them as best I could," he informed. "Frames are

silver and should hold up a might better than those copper ones you had. Can you see okay with them?"

"Perfect!" she declared. "These are wonderful!"

"Finished them about a month ago and hoped you'd be here to claim them." He smiled a little. "You pulled me daughter through a difficult illness, Lass. I'll not forget that."

Malkar reached into a pouch on his belt and asked, "What do we owe you for those?"

Looking to him, the craftsman replied, "She pays me in full each time I see my daughter smile at me, friend." Looking to Ellianta, he motioned to Malkar with his head and asked, "Who's the pretty bloke with ye?"

She took his arm and replied with a smile, "This is my fiancé, Malkar. He is also a healer."

Braiton nodded to him, then regarded Ellianta with solemn eyes. "I wish you were still here, Lass, or a healer with your touch. We've had none since you were taken. Everyone in the village thought you dead, devoured by that black beast that took you."

She nodded. "I would love to tell you the story sometime, but we must get away from the village before we are discovered."

"I understand," he said softly.

Looking around him, Malkar observed, "You know, we have no one in our village who does work like this. Perhaps you would make the journey there some time."

Braiton shrugged. "I've much to do here and me whole family to consider, debts I owe and debts owed to me."

Malkar informed, "There are no such debts in my village, and no currency to exchange. It is a simple life of barter and people who watch over one another."

"And no dragon awaiting your virgin daughters," Ellianta added. "You were my closest friend here and… Well, I just wanted to offer."

"Everything by barter," the craftsman pondered.

"And a store that stands empty on the market square,"

Malkar informed. "Been vacant for over a season now."

"We would welcome you," Ellianta said straightly, "but we will not pressure you."

"Got a map?" Braiton asked, watching as Malkar produced one from another pouch on his belt.

"Just tell no one where you're going," Malkar advised.

"No problem," Braiton replied, looking over the map. "That's quite a journey to take." Looking back to Ellianta, he winked and said, "See you by the end of fall."

She smiled back, then pulled her hood back over her head and turned to leave.

"Take those spectacles off," the craftsman advised. "You'll be easy to recognize with them on. Just take them out in the box."

She nodded to him and pulled them off of her face, placing them into the box as Malkar opened it. Looking to the craftsman once more, she softly said, "Be well, my friend. I hope to see you very soon."

They left his shop and walked back the way they had come. There was a fountain in the center of the village that reminded them of the fountain at their own village, and here is where they wanted to pause before going on their way.

Once there, they found the place bustling with people. It was a large open area, a place where cart merchants parked to peddle their goods, people met to trade and talk over matters. Fifty paces in any direction were two or three level structures that reminded Malkar of the market square at their own village.

They arrived at the fountain and the walled pool that surrounded it, and Ellianta squinted to see it more clearly.

Slipping his arm around her, Malkar said softly, "Thank you for bringing me here."

She smiled and snuggled into him, laying her head on his chest.

"Well, well," a familiar and unwelcome voice chided from behind them.

Ellianta closed her eyes and blew out a deep breath, finally greeting, "Good day, Mayor Trogden." She and Malkar turned toward him, seeing him standing there with six guards behind him this time.

His arms were folded and he wore a smug little grin. "Looks like you survived your day of sacrifice after all, witch."

"Wiccan," she corrected. "I don't want trouble, Mayor."

"Oh, but you have it," he corrected. "You were sentenced to death, my dear, and now you are a fugitive, but a fugitive no more." He snapped his fingers and the guards stormed forward, two of them taking her arms. When Malkar tried to intervene, two more took him as well.

As he struggled against the guards, Ellianta looked to him and shook her head, and when his struggles ceased, she looked to the Mayor again and shook her head again. "You still haven't taken my advice, have you?"

"No," the Mayor confirmed, "and since your hasty departure the dragon has been worse than ever. He has come right into the village a number of times, just as I said he would. Now we have to sacrifice two girls a month to keep him where he is, all because you would not obey the law and chose to anger the beast more by denying him his right to you."

"He had no right to me, Mayor," she informed with narrow eyes, "and he still doesn't."

"He has what I give him, little girl," the Mayor countered, "and you are his now. You refused to help us, and now it is time for you to fulfill your purpose and your responsibility to the people of the village."

Ellianta refused to show any fear to him, then she looked aside as her Wiccan senses felt something and she almost smiled. Turning her eyes back to the Mayor, she advised, "You should tell your dogs here to release us and let us be on our way before it is too late."

He shook his head slightly and said under his breath, "Foolish little girl." Looking to one of the guards, he ordered,

"Bind their hands and we'll see if the dragon is of fair appetite today."

Two of the guards went to work with their orders, binding Ellianta first.

She smiled slightly and informed, "You won't have to take me to the dragon today, he is coming here."

Everyone else present suddenly showed a little fear which showed a little more as screams erupted from the other side of the market. The guard tying her hands did not get the opportunity to finish his task as he turned and saw the copper dragon charging right toward them.

Running like some kind of giant monitor lizard, the dragon's steps were swift and almost clumsy as he sped toward them from less than fifty paces away. At his speed he would be upon them in only a matter of seconds.

The Mayor grabbed Ellianta's arm and pulled her toward him, then he pushed her into the dragon's path and they all retreated to the other side of the fountain, leaving her and Malkar to fend for themselves.

Ellianta backed away a few steps, then she noticed the dragon look behind him and she smiled a little more. Malkar took her shoulders from behind to pull her away, but she looked back at him and assured, "It will be all right, good sir."

Heavy steps and more screams could be heard from that side of the square.

Only ten paces away, the copper dragon looked behind him again.

Racing from behind two large structures, the black dragon strode into view, looking less like the highly intelligent and wizard trained dragon Ellianta knew and more like a prehistoric predator from long ago. Running on his powerful hind legs, his body was almost parallel to the ground and his wings were folded tightly to his back. With a turn of his head, he spotted the smaller copper dragon and growled, his strides growing longer and into a run in pursuit.

The copper dragon shrieked and ran by Ellianta at his best

speed.

With a mighty roar, Ralligor closed the gap quickly and, nearly to the other side of the square, he swung his jaws open and slammed them shut only a couple of paces behind the smaller dragon before he stopped and allowed the copper dragon to be on his way through the village. He held his body low as he watched the little copper dragon's flight to the other side of the village and toward the forest beyond, then he growled and turned back the way he had come, his eyes finding Ellianta very quickly. Everyone had fled the square by now, everyone but the Mayor and three of his guards, and they were ignored by the black dragon as he strode up to Ellianta with the slow, deliberate steps of the super predator he was.

Trying to wrench her hands free, she offered him a smile and greeted, "It's good to see you again. You almost got him that time."

He stopped ten paces away from her and raised a brow. "It's not always about the catch, little Wiccan. Sometimes it's more about the chase." His eyes slid to the Mayor and narrowed slightly, and his head slowly turned that way

Frozen by the terror coursing through him, the Mayor just stared back with wide eyes, as did his guards.

Looking back to Ellianta as she finally freed her hands, the dragon observed, "I see you made it okay. Did you get what you needed?"

Malkar picked the box up from where he had dropped it and handed it to her.

She showed Ralligor the box and confirmed, "Got everything right here, so I guess we should get back to our own village now."

"Not just yet," the Desert Lord corrected. "There is someone here you will need to speak with first." He motioned behind her with his head.

Ellianta turned around and gasped, covering her mouth.

Leedon was only two paces behind her, and smiled warmly

as he greeted, "Hello there, little Ellianta."

"Papa!" she screamed, tossing the box to Malkar as she charged forward and wrapped her arms around her father.

He hugged her back and tenderly stroked her hair. "You've run my apprentice weary, my little healer, almost as much as that bothersome unicorn he calls his friend."

Ralligor grunted and turned his eyes up.

Turning her head, she kissed his cheek and then buried her face in his neck, weeping a little.

Looking to Malkar, the wizard smiled and nodded once.

Ellianta pulled away and turned to Malkar, extending her hand to him, and when he took her hand she introduced, "Papa, this is Malkar. Malkar, this is my father." She winked at him. "And I think you have something to ask him."

Malkar swallowed hard and took another step toward the wizard. He found himself nervous all over again, even as the wizard smiled at him. "I, uh... I would ask for your..."

"Just ask, lad," Leedon advised with a nod.

Drawing another breath, a deep one, Malkar finally mustered his courage and said, "I want to ask for your daughter's hand in marriage, and I would ask for your blessing, Sir."

The wizard glanced at Ellianta and nodded again, then he looked to Malkar and replied, "My daughter is very happy in your company, and her heart is already with you. She knows you have a good heart, and I know as well. You have my blessing, my boy."

Ellianta hugged him again and squealed through a big smile, "Thank you, Papa!"

"This is all very touching," the black dragon snarled, "but I have business elsewhere. *Magister*, that witch will find you in short order, but it will take her considerable time to muster her minions and get them here. I think you have the day at least. Perhaps you should take the time to converse with your daughter and her future mate." He looked down at the Mayor with narrow eyes and finished through bared teeth, "And I'm sure the village would be happy to treat you and your family to a meal, wouldn't they?"

Still wide eyed, the Mayor nodded in quick movements.

"Because," Ralligor added, his sword sized, pointed teeth still bared, "I might be very annoyed if they are not, and much more annoyed if anything happens to you and your family while you visit here, very annoyed, village destroying annoyed."

"I know just the place!" Ellianta declared. "Papa, you..." Something more serious took her eyes and she asked softly, "You won't be able to come to my wedding, will you?"

"He'll be there," the Desert Lord assured. When he had their attention, he nodded to the young woman and said, "I think we can manage a day without her finding you two together. Just leave it to me."

Tight lipped, Leedon nodded to the dragon and offered, "Thank you, Mighty Friend."

The dragon nodded back, then he turned and opened his wings, lifting himself into the sky.

With a broad smile, Ellianta, took her father's arm with hers and her fiancé's with the other and led the way. "I know just where to go." She stopped and squinted. "Can't see."

The two men looked to each other, and Malkar slipped her spectacles into place.

She offered him a warm smile and gave him a kiss, then led on again. "After everything that's happened the last month or so, I'm ready for some happiness in my life." She looked over her shoulder and called back, "Come on, Mayor, you heard the dragon. You're buying."

It would seem that Ellianta's life had finally come full circle. Little would she know that more turns were in her future, and that the fates were far from through with her...